THE DARK AT THE END

Also by Susan Adrian

Tunnel Vision (St. Martin's Press), 2015

Forthcoming by Susan Adrian

Nutcracked (Random House), 2017

SUSAN | ADRIAN

THE
DARK
AT THE END

A TUNNEL VISION novel

Cover image by Arsgera, istockphoto.com

ISBN (paperback): 0692777954

ISBN (ebook):

www.susanadrian.net

SALTO

For the dedicated readers of TUNNEL VISION,
who wanted the rest of the story

1

JAKE

Vladimir by Royce

The van rattles to a stop across from Vladimir's house. All of us stare at it, silent except for the occasional noisy slurp of ice cream.

The house is straight out of the 1950s: a tiny, sun-yellow box with white windows and door, a porch on one side and a shaded carport on the other jutting out like bookends. A jewel-green lawn stretches all around it, mowed to a half-inch flattop. Little bushes clump across a bed in front. Neat, precise. Like most of its neighbors on this street, like most of the houses we've driven past. I guess if everybody's retired they have more time to maintain their houses. Or maybe they have really good lawn care service here.

No, if this Vladimir guy is anything like my grandfather, Dedushka—and I bet he is, since they come from the same twisted Russian background—he does it all himself. Dedushka studies the house through binoculars, tapping one finger on his knee. He's been dodging spies and governments all his life, since he got injected with a superpower in a Russian lab in the 50s, and successfully escaped. Vladimir was there too. They've

1

kept in touch, with their dodging-spies methods, but Dedushka hasn't seen him in person in years.

My sister Myka sucks on her Bomb Pop, and he glares at her, briefly. I take a guilty lick of my fudge bar. It was Myk's idea to stop at the ice cream truck a few blocks back, and she was persuasive.

Okay, she was a pest. But she's thirteen, and summer should still mean ice cream. Rachel and I gave in and got something too. Dedushka grunted and muttered about time, and wanting to get to the house already.

There are two other cars and a Jeep on Vladimir's street, but they haven't moved. There's no one in sight. But we'll sit here and wait until Dedushka is sure it's clear...so we might as well have treats. It could be hours, knowing him. He's cautious, but he knows what he's doing.

All we need is the serum this Vladimir is hoarding, that he, Dedushka, and my grandmother made after they got to America. It wiped out Dedushka's power. Personally, I'm aching to bust the door down, swallow it all in one gulp, and finally lose my own powers. It feels like normalcy and safety are at my fingertips, for the first time in my life. If this old guy really has the stop-power serum in there, if it works, I could be a normal person five minutes from now. If it works, I won't be hunted anymore. My family could go back to school, work. I could have a real life, instead of running and hiding and living in a van.

Maybe. A lot has happened. But it's more of a chance than we have right now.

"It looks like a dollhouse," Myka says, at my shoulder. She peers through the window, popsicle dripping on my seat. This van has its own windows in back–I didn't want anything that reminded me of DARPA and its windowless government vans, thank you very much–but Myk doesn't stay back there very often. If she doesn't have to be in the seatbelt, she isn't.

I poke her side. "You're too young to remember when we were in military housing, but most of it looked exactly like that."

"I remember military housing," Myk says indignantly. "I remember everything."

"She's right," Mom says from the back. "She does."

I look in the rearview mirror. Mom's in her seat in the back row, feet on the floor, hands in her lap. Eyes locked on the window next to her. She's still a little lost. Five weeks ago she thought I was dead, that Dad had been dead for two years. She didn't know anything about my tunneling—my ability to connect to people through a personal object of theirs—or...anything. But I wasn't dead. Just being held by a secretive government agency, DARPA, while they used me to spy on people, while they pretended to protect my family. Then on the run with Dedushka and Rachel, my sort-of-girlfriend, while DARPA and their rivals, good guys and nasty guys—like Gareth Smith— hunted us so they could use my powers too.

It turns out not only could I see what people were seeing and hear what they're hearing when I hold an object, which I always knew, but if pushed I could control people through that object too. I could control anyone, long-range, without their knowledge. That was too much of a temptation for any government agency or bad guy to resist.

The kicker, the one that punched me in the gut, was that Dad was alive too, and turned out to be running his own lab trying to create powers like mine. He'd left me out of it until DARPA recruited me, but then he was happy enough to use that as an excuse to take me underground himself. To use my power, just like everyone else, to spy on people. To control and spy and run the world. But Rachel helped me get away.

Myk told Mom all of that when they had to run away too, so they couldn't be used as leverage...and all of a sudden she found herself hiking the Appalachian trail for three weeks, hiding out from the very government she works for.

It's all been a bit much. Sometimes she has that long-distance stare I've seen in vets when they come home. She and Myk met up with me, Dedushka, and Rachel a week or so ago, and now we're together, hiding from DARPA and Dad and Gareth Smith, and who knows who else. But we're here in Sarasota to finally end it.

She looks up and I smile at her, through the mirror, fudge all over my teeth. She smiles back, thin, then looks away again, and runs a hand through her curls. She has a smudge of dirt on her cheek.

I wish she could be home. That we all could.

It's getting hot in the van with the engine off, without the air conditioning constantly blasting. Our ice cream is melting fast. We'll all be sweaty puddles by the time we go in there.

Sarasota, Florida, July: the kind of hot where somebody's got their fingers on the oven knob, considering how much to roast you before you're done. With a humidifier added in to keep you moist and juicy.

"Why aren't we going in already?" Myk asks, rubbing her knuckles up, down, up on the vinyl seat.

"Exactly my question," Rachel says. She licks the rest of the vanilla off her stick, raises her eyebrows at me, and I shrug. It's a boring Florida street, everybody in their houses watching TV away from the sun or out somewhere playing bingo. We haven't been followed—we've been keeping careful watch of that—and as far as we know nobody has any idea where we are anyway. Dedushka and Vladimir are the only ones who know about the serum, as far as we know. Of course I can't tunnel and find out. I don't have personal objects for anybody except Dad.

It all seems pretty benign. But I know by now to trust Dedushka with things like this.

"Not yet," Dedushka says, lowering the binoculars. "We wait a few more minutes. Then me and Yakob, we go in and talk to him."

"And me," Rachel and Myk say at the same time.

I look at them both. Not Myk, not for a first meeting with an ancient, possibly crazy Russian dude. I don't know what she'd say, what she'd do. She is still only thirteen, even if it's a crazy-smart thirteen.

Rachel, though. She sees things I don't, thinks of things I don't.

"And Rachel," I say.

Myk groans, but Dedushka grunts agreement. I get up, ceding my sticky seat to Myk, and go back to sit with Mom for a second.

She glances at me again, then back out the window, as intent as Dedushka.

"You okay?" I ask.

There's a long pause, so long I start to wonder if she heard me. "I'm okay," she says, her head still turned away. She pauses again, runs her finger down the glass. Then she finally turns to me. "Are you sure you should get rid of it? Your…tunneling? If it's always been part of you…."

"Hell, yes." I swallow. "Sorry. Yes. I'm sure. I can't wait."

She raises her eyebrows. "Really? Just think about what you could do…"

"It is time," Dedushka cuts in.

Myka groans again, and flops on the seat next to me. "Be right back." I touch Mom on the shoulder, then tug on Myk's hair, the dark curls flipping under her chin. "Watch the van for us."

"And wish you luck?" she says, sulkily. "Fine, good luck. Get the serum, so we can get out of here. I'd like to get back home before school starts."

You and me both, kiddo.

Dedushka and Rachel and I hop out. The heat slaps me in the face. I don't know how people live here.

We cross the street, and Rach and I hang back while Dedushka knocks on the front door. They're the old friends. Vladimir's expecting us. But Dedushka has to take the lead, make it a reunion.

Nobody answers.

Dedushka stares at the door, frowning. He knocks again. Rachel slips her hand into mine. It's damp—everything's damp. I can feel the sweat dripping down my back. But I squeeze.

We wait, listening for the sound of footsteps coming towards us. It suddenly reminds me of Halloween, standing on a porch with Myka holding my hand, both of us in ridiculously complex costumes courtesy of Mom. Waiting for footsteps to bring us candy.

This is a different kind of candy, but I still want it.

I step forward and try the door. Locked. I glance at Dedushka.

"Perhaps he waits for us inside." He scratches at his beard. "We try the back."

He strides down the steps, around the carport side. We follow, slower. Looking everywhere.

"Yakob." Dedushka's voice is spiked with urgency. When we get to the back, Dedushka stands there holding the door open, looking in. "It is wrong," he says. "Be careful." He goes in,

6

stepping lightly. I go up, see what he means, and let go of Rachel's hand.

Shit.

It's trashed. Unless Vladimir is a really messy housekeeper, someone's been here before us. The door opens into a kitchen, and every surface, almost every inch of the floor, is covered with silverware, shards of glass, scraps of paper. The drawers and cupboards are open. Even the refrigerator is open, pumping cold air uselessly into the room. I close it, then follow Dedushka. Rachel follows me.

There's a bathroom on the left, the light on. Not as bad, but still rifled through. It smells sharply of mouthwash, a green puddle on the floor. The living room is thrashed too. There are papers on the floor, on the battered green sofa, and a whole bookcase knocked over, books spilling out. But there wasn't as much to go through in here.

They were looking for the serum. They had to be, with everything searched through like this. Jesus, how did they know about the old man and the serum?

Dedushka keeps moving forward, slowly. I move too, even though every cell in my body wants to stop and run away like my legs are on fire. They might still be here. They might take me again, shove me underground again. End everything.

Rachel is silent behind me.

I keep walking. Dedushka looks in a front bedroom, left off a short hall. He moves on, to the last room. I poke my head in the front one too. It's a trophy room, or it was before it all got turned over. Baseball stuff, bats and balls and gloves and tickets, hundreds of tickets. I can see spaces on the wall where frames must've hung, but now they're on the floor with everything else, shattered.

Dedushka makes a strangled noise from the back bedroom, and I jump for the door. I stop short when I see, Rachel at my shoulder. She screams, small, before she cuts it off.

Vladimir is sprawled on his back across the bed, a gunshot hole in the middle of his forehead.

Dedushka puts two fingers to Vladimir's neck, but even I can tell it's useless. The guy is dead. I've seen exactly one dead body before—Eric, a government agent who had been my friend before he turned on me—and he looked the same. Empty.

"Cool, but not stiff," Dedushka says. He kneels by Vladimir's side, takes his hand. "It has not been long."

Rachel's breathing fast behind me, panic-breathing, and I turn, move her gently back into the hall. She's seen zero dead bodies before. Her eyes are wide, wild, her fists clenched.

"It's okay," I say, even though it isn't. At all. If someone came here and trashed the place, they know about the serum. They know about us. They're not far ahead of us. And they *killed* Vladimir. If they went through the house after they killed him, they could still be nearby. We could have missed them. They could've been watching us....

Fucking hell. Mom and Myka, sitting outside in the van. Alone.

I run. Down the short hall, through the living room. I grab the door handle, yank. I forgot, it's locked. I fumble for the lock button, find it, throw the door open. Launch myself down the steps.

The van is gone. There's nothing but an empty street, no one moving.

Mom and Myka. Gone.

2

JAKE

Kidnapped, North by Northwest original score

I pound across the street and stand where the van was. Where I left them alone, unprotected. I spin in a circle, like it will make them reappear. There's nothing. Not even an ice cream stick.

Rachel stands on the front steps, her face stark white.

I stare vacantly at the steaming black pavement. They can't be gone. They have to be close. We were only in there a few minutes....

I take off running, north. Maybe they're just ahead of us, around the corner. Maybe I can still catch them, see which way they went.

It had to be Gareth Smith. The man is a complete psychopath, an ex-DARPA agent who went rogue and started selling information freelance. The first time I met him—Rachel and I together—was at gunpoint, when he decided to scoop me off the street and sell me to the highest bidder. I still can see him laughing while his men sliced Rachel's cheek with a knife, just to get me to talk. Who else would kill an old man like that, heartless? Who else would steal my family like that? If it was the government they would've just charged into the house and taken me, not them. I don't even understand why Smith would've taken them.

To hurt me? To make me turn myself in? He likes to play games.

"Stop!"

It's Rachel, running behind me. But I'm almost at the corner. I at least have to get to the corner, see if I can see them.

"Jake, stop!"

I get to the corner and finally stop, look both ways. One car, far, heading away from us. A little blue car. Not the van. Not my mother and baby sister.

Rachel catches up to me, panting. I look towards her, not even seeing her. I only see Myka's face, trusting me. Wanting to come with me. I should've brought her inside. I shouldn't have left her. *My fault.*

"I can't tunnel to them." I look up the street again, down, in case I missed something. "I don't even have any objects of theirs. It was all in the van. I can't..." I feel off-balance, like I might fall down. "I was supposed to protect them."

"I know," she says, so quiet. "But you couldn't stop this. There was no way to—"

"I could've not left them alone in the fucking van."

She shakes her head, but I see it in her eyes. She knows I'm right. It was a mistake. It would've been safer to stay together, in an unknown situation. I want to hit something. Smash something, anything, into tiny unfixable pieces. I clench my fists, but it doesn't help.

"I need to find them." My voice breaks. Damn it. "It's Smith. It has to be."

She opens her arms to hug me, but I push her away. If I hadn't agreed for her to come, she'd be gone too, vanished. I stride down the street east, turn, west. Nothing. Loop back. I stare down at the yellow house, and where the van was, fists still clenched. Dedushka's there, out on the sidewalk. He gives a quick glance around, then disappears back inside again.

"If it's Smith, he won't kill them," Rachel says. "He wants them for something. Bait."

"Maybe. But he might hurt them. Jesus. Remember..." That knife, pressing into Rachel's cheek, when I could do nothing. There's still a little mark there, a white ghost of a line on her cheek. I close my eyes, breathe, press my tongue against the roof of my mouth hard. I always think it will help. It never does.

She touches my shoulder, like I just did with my mother. Moments ago. And now I don't know where she is.

"We need to go back and help Dedushka search the house," she says. "There may be clues to where they are. And Vladimir might have left something about the serum. This may be our only chance."

Screw the serum, I think, but I don't say it. I still need it if I want to end all this mess, take away the reason this happened. And she's right. There may be clues about where Smith was going, what he's doing. If I'm really lucky Smith's people left something I can tunnel with. Find out where the hell they are. It feels like giving up to go back, but we walk down the street. Not as fast. The Jeep is gone too, I realize. Not that that means anything. Not that it matters. The van is gone, and that's all I care about.

"I can't tunnel to my dad anymore either," I say, almost under my breath. "Myka had the picture of him, in the van. I can't tunnel to anyone. We have no warning."

She takes my hand. I don't want her to—it feels wrong to accept any comfort—but I don't pull away this time. "But that's what we want, in the end," she says. "If we get this serum, and it works for you. You won't be able to tunnel at all."

Is this what that would feel like? Blind, helpless? Is it crazy to hunt down a serum that would take away my only tool? But then no one would want to steal my family right from under my nose, would they? They wouldn't be bait anymore.

We go back up the steps into the little yellow house. Where I'd almost forgotten that Vladimir is dead.

It's hard to concentrate on searching, but I stumble through. Dedushka searches the baseball room, Rachel the living room. I take the kitchen. Dedushka says he already searched Vladimir's bedroom, and we don't need to go in there again. The door is closed.

He rests a hand on my arm. "We will get them back," he says, certainty in every word. It's the only thing that's made me feel any better. It's hard not to believe him when he talks like that.

I look through every bit of the kitchen, even things that weren't smashed. I'm hoping maybe Vladimir hid the serum, or a clue to it, taped to a flour container or something. Or Smith's men dropped a ring, or a key, or a pen, something that stands out. All I need is one object of theirs, and I could tunnel to them, find out exactly where Mom and Myka are right now.

Nothing. I don't think Vladimir even ate anything except eggs, bananas, and sandwiches—there's two containers of peanut butter, two kinds of jelly, and a new loaf of bread. The only thing in the freezer is another loaf of bread and some ice.

Jesus. Here's this old guy sitting alone in his house eating peanut butter sandwiches and watching baseball, and he ends up shot in the head. For a 50-year-old secret. For me.

No, I do need to go in that bedroom again.

I stride down the hall, past Rachel, past Dedushka, and slowly open the door.

Dedushka's laid him out on the bed, his hands folded on his chest, his eyes closed. If it weren't for the angry hole in his head, his faint blue color, it'd look like he was sleeping. It smells odd, musky. Ripe.

Dedushka stands in the hall, his eyes questioning, but I shake my head and close the door. Turn back to the old man. Just me and him, in a blue-painted room bright with sun even through closed blinds.

"I'm sorry," I say to Vladimir. My voice sounds too loud. "This is because of me, because you were going to give us the serum you've been sitting on for this long. It must've been, right?"

If this was a horror movie, he'd open his eyes and leap at me. If it was an action movie, there'd be someone hiding in the closet with a gun. I look around, just in case. But it's quiet, only the sound of my breathing. Painfully quiet. I'm the only breath here.

"I hope—" No, that's dumb. He doesn't have any hope left. "I guess that's all I can say. I'm sorry. I'll do my best to make them...sorry too."

It's not much, but it's all I have. I look one more time at his still face, then go, closing the door behind me.

13

"I may have something." Rachel's sitting on the sofa, bent over something in her lap. She holds it up when Dedushka and I come in. "This was out here, under the coffee table." She lays it out for us on the table, smoothing the folds. "It's a map of the baseball stadium here, where the Orioles do spring training."

"He's got all sorts of baseball stuff," I say. "The house is full of it."

"No, that one *room* is full of it," she says, eyebrows high. "It looked like everything was organized, neat, before they messed it up. All of the baseball paraphernalia is in that room. Except this." She taps on it. "There aren't any other paper things out here except this newspaper, and what they pulled down from the bookshelf. This is out of place. He knew we were coming, right? So what if he had this out so he could show us?"

I look at Dedushka. He runs a hand over his beard, rhythmic. Nods. "It is like him. He did nothing without a purpose, Vladimir. And I have found nothing else out of its place, that these *zlodey* did not do themselves."

"Have we looked over everything?" she asks. "Nothing else?"

"Kitchen is clean," I say. "No clues."

"Clean," Dedushka echoes.

I stare down at the newspaper, the only other thing on the table. It has one of those four-inch screaming headlines they only use for big news. LOCAL GIRL STILL MISSING, FBI CALLED IN. I pick it up, scan the story. A Sarasota girl, 10 years old, missing since last week. Believed to have been abducted by a stranger, and taken over state lines. Exactly the sort of case Liesel would've brought me, in Montauk. If someone brought me an object of that girl's, I'd know where she was in three seconds. Or I'd know if she was dead. But someone would have to ask me.

14

Dedushka nods again, tapping the map. "Let us go to this stadium and see where it leads us."

It's not what I want to do. I want to run screaming after Mom and Myka, in every direction at once, until I find them. But I can't. I have to follow this possible clue, one slow step at a time.

We go out the front door, leaving Vladimir and his little house behind us.

3

JAKE

Say Goodbye (A Tough Decision) by Una & The Sound

Without the van, we have to steal another car or find some other way to get to the stadium. There aren't any cars handy—and this isn't the kind of place where people leave them unlocked. We walk out to a main street and try to find a bus that will take us, but there isn't one. So we walk. In the broiling afternoon sun, about three and a half miles, according to the map Dedushka found. In silence, each in our own heads.

I'm not having any coherent thoughts. My head is stuffed with rage, sheer helplessness, and guilt. A lethal mix. I want to run and hurt mindlessly, like a bear when you're aiming at her cubs. Or worse, you've stolen her cubs. My mind is all fangs and claws.

About a mile in, I stop dead, in front of a nail salon. Rachel and Dedushka stop too, with a glance at each other.

"This is wrong." I clench my fists at my sides. "The serum isn't the most important thing right now, by a long shot. We need to go look for Mom and Myka."

Dedushka bites at his beard, then sighs. "How would you look? We do not know where they are taken. No direction. No objects for you to tunnel with. But this stadium—" He points south. "Right there. Vlad may have hidden the serum there, yes? We must look. If we find it, we have something to bargain with."

I frown. "You mean...trade Smith the serum for Mom and Myka?"

He throws his hands up. "I do not know. I do not even know if he wants it. It is more likely he wants you. I am as upset as you, *malchik*. It is Abby and Myka. I *understand*. But I want choices. The only other way is to try to get object for them, yes? At your house, 900 miles away, which is watched and guarded. This is first. Closer."

I turn to Rachel, though the pity on her face makes me want to shrink away.

"We should at least look," she says.

Dedushka steps toward me. "I promise, if we find nothing, we head to Virginia, for objects. We will not give up until we have them with us."

I nod reluctantly in agreement, and we walk again. I stay a pace behind them, though. I feel so alone. When I was being held in Montauk by DARPA, I thought I'd never see any of my family again. It was all I wanted, ached for. I can't believe I finally got together with them, and now they're gone. In an instant.

Even being with Dedushka and Rachel isn't helping me not feel lost.

A little while later, the stadium rises ahead of us. From the outside it's massive, a whole block. The stone is cream-colored, rich, with palm trees lined up out front. It reminds me of a big plantation house, except new.

We pause in the shade of an awning and look at it. There aren't many cars in the huge parking lot across the street, and I don't hear any noise inside.

"No game today," I say.

"They only use it for spring training." Rachel's hair is tied up in a knot now, damp tendrils on her neck. Her face is bright red. Too much Florida sun. "It said that on the map. There was a team, but they don't have it any more. It's a waste, this big place."

What's a waste is coming here. The serum is a side venture right now. But I agreed to try.

"So do you want to break in?" I ask.

Dedushka shakes his head. "I will ask them about Vladimir. That is first. Why steal when you can be given?"

He walks forward, and I start to follow, but Rachel puts a hand on my arm. Her eyes search mine, worried. "You doing okay?"

"No."

She squeezes, brief, then lets go. "I wish there was something I could do."

I want to do something too, more than anything. Take action. Find them *now*. Dedushka is up at the ticket booth, asking about Vladimir. I stare up at the sign above us. HOME OF THE BALTIMORE ORIOLES. Above that—I have to crane my neck to see—ED SMITH STADIUM.

The name burns into my brain, imprinting like a neon brand. SMITH. It's mocking me. Again I see Smith ordering his goons to press that knife into Rachel's cheek, to get me to give up Dad. Holding guns on us in that train yard, threatening to kill Rachel for no reason. He's a sadistic son of a bitch with no regard for anything except what he wants. And what he wants....

Dedushka's back. "Vladimir works there," he says, his voice hopeful. "As a cleaner. I have asked to see his locker, as an old friend he sent to fetch something. Not today, they say, the manager is not here, but tomorrow. He will let us in—"

"Tomorrow?"

There's a silence.

"We can plan," Rachel says. "What we'll do next. We can get out of the freaking sun—" she swipes at her face "—get something to eat, and get some rest. Then tomorrow we can start fresh."

I stare at the ground, at my useless hands in fists again.

But they're not useless, are they? I can do a lot more than most people can.

Dedushka is smart. Trading something for Mom and Myka— it may be the only way to get them back. It's what Smith understands, how he deals with people. He's always looking to trade.

But it's not the serum he wants. Or money. It's me. I bet you anything he'd trade them back for *me*.

That's why he took them. To play one of his weird mind games, and make me turn myself over to him.

I don't say anything to Rachel or Dedushka. But it's a thought. A little flashlight of a thought.

I know it's what I've done before, sacrifice myself, and it hasn't worked out. But maybe I can make it work this time. I'll have to think about it more, tonight. But it might even turn into a plan.

＊

About 2 am, I quietly close the door of the motel room and step outside. It's still warm—probably 70 degrees—but the relative coolness, the breeze, are a massive relief.

I can't stay in there anymore, in a hot, stuffy room with Dedushka snoring in one bed and Rachel curled up on the other. I can't believe they can sleep. I feel like I'll never be able to sleep again. There's a hamster wheel in my brain, spinning away, and I can't stop it.

The parking lot is full, but still. Silent except for the endless clicking of night bugs, the hum of the freeway.

I'm itchy in my skin. I have to go…somewhere. Anywhere. A walk.

There's a Taco Bell across the street, still doing business, and I'm tempted. But it costs money, which we don't have a lot of. More, I'd have to interact with someone. I don't want to talk to *anyone*, unless it's Mom and Myka. Or Smith.

If only I could find a way to talk to Smith, to…deal with Smith, this could be over.

It's insane. I can't do that.

I walk. There are a few cars, not enough to bother me. Mostly closed shops and other fast food places. Still too bright, too distracting. When I come across a park I veer straight in. It's big, with lots of trees, and in the daytime it's probably great for shade. At night it's creepy and forbidding, and entirely deserted.

Perfect.

I stop somewhere around the middle and sit, on an exposed root under a big tree. I wrap my arms around my legs, stare into the dark, and try to let my mind settle a little. Just enough to think.

First: I have to try to clear the guilt away, long enough to figure out what to do. Leaving them in the van was a viable plan, and should've been safe. We must've missed something, clearly, and I really want to know *what*. But Smith is the one to blame. He's the psycho who did this.

Is he? Do I know that for sure? I flip through the possibilities. DARPA. Liesel Miller is the agent I dealt with there. She started everything, six months ago. She came to my house, told me she knew what I could do, and could protect me and my family. She could help me. All I had to do was cooperate. I had two agents worm into my life—Ana and Eric—and for a while, it worked. I could tunnel and balance everything else, living at home. But then they claimed another group, a foreign agent, was threatening my family, and I had no choice but to go underground. They sealed me up in their base at Montauk and made me work for them, lying to me the whole time. So DARPA and Liesel are manipulative. They can even be violent. Eric went crazy after I controlled him through tunneling to escape. He threatened Dedushka. And then Liesel shot him, right in front of me.

I hug my legs tighter. I don't like to think of that, or it takes over.

But Liesel shot him so he wouldn't shoot ME.

I picture Vladimir again, harmless, shot defenseless in his bed. It has to be Smith. No one else in this game—Liesel or other people at DARPA or Dad—would do that. And Smith's the only one who would search for this serum, which is only good to me. Only because he wants to lure me. He happened upon something even more valuable to me, my family, which he saw instantly and snapped up.

It's Smith. And he really wants to trade. He wants to sell me again.

I take a deep, strong breath of night air and let myself imagine it. Captive. In someone else's hands. Last time Smith sold me to Dad, and I thought I was saved, only to find out Dad wanted to lock me up too. Everyone wants to lock me away and force me to tunnel for them. With Liesel it was tunneling to fugitives, terrorists…and occasionally kidnap victims, like that little girl. Locating them fast before something even worse happened. That part wasn't so bad. I was helping people. Could I do that again? Could I consider doing that, voluntarily, to save my mother and sister?

I let my hands fall, feel the damp, alive grass under them. The tree at my back. Look at the sky, stretching wide behind the trees, the few dots of stars.

In Montauk I was never allowed outside. I couldn't even see the sky. Dad wanted to keep me underground too, for "safety." He wanted to experiment on me. I shudder. It was worse, when it was Dad. It was betrayal. I hate him for that.

If Smith sold me to either one of them I could be shuttering myself away from sky forever.

But it's my *family*. It's Mom and Myka. I hurt them before, letting them think I was dead. I hurt them now; they were taken because of me. To stop that, to make it right, I could give up everything again. I'd never forgive myself if I didn't.

I have the hope that I could figure a way out, eventually. After all, I got out of Montauk, a maximum security facility. I could probably get out of most places. So maybe it wouldn't be permanent.

But even if it was for a long time—God—I have to do it.

I really have to do it.

I stand, pushing up against the tree. I have to find a way to contact Smith. Now.

I could probably get to him eventually if I pushed my face in front of a bunch of cameras at banks, at gas stations. He probably monitors that stuff. But so does DARPA, and Dad. I don't want someone else to find me first. The most important thing is getting Mom and Myka back.

There's a more direct route. I know he has a company, Smith Enterprises in DC. I bet they have a phone number.

I head back out onto the street, back to the few places that have people. This time I'm crammed with purpose.

I find it in about an hour, the other way from the motel at a little gas station. A cell phone sitting on the console in an empty car, the driver inside paying.

I reach in through the window, grab the phone, and keep walking, around behind the station, off into some bushes in a ditch. Sit and stare at it, my heart pounding.

It doesn't have a lock code, the owner entirely too trusting. They may be able to trace it, soon, but I only need it for a few minutes anyway.

I search for the number, find it way too quickly. Breathe once, bite my lip, and hit the screen to dial. Leave a message that Smith will understand, with a place to meet me tomorrow.

Then I leave the phone in the bushes and make the long walk back to the motel. It's done. All I have to do is show up tomorrow, and if everything works, they'll be safe, all of them. I can forget about the serum for now, my chance of getting rid of this power. I need to tunnel for a little while longer.

When I open the door to the motel, and they're still there, sleeping, I almost want to cry. But I don't. I curl up, gently, behind Rachel, on top of the sheet. She's warm, and it's too hot to be touching, but I don't care. For tonight, it's what I need.

It's all I need.

4

RACHEL

See You Again by Elle King

Jake's leaving. After all we've been through. All he went through at the hands of those people. He's turning himself in to that *psychopath*?

Dedushka and I sit on one of the motel beds, facing him, like he's trying to defend himself in court and we're his jury.

I would find him guilty of being a fool.

"No," I say, flat. "No no no *no*. It's dumb. I won't let you."

Jake raises an eyebrow, and I kind of want to punch him. Like I couldn't stop him if I really wanted to.

"It's already done," he says. "It's arranged. If I don't show now, he'll track me down anyway...and I won't have him find you."

"Then un-arrange it!" I look at Dedushka, who's being oddly silent. "You don't need to protect me. How will this help Myka and Abby? How will it help for you to be locked up again, who knows where, with that freak?" I take a deep breath, and close my eyes for a second. Those were the worst moments in my life, with Gareth Smith. When I saw Jake in the library and went

24

along with him that first time, it was mostly because I was shocked he was alive...and curious. It was a puzzle I wanted to solve: where he'd been, why everyone said he was dead. That I needed to solve. I didn't honestly think there would be any *danger*. Then I had a gun in my face, a knife cutting into my skin, and it was all different.

He crumples the comforter. "If I go, *they* won't be locked up with Smith, for doing nothing. That's how it will help." He looks at the clock. "I should go soon."

"You're so anxious to give yourself up?"

He meets my eyes, shakes his head, and I turn away. I can't look at his face anymore. He doesn't want to do this, I can see it. It looks like it's killing him to do this. And yet he's doing it anyway.

"Dedushka," he says, soft. "I'll be okay. I have to try."

I glare at Dedushka, willing him to say no. Jake would listen if he did. He nods, a tiny tilt of his head. "I do not like it. But..." he shrugs, and my heart sinks. "If he will trade, it is a good start. You can tunnel to me without any object. They do not know that. So you stay in touch, yes? You tell me where you are, we come get you."

"Are you insane, both of you?" Two pairs of identical gray eyes look at me. I thrust my chin up. "Mr. Smith has a ton of men with guns. He has security. You don't just put yourself in that situation, on purpose..." My eyes burn with tears, and I swipe them away. "Don't leave," I say, quietly.

He left before, when he went underground, without telling me. Like Dad left. People are always leaving. I'm sick of it.

"I have to," he says. He reaches out for me across the bed, but I fold my arms and turn my back. No.

Dedushka clears his throat. "We will go and look for the serum, Rachel and I. Then we will have it when you see us again."

"Speak for yourself," I snap. I stare at the motel wall, hard, the tiny bumps and smudges. The terrible painting of boats on the bay. "I may not be here when he comes back. If he comes back. If he's going to be this much of an idiot..." My voice wobbles, and I stop.

I mean it, I realize. Maybe it's time to go home. If he's just going to leave too. This is so wrong.

"Enough." Dedushka reaches out and squeezes Jake's hand. "Be safe. Contact me as soon as you can, and I will help."

I hear Jake stand, shuffle his feet. He circles around the bed to face me, but I stare down at the comforter. I can't look at him. I can't watch him leave on a suicide mission.

He stands there for a second longer, then turns and leaves. I watch his feet go out the door.

Dedushka pats my leg, awkwardly. "He will be all right."

"Will he?" No, I don't think so. And I'm not going to just sit around and do nothing. I stand, my legs wobbly. "You might be sure of that, but I'm not. I'm at least going to see what happens, witness this meeting. And if Abby and Myka are there, if Smith releases them, they won't know what's going on. They need us to help them. Did no one think of that?" I take a deep breath. "I'm going to follow him."

Dedushka sighs, but he nods. "I will go with you."

I guess I'm not ready to go home quite yet.

We follow Jake at a distance as he takes a crazy route, doubling back on himself and stopping often to check behind him. If Dedushka wasn't here, and leading, Jake would have totally spotted me. It's 9 am, and it's already a thousand degrees out here, plus steamy. I wipe the sweat off my face with the back of my arm, trying to keep Jake in sight.

Why am I here? The thought nags at me. Why don't I just walk away, go back home?

Jake stops again at the edge of a big park, a long stretch of wiry grass and random trees. When he looks back I spin on my heel and head the other direction for a minute or so before I turn again and look back. He's still staring this way. I think he sees me. Dedushka, as usual, has melted into the crowd. I don't know how he *does* that.

Jake and I lock eyes for a long second. Then he smiles a little, and dives into the park.

For this very moment, I'm here still because of him. First it was just curiosity. But now...I try to imagine life at home, without having any clue where he is and that he's okay. Life with Mom.

I can't.

Dedushka and I push forward, and cross the street to the park. I don't see Abby and Myka, or Mr. Smith, or any of his guys. Just Jake, an old lady slowly shuffling down a path a ways off, and a couple on the other side on a bench, kissing.

Jake lopes around the park, scanning everything, while Dedushka and I stay at the edge looking in. Eventually Jake leans against a tree, arms crossed. Nothing happens for a long time. Maybe nothing is going to happen. Maybe this was all just a false alarm, and Mr. Smith didn't get his message at all.

Then I see movement.

It's not Mr. Smith, or Abby and Myka. It's a single huge man in a blue suit and tie, walking slowly towards Jake. He says something, smiles, and holds out a hand for Jake to shake.

I don't think this is what was supposed to happen.

"Dedushka?" I say.

"I see," he replies, tightly. "It is not good."

Jake says something else, his hands up. A plea. Another man, also in a suit, appears beside the first. The big man holds up his left hand, and I see the glint of a needle. I start to step forward, to stop it somehow, but Dedushka puts a hand on my arm.

"It was not the plan," he says, low. "But it will still get him where he needs to be."

Jake turns to run. But the man is fast. Jake slips on the grass, and the big man tackles him, and shoves the needle in his arm. I press my hand against my mouth, to keep from screaming. Jake slowly closes his eyes, and the two men pick him up and carry him between them, off the other direction.

27

No one sees, except us. No one cares. But Jake is really gone.

5

MYKA

Taken by One Direction

Mom and I huddle together on the floor at the back of the van. They still won't tell us where we're going, or what's going on. The two men, big military-type guys, jumped in the van at Vladimir's house. One hot-wired the van while the other threw handcuffs on us in two seconds flat, laid us down on the floor, and told us not to scream. He said we were safe, and they weren't going to hurt us.

I screamed my head off. He slapped his hand across my mouth and nose until I had to stop, because I couldn't breathe. His hand smelled like hot metal, like fireworks. Mom was so scared she started crying. When he let go, I cried too. My face still feels puffy.

Of course we're not *safe*. He's only saying that so we won't panic. Someone took us because of Jake, and none of the choices are good.

From what Jake told us, I'm guessing it's Crazy Smith. He's probably going to torture us or something...until what? We don't know anything. Maybe just until he gets Jake to come to him.

We've been driving all night, though I can't see where. I think it's north, because of the sun. But I remember Mrs. Wynn's geography class, and the giant puzzle of the U.S...everything is north of Florida. All I can see from the floor is sun and blue sky, and then stars, with trees flying past. The men take turns, one sitting in the chair looming over us and one driving. They won't let us talk to each other at all. We pulled over for a while in the middle of the night so the driver could sleep, and Mom whispered to me to just keep calm, and we'd be all right.

That made me cry hard, somehow, which made the watcher guy tell me to shut up, which woke the driver guy up, swearing.

It's better just to keep quiet, I guess. Until we get wherever we're going.

It doesn't make any sense. Why take us? Why not take Jake, when he was right there?

I wish Dedushka was here. Out of all of us, he would know what to do, even more than Jake. He would protect us.

I finally fall asleep after a while, curled up next to Mom. I forget where we are, and dream about home, about being late for a chemistry test. And then I get there, and there's a list of procedures I need to do, but I don't have any equipment, and no one will help me.

The watcher guy pokes me in the side. "Wake up," he growls. "We're almost there."

"Where's 'there'?" I ask.

He doesn't answer. He pulls us up, one at a time, and sits us on the back seats. Mom helps so I don't fall off. Finally, I can see out the windows.

We're in mountain country, the road crowded by huge pine trees. I can smell them a little bit, a fresh scent that reminds me of camping. Back when we were all together as a family, Mom and Dad and me and Jake, Dad would pack us up in the car and drive to the mountains, put up a tent and build a campfire. I loved it. It made me so happy, sitting around the campfire at night looking at the stars, talking about nothing. Or Dad quizzing me on the elements, or constellations.

And s'mores.

It was only two years ago, but everything has changed. I still can't believe Dad's not dead. Jake says it's true, that he saw him, but it doesn't *fit*. Why would he lie to us like that? Why would he go away if he didn't have to?

If he were around, if he hadn't left, would any of this have happened?

I press my leg up against Mom's. She presses back, silently.

We turn off onto a dirt road that winds up into the hills. After a long time the road gets narrower, then goes between two big hills into a little valley. The road ends at another hill. Seriously, there are no buildings or anything. The road just ends.

"Where *are* we?" I ask.

The watcher guy looks at me, but doesn't reply. The van pulls up in front of the hill, and suddenly I see it: there's a door. A truck-size square metal door, set right into the hill, painted the same color as the dirt. It's really hard to see unless you're right next to it. The driver says something into a radio and the door starts to slide up, the metal grinding.

It's like the Doors of Durin in *Lord of the Rings*. It'd be really cool if it weren't terrifying.

Mom and I look at each other, eyebrows up. My heart starts thumping. Who would have a place like this? Smith? Some crime lord? Why would they bring us here?

We drive in, to a massive garage full of military vehicles, most in camo. There's even a helicopter, parked on a truck. The van stops, and I expect something to happen. But there's a long wait, while Mom and I just sit there. Then, finally, the back doors open.

There's a little group of men in military uniform standing there waiting for us.

31

Standing at the front, watching us coolly, is Dad. Mom gasps, but I just stare, my brain locking. That was the last thing I expected.

It wasn't Crazy Smith who took us at all. It was Dad.

6

JAKE

Judas by Cage the Elephant

I wake up slowly. That drug disorients me. It takes a while to figure out where I am, what's going on. But I remember, before I open my eyes. Smith. I gave myself up, for Mom and Myka. He tricked me, didn't do it the way I asked, but his man came. I should be with Smith now.

I have to step very, very carefully here.

"I know you're awake, Mr. Lukin. You may as well join the party."

At the sound of his voice a wildfire of rage flames through me, almost uncontrollable. Almost. I have to be smart.

I open my eyes, expecting a gun, a cell. Instead I see a fancy chandelier, high above. I seem to be lying on a sofa. I try to move my hands, but I can't. They're handcuffed in front of me. Well, I suppose that's not a surprise.

It smells, oddly, like cinnamon.

I swing my legs down to a carpet—my feet are bare; I can feel the soft fibers with my toes—and sit up, woozy.

"That's a good boy. Your breathing changes when you wake, you know. I can tell. And I do so hate deceit, even passive."

I blink two times, three, and he comes into focus. Salt-and-pepper hair, strong chin, crazed pale blue eyes. He's in a perfectly tailored three-piece suit, sitting behind a gigantic wooden desk. His fingers tap impatiently.

"Where are my mother and sister?" I growl. "You were supposed to bring them with you, let them go when you took me. What have you done with them?"

He stares at me for a long second, frowning. Then he lifts his chin. "I have them somewhere safe." His voice turns mocking. "Why, were you worried?"

Smart. Stay smart. Stay...

The rage wins, and I leap for him, arms raised. Powerful, meaty hands grip my shoulders before I even get to standing, and press me back into the sofa.

"Now, now. None of that."

I twist my neck to look back, up. A goon I've never seen before towers above me. From here he looks at least 7 feet tall, with shoulders like planks. Different than the one who brought me in. He looks down at me impassively. Okay then. Back to smart.

"To what we were discussing," Smith says. He pulls a yellow pencil from an artfully arranged cup and rolls it on the desk with the flat of his hand, up, back. Up, back. The desk is dark wood, cherry maybe, polished to a high gloss. Totally empty, except the cup and two manila folders. "Your mother and sister will remain safe as long as you do exactly what I want."

"No." I swallow bile, my voice rising. "You let them go. I'm here like you wanted, why you took them. Why you killed Vladimir in cold blood. That's why I called you. Let them go *now*."

He raises both eyebrows. "I made no agreement with you, Mr. Lukin. And remember, I have no rules. I told you that explicitly, when we first met. I *have* to do nothing. However…" He pauses, takes a deep breath. "I will make an agreement now, for clarity's sake. You stay here, tunnel for me…and do me no harm…and they will stay safe and well."

Stay with him? He doesn't want to sell me? I shake my head. The hands press slightly harder, pushing me down. "No. I'll stay. I'll work for you. Whatever. But I want them freed, now."

"But think, Mr. Lukin. For just a moment, try to *think*." He picks up the pencil, snaps it in half with one motion, and throws the jagged pieces at me. I flinch away, startled, and one bounces over the sofa behind me. Casually he pulls another pencil out of the cup, starts rolling it across the desk like that never happened. "Why would I release them? They are my leverage that you will work, and work well." He stops, narrows his eyes. "Speaking of leverage, where is that pretty girl who was with you last time? Aw. Did you have a falling out?"

I try not to think about Rachel, where she is. Like he's some sort of mind reader, and if I think of her location he'll know.

Maybe she went back home. I almost hope she did, so she can be safe. Though what's to prevent Smith from snatching her up too? As "leverage"?

He pretends to pout. "Too bad. I would've liked to see her again."

I stare down at the white carpet. The sofa is red, crimson, like blood. The whole room is decorated like an old-time mobster's living room. I bet he gets off on that. "Where are we?" I ask, through my teeth.

"Oh! Yes. I did not properly welcome you." He stands abruptly, walks around the desk, and leans back against it, ankles crossed. Every move seems calculated, posed. "My apartment in Washington, D.C. I find it so handy to be close to the...centers of influence. That's why I have decided to keep you to myself for a while. Everyone in this town has secrets they're trying to protect, are willing to pay, or trade, to protect. You will be very useful."

"Like a chained dog," I snap. I won't admit yet that this isn't working out the way I thought, that I should've come at it another way. But the knowledge is settling in my gut. He can't keep me *and* Mom and Myka. That wasn't the plan.

He brightens. "We can get you a collar if you like." I glare at him, the hands still heavy on my shoulders. "No? Too bad. It was a good image. In any case, I'll sweeten the deal, offer you something else." He waves a hand at the guy behind me, and the hands suddenly lift. I breathe like I'd forgotten how, and roll my shoulders. I can still feel him, though, looming above me. "No, no, I know that your mother and sister being free is all you want. Blah blah blah. But if you can't have them free, you want them well, yes? If you stay good and work for me, I won't hurt them. Not even a little bit."

My fists clench, involuntarily. "Incentive," I say, hoarsely. "And you'll hurt them if I don't do what you want?"

"That's right." He smiles, like a businessman in a meeting. It's unnerving. "See, I'd like to not be forced to lock you up somewhere. It's so much easier if I can let you roam freely, not have to deal with handcuffs and prison cells and such. Liesel may like those things, but I do not. I feel, with the way you are, that I can only give you freedom if you have an

36

incentive to play along." He folds his arms, stares down at me with his spooky blue eyes. "Do we have a deal, Mr. Lukin?"

I hate this man, more than I thought you could hate anyone. More than Dad, more than Liesel. But it's another one of those impossible situations. I have no leverage except the work I'll do.

I hold out my hands for him to take the handcuffs off. "Don't you touch a hair on their heads, you bastard."

He smiles again. "We have a deal."

7

JAKE

Back in the Saddle by Aerosmith

Smith leaves me to sit for a while, while he "prepares a fun treat" for me. I don't have the handcuffs on anymore, but Mr. Super Big still stands behind the sofa, ready to lean on me if I try anything. I realize he has the exact same suit as the guy in the park: navy with brass buttons, a blue and white striped shirt, and a pale blue tie. Their uniform, I guess.

I wonder if it would accomplish anything to try to attack this guy while he's alone, to choke his thick neck until he tells me where Smith is holding Mom and Myka. But even if I could, he has a gun too—I saw a flash of it under his coat. It doesn't usually work out well to go me vs. a big man with a gun. Or even a big man with a needle.

He's humming, low in his throat. It takes me a while to figure out even what the sound is. I can't tell what song it is. I don't think he knows he's doing it.

I sit there like a good dog and stare out the window. It's getting dark, showing the lights of the District and the Washington Monument, glowing white and tall in the distance. It's almost home—but I don't have a home anymore. I gave that up when I went underground with Liesel. I was getting used to

38

that van being home, sleeping in a jigsaw puzzle of sleeping bags, Myka on one side and Rachel on the other.

I close my eyes, wishing I had the power to time travel to yesterday morning. Or to find a portkey to the house in Virginia, grab Myka's old stuffed animal Horse, or something else of hers so I could tunnel to her. Is she in this building? Or somewhere else entirely?

Or Dedushka. I can at least tunnel to him—only him—without an object. But I can't do it now, with someone watching. I can't let Smith know I can do that, or it will make everything worse. He'd never let me be alone.

"All right, my pet." Smith charges into the room. "Time to do a little test. See what you can get out of this." He opens a glass box in his hand, pulls something out, and places it in my palm. It's a keepsake coin, with John F. Kennedy on the front. It's cool to the touch. The air conditioning in here is cranked up high. He folds his arms. "Impress me."

Tunneling under pressure again, just like when the government held me, almost like I never stopped. Here we go. I rub the face of the coin with my thumb, close my eyes, and let myself go. I say what I see aloud, because I know he won't accept anything else. The familiar tingling, the warmth, starts at my fingertips, then sweeps up my body in a rush. Then I see the owner of the object. I'm there with him. I can see what he's seeing, feel what he's feeling.

It's a man, black, head shaved shiny, in army green. An officer, specialty Electronic Warfare. He's in the Pentagon, office 3C710. He's working, the fluorescent lights flickering above him. He taps at his computer, references a folder splayed out in front of him, taps again. He's worried. This isn't good, and the General isn't going to be happy. But there's no other way to spin it. We're vulnerable, and they're close to figuring it out.

39

I pull out of it, wiped. It's been a while since I've done that to a stranger. I've tunneled to Dad a few times since we left the base, just to see where he was, but never got anything useful. And now Smith has me outright spying, on the Pentagon of all places. Who's he going to sell that info to?

I reach out to give the coin back to Smith.

He leaves his arms folded, eyebrows down. "Why did you stop? Did I tell you to?"

I frown. "I have to come out when I do. I can get stuck, otherwise."

He just looks at me.

"It's nothing you can tell me or not tell me," I say, annoyed. "I come out when I have to."

"That's not the way it's going to work with me," he snaps. "Half-seen thoughts won't cut it, Mr. Lukin. You stay until you see something useful, until I tell you you're done. Come out too soon, you go back in." He jerks his chin at the coin, still in my fingers. "Go on. See what's in the folder, or on the screen."

"But I can't—"

Mr. Super Big's hands lower onto my shoulders. Not pushing, just resting. For now. "Go!" Smith bellows.

I go back in.

He stops typing, staring at the screen with his chin in his hand. VULNERABILITY OF U.S. DEFENSE SYSTEMS TO ELECTRONIC ATTACK, it says. 'After a long and complete study, the task force has determined that U.S. Defense systems are not well protected against the type of attack we have seen recently from the Chinese on private targets. The task force believes they are practicing infiltration methods, and will attack defense systems soon. The task force believes they will succeed, unless...' The cursor blinks at him, mocking. "Unless what?" he says to his empty office. "You gotta give 'em a solution." But he sits and stares, and the cursor still blinks.

I'm sticking, feeling claustrophobic in this guy's skin, and I don't want to stay anymore. I come out, open my eyes defiantly at Smith. He stares at me, unblinking.

"Better," he says. "But that one doesn't get you a gold star."

I shake my head. "You're spying. Actual spying on government weaknesses."

He raises an eyebrow. "No, I'm not. You are."

I shake my head. "Are you going to sell that info to someone? Leave us open to attack?"

Smith stares at me, his head just a little tilted. "Jones, take him to his room."

"His name is Jones?" I ask, so frustrated I can't even stop myself. "Smith and Jones? Could you come up with some more original aliases maybe?"

Smith slams his hand on the table, so loud I jump. He pauses, for a long second. "Do you WANT me to kill you?" he whispers. "Are you asking for it? Or do you want me to kill your precious little sister instead?"

I grab the edge of the sofa, in instant full panic mode.

"Respect," he whispers. "It's all I ask. No, I suppose I ask rather a lot, actually." Then he laughs, a little giggle.

Right. He's totally insane. I'd almost forgotten that.

There's a headache forcing itself into my head. Shit. It's my side effect. It doesn't happen every time, but when it does it knocks me flat.

I press my hand against my forehead, trying to brace myself for the brain-splitting pain. Though nothing works for it,

41

not anymore. Liesel used to give me an experimental drug, T-680, which stopped them cold (and made me high). But the side effects of *that,* long-term, were far worse. Hallucinations. Then insanity.

"Headache," I say, my voice choked. Here it comes, the giant hammer smashing, eclipsing everything else. I scream, my throat raw.

A hand opens my mouth, and I taste the familiar Froot Loops flavor of T-680. No. It can't be. I try to spit it out, try to struggle, but the hand holds my jaw shut, and I swallow. The headache dissolves at the edges, gone within two minutes.

Damn, that drug. I forget where I am, smile, and fall asleep.

8

RACHEL

Say Hey (The Willie Mays Song) by The Treniers

I watch the water roll down the side of the Coke glass, expanding the puddle it's sitting in. It makes me more angry. Why is it so irrationally hot?

Why did Jake abandon us? Abandon *me*. And to see him taken like that, drugged and dragged off like a puppet. I want to smash my drink, feel the satisfaction of being the one to do something for once. I can't believe he'd give himself up like that. On purpose. "We can't just leave him with Mr. Smith," I say, to Dedushka.

We're sitting at a cafe, trying to eat lunch. There's a plate of uneaten fries in front of me. The fried smell of them, so good when they came, is making me feel nauseous.

Dedushka looks at me sharply. "It is done. And it is for Myka, you see, and his mother. He cannot think of anything else, until he does all he can to get both of them back."

I swallow, tears pricking the back of my throat. Little Myka. I've only known her for a week, but if I let myself think of it, her with Mr. Smith...I can see why Jake would do crazy things to stop it.

I can also see that Jake is gone again. Like the months I thought he was dead, when he was really locked in a government prison. Only who knows what Mr. Smith will do with him. Mr. Smith's face is in my nightmares still, staring down at me. He's

43

crazy. Last time all he wanted was to get Jake to give him enough information so that Smith could make a quick sale. What if he wants more this time?

"You shouldn't have let him do it," I say. "You have better sense. You should've known it wasn't going to be a trade like Jake thought. That they'd trick him."

"Perhaps," Dedushka says, his voice as gentle as it gets, "it is time for you to go home."

I jerk, knocking the almost-empty glass into my lap, ice sliding all over my bare legs. I bolt to my feet and push the sticky ice off, wiping at my legs. Dedushka waits, gaze fixed on the table. He's nothing if not patient. He's the only one of us.

"Why would you say that?" I sit, gingerly, on the chair. "Because I think *you* did something wrong?"

Dedushka's eyes—the same as Jake's, which is weird sometimes—look steadily into mine. "You came to help him find his father. You did that. You saved him. You stayed with him until he was united again with his family. It is more than was expected." He waves a hand. "But now it is different. He is gone. Perhaps now is the time to go back to your mother, prepare for college. It would be safe for you."

"It's safe for me?" I laugh, without any humor in it at all. "You realize that if I'd stayed in the van, which I almost did, I'd be with Mr. Smith too? That he—and maybe John too, or Liesel, I don't know, all these lunatics—would be perfectly happy to use me as bait, if they thought it would bring Jake to them? How am I *safe*?"

I hadn't even realized that, consciously, but it's true. Even if I'm not with Jake, I'm not safe anymore. Because of choices I made. One choice, really.

When I think back to that moment in the library, when I saw Jake was alive and confronted him, I wonder if I would make that choice again. Knowing everything I know now, everything I've seen, would I stop him? Or would I let him walk right by?

That poor old man, dead in his bed. That was *yesterday*. And Jake crumpling to the ground, unconscious. I'm in a world now where people are killed, drugged, used mercilessly.

44

But If I'd let him go past in the library, I'd still be working my summer job, mourning my dad leaving us, and trying to deal with my mom's oppressive craziness. She was getting bad before I left, screaming at me about everything I did. So much worse since Dad left. She'd yell at how I loaded the dishwasher. How I folded the towels. How I was wasting my life staring at my phone. A hundred times a day she'd yell "RACHEL!" at the top of her lungs, scream for me to get my butt over there so she could explain in detail what I did wrong. Or drink a whole bottle of wine, and cry.

I hated every second in that house. It would've been miserable trying to ride it out until I could get away and go to college. Safe...maybe...but absolutely miserable.

And without me, Jake would probably be trapped with his dad right now. I was the one who got us out of that, away from John. Alone, I don't know how he would've managed it.

I think of kissing Jake, the flood of emotion between us. The way I feel awake when I'm with him. The way my pulse thumps every time we touch. It's just starting, whatever this is between us. We've only kissed a few times. But it's *something*, a connection I've never experienced before.

I can't go back. Not now. Not yet.

I meet Dedushka's so-calm eyes. "I can't go back to my mother, back to 'normal.' Knowing he's out there, with Mr. Smith...how could I? Just pick up my toys and go home, and never know? Never see him again?" I shake my head. "I said I could, but not after seeing him taken like that. We have to find the serum. It's the only way it'll end, the only way any of us will be safe. And then I *will* go back to normal, as normal as I can...and Jake can too."

Dedushka's thick eyebrows rise, which means he's listening to me. I think. He doesn't say anything, so I keep going.

"We're close, right? Maybe. We think Vladimir pointed us to the stadium. So if Jake's gone, for now, then you and I need to keep working to find it. We find it, and then we bring it to him, wherever he is, and get him out of there. And then all of this stops for real. Okay?"

45

Dedushka smiles, and sets his hand on top of mine. "It is well done, *milaya.*"

I tilt my head. I get the feeling that's what he wanted me to say all along. "Were you playing me, Dedushka? Did you really want me to stay?"

He shrugs one of his big Russian shrugs, and smiles a little through his beard.

"Tricky. What does '*milaya*' mean?" I ask.

"You." He stands, brushing off his pants. "Shall we go find a vehicle? It is too hot for an old man to walk in the sun, and the streets are too wide and too long here. Then we will go to this stadium, see what we see."

"Sounds like a plan." I feel better doing something, anyway. We're not helpless. Dedushka and I will find the serum that Vladimir left, and we'll hook up with Jake again—and then we'll make it all stop. Then Mr. Smith, and the rest of them, will have no reason to keep Abby and Myka. To try to grab me, or Jake, or anyone.

The thought crosses my mind that we still know an awful lot, about government secrets. Will they really let us walk away? Will I be able to go to Berkeley in the fall, like I'm supposed to?

Well. It's a plan. Far better to have Jake with no power at all, and give us a chance.

It only takes five minutes for Dedushka to convince the stadium manager to let us see Vladimir's locker, saying he's ill and he wanted his things. There's something about Dedushka when he turns on the accent full-bore, a charm that's hard to resist. It's easier for people to just give in and agree to him. I'd say that's his gift, that and hiding out successfully, but Jake said he used to have another power. A darker one. If he heard a dead person's voice, on TV or the radio or whatever, he would experience the last moments of their life.

I think that's a terrible power. But he and his wife made this serum, with Vladimir's help, and they stopped the power completely. The magic, remote serum. Dedushka says there's only one bottle of it left. The holy grail for us.

We walk through a maze of hallways, following the manager. Everything is well-lit, cream paint and spotless, even in the tunnels. It smells stale, but still clean. Newish.

'Tunnels' just makes me think of Jake again. Where is he right now? What is he doing? If I had an ability like his I'd be able to find out. But Abby and I are the only ones without some kind of power, if you count Myka's super-brain. Myka joked that I'm like Lois Lane, the normal mortal. Except Jake doesn't have to go around rescuing me. Thank God.

Maybe more like Xander in Buffy. At least he was helpful, most of the time.

The hallway gets darker, smaller and less fancy, and finally we're at Vladimir's locker, in a row of about 20 others. The manager reads the combination from a little piece of paper, opens the locker, and steps back.

I'm half-afraid it will explode or something, that it was a false clue for the bad guys and he rigged it with a bomb. But Dedushka steps forward and looks, and I guess it's okay. I peek over his shoulder.

There's a light jacket hanging on a hook, and a pair of cleats. That's all. My eyes fill at the sadness of it, these two lonely items. That's all that's left of a whole life.

"Thank you," Dedushka says, like it's exactly what he expected. He hands the jacket to me—a pale blue windbreaker, so old man—and takes the cleats himself. "He will be glad to have these."

I swallow hard, try to blink away the vision of Vladimir's body. No. He won't.

I check again, but the locker is definitely empty now. No secret panels or a hidden shelf or anything dramatic. It's a dead end. Clothes from a dead man. We have no idea where to look now. We get to sit back and worry until we hear from Jake. Or I go home, alone.

The manager offers to show us the field since we're here, and Dedushka enthusiastically accepts. I follow along, half-hearted, the jacket folded over my arm. I never liked baseball much, though Dad was into it for a while. I like volleyball, which I played until sophomore year. And football. If this was the Dolphin's stadium it would be much more interesting.

The clouds are low and dark, even though it's almost 90 degrees. The air sparks with electricity, and the field looks strange in the light: wide and otherworldly. It's going to rain, soon.

"Of course today wouldn't be a great day for baseball," the manager says, with a grin. He has yellow teeth, and eyes with lines radiating around them. His gray hair is pulled back into a ponytail. He seems happy to have a chance to talk to someone. "But Vladimir would've been here anyway. Every day, that guy, cleaning the stadium, sometimes even when he was scheduled off. I'm sorry to hear he's not well. I hope he'll be back soon?"

Dedushka makes an affirmative noise. I hold the jacket close. It smells faintly of peanut butter. I gag, thinking of him still lying there in his house. He'll probably be found soon. We did this just in time. There'll be police crawling all over Vladimir's little house. But I can't think of that, or I'll lose it.

It's then I feel something in the jacket. Not in the pocket, but in the lining. The crinkle of paper.

"May I use the bathroom?" I ask, too loud. The manager looks surprised for a second, then nods and points around the corner. Dedushka narrows his eyes at me, and I smile, bright and fake, and hurry away. I guess I should get better at the subtle spy tricks, but it worked.

I bundle into a stall in the bathroom, lock the door, and examine the jacket. Sure enough, the pockets are empty, but there's something hidden inside the back. I can see tiny, neat stitches around a long slit in the liner.

Oh my God. There really is a secret pocket.

I stick one finger in the stitches and tear, with a silent apology to Vladimir. Inside is a single sheet of yellow paper, folded in half. I open it, my hands shaking.

It's a note, handwritten. "Выпейте на старом соленой собаки." It's in Russian.

48

Of course it is.

I fold the note again, carefully, and tuck it in my shorts pocket. I check the jacket for anything else, but that's all it was hiding.

I found a secret message. I have to admit, that's pretty cool.

When I return to the field again, the rain is coming down in sheets. Dedushka and the manager are talking in the hallway, something about baseball and the Orioles, like it's not torrential two steps away from them.

"Shall we get these back to Vladimir?" Dedushka says to me, a question in his voice. I nod, and he says polite goodbyes. It's not till we're outside, under the shelter of a bus stop, that I show him the note.

"Vlad, he is sly," he says, nodding, pinching it in his fingers. He looks a tiny bit excited, which is saying something for Dedushka. "I checked the cleats, but there was nothing. Well done." He reads it, and laughs. "Drink at the old salted dog?"

I frown. "A bar, maybe?"

"A silly bar name," he says. "But a good guess. Let us go to the car and see if we can find it. Are you not now glad we took the time to steal a car?"

I snort. Life with Dedushka is so far from normal. From home, with Mom. I like it, most times. I just wish Jake, Abby, and Myka were with us too.

9

MYKA

Confessions of a Broken Heart (Daughter to Father)
by Lindsay Lohan

Dad is *here.*

This is his secret military base, somewhere in West Virginia. He's the one who grabbed us off the street, without telling Jake or Dedushka or even telling us where we were going. For our "safety," he says.

He hugs me when we get out of the van. At first I'm so surprised that I let him—and it feels nice. He smells the way I remember, Old Spice and fresh-pressed clothes and *Dad.* I want to fold into it like I used to, let him make everything okay.

But he left us. He pretended to be dead. He tried to keep Jake in an underground base, and now he brought us to one too.

I push him away and Mom draws me into her arms, like she's protecting me from him. "What did you do?" she asks, high, her voice cracking. "Tell me, John. What have you done?"

Dad doesn't answer. He and a couple of his soldiers escort us through a maze of tunnels—metal and undecorated and boring, nothing to mark one from the other except signs—and into a weird kind of lounge room.

50

It's pretty big, with about ten hard metal chairs, two low tables and a high table, a plain tan sofa, and a fridge. Dad dismisses everyone and sits on the sofa, gesturing for Mom to sit next to him. She sits on a chair. I drop onto a different one, across from them. And then they start arguing. She tells him he has to let us out of here, that he *kidnapped* us. That Jake and Dedushka and Rachel must be frantic.

"They'll be here soon enough," he says.

"Why?" I jump in. "Are we bait? Why didn't you just take them too, if you wanted them here?"

He smiles. There's something wrong with his smile, with him. It's off. It's not how I remember him at all. "Not to worry. It will all work out as planned."

Whenever anybody says that in a movie, or a book, they're the villain. They're always talking about their evil plans. But he's my *dad*. He's the one who taught me how to play cards. He helped me with my math homework. He gave me big squeezy hugs. How could he be a villain?

It's confusing.

I just watch him after that, talking to Mom. He explains that he's only acting on our best interests, all of us. That he's only trying to protect us from all the scary people who could be after us now that Jake's secret is out.

"I'm running a very important operation here, Abby. We're trying to enhance—or even create!—powers like Jake's."

He looks hard at me when he says that, and I shiver a little. He knows I don't have a power like Jake does. Dedushka did—though I didn't know that until recently—and Jake does, of course. But Dad and I don't. I bet he always wanted one, and that's why he's doing this.

I bet he thinks I want one too.

I did, when I was little. I would have traded anything, when I was six, for a power *even better* than Jake's, something spectacular. Invisibility, maybe. Or the ability to

51

control light and dark. I always thought that would be a good one.

But lately? After seeing all the trouble Jake's landed in, and all he's had to go through, I don't want that anymore. Unless absolutely no one knows about it, it's just not worth it.

Dad keeps on talking about his base, and what an impact his research is going to have. It's so weird to see Dad in person again when we thought he was dead for so long. He looks old. Older than I remember, anyway. The skin on his hands sags. The wrinkles in his forehead are deeper. It felt like I was so much younger when he died. I was nine, at the funeral. The fake funeral for a fake death.

I turn away. I don't want to look at him anymore.

I want Jake, and Dedushka. And even Rachel. I want to be back in the van, sucking on a popsicle with everyone together. Or even better, back at home, in school, before this Liesel Miller even contacted Jake.

I guess it would be nice to have a power, right now, just so I could time travel, back to when none of this had happened. Or reach out and tell them where we are.

I curl up into a ball on the chair. I wonder what they're doing right now. Where do they think we are?

I'd bet my whole bookshelf at home that they don't know we're with Dad.

10

JAKE

Can't Find My Mind by The Black Keys

I wake up still on the sofa, stretched out, alone. Not even Jones the babysitter is here. It takes me a couple minutes to figure out what happened, shake off the drug.

T-680. Damnit. The drug that Liesel was feeding me to control the headaches, not knowing that it caused nasty hallucinations too. Smith must have kept the bottle I snuck out of Montauk when he captured me last time, in the train yard. I don't even know why I took it with me in the first place. I never wanted to have that crap in my body again. I was finally almost done with the hallucinations, with it all out of my system, and here I am back at square one. Like an addict fallen off the wagon.

I sit up carefully, but I'm fine. Probably better, now that I got some sleep. The stuff works. It just has horrible side effects.

And there it is. The green glass bottle, sitting on the edge of his desk. I'm surprised he left it out. He seems like an "everything in its place" kind of guy. Maybe he didn't know whether I'd need more.

It's my chance. He probably wants to keep me dependent on this stuff, keep me crazy, hallucinating all the time. I'm not going to accept that.

I jump up, snatch the bottle. Take off down the hall to the bathroom before anyone can stop me. Sure enough, I hear footsteps as soon as I move. I was being watched. But I'm too fast. I open the bathroom door, pull off the toilet lid, and dump the whole contents, all those little white pills, into the water. Smith appears at the door.

"Stop! What are you—"

I flush it, watch all the pills swirl to oblivion. No more. I won't be their guinea pig anymore. Not that way, at least.

Smith leans against the doorjamb, frowning. He waits for the flush to finish before he talks. "Those help you. Tell me why on God's green—well, *my* green earth—you would destroy them?"

It sounds like he's sincerely asking. I give him a what-kind-of-idiot-are-you look before I can stop myself. "The hallucinations? Not worth it. Never again."

His frown deepens. "Hallucinations?"

I step back from the toilet, tilt my head. "You didn't know about the hallucinations?"

There's one more second of complete bafflement before his mask clicks in, and he shrugs. "Of course." He steps back, away from the door. "Would you kindly get out of there, please? I am tired of staring into a crapper."

But it's too late. He let something slip. He knew about the T-680, but not the hallucinations. That means something important. But what?

I follow him back into the main room. He goes straight to his desk, starts rummaging in a drawer. I don't go to my place on the sofa. I walk to the window and stare out at the view, big clouds piling up over the familiar D.C. buildings. I'm not sure what time it is, how long I was out. Late afternoon, maybe. Or even early evening. Sometimes it puts me out for hours.

A different big guy appears in the far doorway and shuts the door behind him, blocking it with his football body. The blond guy who tackled me in the park. He smirks, the big jerk. I note for later that they don't want me to go in that door.

I should go in that door as soon as I get the chance.

"Why didn't you know about the hallucinations?" I muse aloud. "You knew about everything else. How the tunnels work, that the T-680 was for the headaches."

"Shut up," Smith says. "You're yapping."

But I've latched onto it now, and I can feel the answer there, waiting for me.

"You had an informant," I continue, piecing it together. "Someone who was right there, closely involved. There weren't very many of those, believe me."

Big man in the corner is watching me like a cat watching a bug, but Smith hasn't told him to move yet, so he doesn't move. Smith is pretending to look in his drawer, but he's listening. I think he's curious if I can figure it out. I cross my arms and take a step closer to the window, my nose almost touching the glass. It's cloudy out there, but I can still see it, the outside world. Which I never could in Montauk, when DARPA was holding me. I was stuck in that underground cell with no windows, no air, no sun. There were people who brought me food and stuff, but probably didn't know who I was. And four other visitors, ever: Liesel, Bunny, Dr. Tenney, and Eric. Well, Liesel wouldn't be his informant, not in a million years. She knows him, and hates him. And Dr. Tenney and Eric certainly knew about the hallucinations.

But Bunny didn't. She was an assistant, a doctor, who ran the tunnels with me. She was there from the beginning. But Liesel kicked her out after I successfully flirted with Bunny and managed to steal something from her, to try to tunnel with. That was before the hallucinations started.

"Bunny," I say, victorious. I spin around and face Smith. "Bunny was your informant."

He laughs dismissively, and shuts his drawer with a bang. "Bunny? The drug has made you insane as well, is that it? Fast-acting. Or were you already insane?"

"Dr. Milkovich," I say, remembering her real name. Bunny was a nickname. "She wasn't there when the drug did start making me crazy, or you would've known about it."

"That is quite enough, Mr. Lukin." Smith stands, licks his lips, and I know I've got him. I'm right. "As you inconveniently slept through the second meeting I wanted you to attend, you are done for the day. Jones, escort Mr. Lukin to his room, please."

The bulky guy comes over to me quicker than you'd think, but I don't move. "Jones?" I ask. "They're both named Jones?"

Smith rolls his eyes. "I call them all Jones, Mr. Lukin. I like to make my life as simple as possible."

Figures.

"Is Bunny—Dr. Milkovich—still working for you? Or did she stop being useful once she wasn't assisting with me anymore?"

His jaw clenches, and I know I've gone far enough. He waves a hand. This Jones grabs my arm like he's going to strip it right off, and shoves me toward the hall. I take one last look at Smith over my shoulder before he disappears. Jones throws me ahead of him down the hall, into a bare bedroom, and locks the door.

I hope that wasn't a mistake. After all, that guy, that *psychotic* guy, is in charge of everything about my life right now. Including whether I live or die. More, whether Myka and Mom live or die. Or are hurt. God.

But I know more than I did before. That's gotta be worth something.

The room is smaller than my cell at Montauk, but not by much. It has an actual window and real furniture: a nightstand and a bed. Not even a cot. A normal bed, like a hotel. It smells like a hotel, detergent and cleaner. I sit on the bed gingerly, like it might explode. It's a ridiculously soft, normal bed, with thick pillows. I don't even remember the last time I slept in a nice bed. Since the cabin it's all been cars, cots, or our Army/Navy store sleeping bags, that always smelled a little like mothballs. That cheap motel last night. Before the cabin...it was my DARPA cot, attached to the wall. The last time I slept in a real bed was my own, before all this started. Six months ago.

It smells faintly of food, something fried. My stomach starts rumbling. I haven't eaten since before I came to Smith. Before we went into Vladimir's house, we all had the ice cream. That night we picked at pizza. That was a long time ago.

I should tunnel to Dedushka, let him know where I am.

Myka appears on the bed, and I groan. Here come the hallucinations again, already. I try not to look at her.

"What the heck are you doing, Jake?"

57

I close my eyes. Don't look, don't look, don't look. It's the only way I can deal with them. Pretend they don't exist.

"We're being held by this guy, *kidnapped*, and you're messing around? You don't even *care*?"

"I do care," I say through gritted teeth, even though I know it's not her. Not real. "I'll get you out. That's why I'm here."

"That's why you're here? Don't even tell me you came here on *purpose*. How dumb are you?" She punches the bed, and I look at her. Her hair is short like it is in real life, not like the hallucinations I used to live with.

I shake my head. I can't engage with hallucinations, or that's all I'll do. I know this. I close my eyes tight, for a long time. When I finally look again, she's gone.

The door opens. It's a Jones, though with the light behind him I can't see which one.

"Mr. Smith has decided to invite you to dinner," he says, in a butler voice, like he was told exactly what to say. Then he snorts. "No need to dress."

My stomach growls in response. Okay, then. "I accept," I say, formally. Because why not? And any opportunity to talk with Smith might give me more information.

Hallucination Myka appears again, and starts to protest about eating with the enemy, but I walk out the door. Fortunately, she stays behind.

11

JAKE

Dinner Party Massacre by the BBC Scottish Symphony
Orchestra

A Jones—a new one I haven't seen before, skinnier than
the others—takes me the other direction down the hall, which is
mildly exciting in itself. Every bit more I can learn, I might be
able to use. We go around a corner, then he opens a door on
the right, with a flourish. At least this Jones has a sense of
humor. I step in. It's a formal dining room, fairly small, with a
floor to ceiling window on one side showing a different
spectacular view of D.C. There's a crystal chandelier hanging
over everything, scattering the light into rainbows.

There are narrow tables and cupboards around the
walls, and a long table in the middle that could seat at least ten.

Right now it's set for three. Smith sits at the head, waving
like a little kid. Sarcastically, of course. Next to him is Bunny.
Exactly like when I saw her last, except without the white lab
coat. Pale, translucent skin, white blonde hair. Tiny bird-like
frame. She's wearing a bright red sweater, which only makes
her look paler. She gives me a small, resigned smile.

I sit across from her, completely thrown. It's one thing to figure something out in theory. It's something else to have it confirmed in the flesh, in front of you.

"Come on, then," Smith says, one hand out to each of us. "Entertain me."

I pretend really hard he isn't there. "Bunny? You really did work for him the whole time?"

She locks her eyes on her empty plate and glances up, quick, then down again. A blush splashes over her face. Still shy. There's a reason everyone called her Bunny. "Yes," she says, soft.

"So that makes you...a traitor?"

She presses her lips together and stares at her plate, but doesn't answer.

"Now, now," Smith says, in a professor voice. "Not at all. It just makes her someone who's smart enough to see there are multiple markets for the same information."

I turn to him. "Like you. Did she tell you everything I did? Everyone I tunneled to?"

"And your sad-sack attempt at seducing her so you could escape." He smiles viciously. "I was encouraging her to let you have the hair clips, to see what you'd do with them."

I shake my head. Jesus. Did she have Liesel talking in one ear and Smith in the other? Was anything in my life ever simple or straightforward?

I know that one. No.

"I would've invited Eric Proctor to dinner as well," he continues, "but I believe something is wrong with his head."

That stings. I flinch. "You mean he was shot in it? Yes. He's dead. But he never worked for you."

"Sadly, no. Though perhaps he would've been interested, at the end."

I can't say anything to that. Eric was one of my handlers, and the closest thing I had to a friend. But I had to mess with him to escape, control his body so it looked like he was taking me hostage. He lost it when the government he trusted accused him of being a traitor...and because he couldn't trust himself anymore, with me out there. I could've tunneled to him anytime, as far as he knew, and controlled him again like a puppet.

He took Dedushka hostage in return, to make me come to him. He would've killed me, if Liesel hadn't shot him.

Simple and straightforward.

A side door opens and the first Jones comes in with a tray of appetizers, stuffed mushrooms and bruschetta. He holds it next to me, and I take as many as I can. Who knows whether he'll even give us anything else.

"Dr. Milkovich was the only one working for me in Montauk, of consequence," Smith says. "A couple other nonessentials. But it was quite profitable for me nonetheless. I was perfectly happy to leave you there, feed you people to tunnel to through Liesel, but you had to go and escape, so then I had to take care of it myself." He takes precisely one of each appetizer and sets them on his plate, even with each other. Like mismatched eyes. "I wonder...what should I do with you when I'm bored here? Shall I sell you to Russia? Or back to Montauk? Or back to your father once more? He was most willing to pay once. That's something. You do manage to make me money. Though he'd really have to keep a better hold on you this time...you were there what? An hour?"

My hands start to tremble, but not from claustrophobia. From fear. Any one of those things would be a nightmare. I stuff a mushroom in my mouth, but it makes me want to puke. I gag, swallow, until it goes down.

He's really not going to let me go. I knew it going in, of course. I was willing to make the trade. But he's not going to let *them* go either. That I can't deal with.

"Leave him alone," Bunny says, quiet, but firm. "He's not used to you."

"As though I want anyone *used* to me." Smith eats his piece of bruschetta, tomatoes tumbling between his manicured fingers, watching me. I kind of want to starve and go back to my room, get away from this Mad Hatter meal. But my gnawing stomach won't let that happen. I eat a piece too, try to figure out what to say next. If there's any way I can use this to my advantage.

It's delicious. I want about twenty more.

"How are you, Jake?" Bunny asks, the blush still staining her cheeks.

I sigh. Small talk. I don't want any of that. "I was great until he stole my family off the street, and I had to come here to get them back."

Her head whips to him. I guess she didn't know he took Mom and Myka. But how could she not know how evil he is? How could she stand to work for him? I finish my last mushroom just as Jones comes in with a tray of fresh dishes. He takes our appetizer plates and gives us the new ones. Caesar salad. He grinds fresh pepper and shaves fresh parmesan cheese over everyone's.

This is surreal. It's like we're eating in a good restaurant somewhere, instead of an insane man's house. But we eat, all three of us, crunching salad. Bunny steals glances at me, and I watch her. I can't believe she worked for him—spied for him. Still does. Still probably works for DARPA or the CIA and gives him information. No matter what he says, that's treason. I think you can get shot for doing less than that.

"How did you get started?" I ask her, curious. "With the CIA and DARPA and everything? You're, um...very young." *To be a traitor.*

"I'm twenty-three." She stabs another bite of lettuce with her fork, viciously. "They like to recruit young. They recruited me when I was 12."

Twelve. Almost Myka's age.

"I was part of a talented kids program—super-smart bunch, you had to test into it—and they had this overnight camp at the Spy Museum? Where you have a cover and all that and pretend to be a spy, crack codes and take on an identity and everything."

I set down my fork. Myka went on one of those, last year. She's part of that group.

Bunny doesn't notice. Smith does—I'm sure he doesn't miss much—but he just raises his eyebrows at me, then turns back to her, chin on his hand, and pretends to be fascinated.

"I won the game, and at the end the organizer slipped me a card. She said they'd keep an eye on me, and to call the number when I was 'thinking about colleges'." She takes the last bite of salad and chews it slowly, thoughtfully. "I called three years later, and Liesel answered. They got me early admission to Yale, and I finished in two years. Then Masters in one year, doctorate the next. I've been working for her ever since. Until she left. But I'm still there." She glances at Smith. "Doing research."

Jones comes in and takes our plates. I only ate half the salad before I lost my appetite. I wonder if Myka won that game too, if she got a card. Before all this happened.

I wonder if that's why they were looking into our family, and found out about me.

No, I can't blame that on Myka.

"And Smith?" I ask.

"Oh, I was slow," he says, with a sick little laugh. "I recruited Dr. Milkovich at Yale when she was 17." He reaches across and pats her hand, like a dad or a kindly uncle, and I am truly creeped out. "Any pick of Liesel's is a good pick of mine. Like you, Mr. Lukin. And now here we are, a team. Hasn't it just worked out so well? It's only a pity I had to twist your arm."

I push back my chair and stand up. "I can't do this. I can't eat with you and pretend to be...what...co-workers? Colleagues? While you're holding my mother and sister *hostage* to make me work."

His eyes glitter in the light from the chandelier. Bunny's face tightens. She shakes her head, but it's too late now.

"Oh, I see," he says, quietly. Dangerous. "So you'd rather starve and be kept in cuffs while I have your mother and sister hostage? You would rather suffer more? I thought I was doing you a favor to ask you to eat with us. To treat you like a human instead of an animal, like you complained about before." He's getting louder and louder as he talks. "But you'd *rather* be treated like an animal?" He stands and slides his arm across the table, sending plates, glasses, and silverware to the floor with a massive crash. Bunny flinches, but doesn't move. Then he strides to my place, does the same with mine, staring defiantly at me. He looks at Bunny, but she has one hand on the table, on either side of her dishes, head down.

"JONES," he bellows. Two come in, from opposite doors. He points to the one nearest me, the skinny one. "Take him back to his...cell. Handcuff him to something uncomfortable. Very uncomfortable. I think that's the only way he's going to feel at home here."

"Don't do that," Bunny says, quiet.

Smith turns to her, incredulous. "What did you say, rabbit?"

64

She clenches her fists, and raises her face to him. "His work is voluntary. You can't force him to do it, and he doesn't respond well when he's...mistreated. He needs to be well-rested, not tortured."

Smith's face is thunder, and I can see he's ready to torture her too. Her cheeks are bright red, but she doesn't stop.

"You made a deal with him, right? He works, and no handcuffs and cells? So if there are handcuffs...." She shrugs. "Why would he work?"

"Because I have his family," Smith growls, low.

She raises her eyebrows, pauses. "You made a deal," she says simply.

There's a long moment while he stands there, staring down at her. Then he sighs, and it's like all the air has gone out of him. "Fine," he snaps. "I honor my word, when I do promise something. Just get him out of my sight." He leaves, brushing past me, without looking at me once. Though he stops next to the skinny Jones. "And don't let him out of yours. He may not be handcuffed, but I don't trust him."

Bunny gives me a small, victorious smile before the Jones takes me back to the room. He slips inside after me and stands by the door, like a sentry.

"Sorry," he says. "Orders."

No tunneling to Dedushka, then. At least not yet.

I lie down, thinking I'll fall asleep in seconds.

Except as soon as I close my eyes I see Myka, hands tied together, gag in her mouth, staring at me. Tears in her eyes. Mom, blindfolded, lying sideways on a hard cot.

I sit up. Those weren't hallucinations. Were they a vision? Something Myk is sending me? I close my eyes again. Now I see Myk on a plane, a knife held to her cheek, as the point digs in.

Not visions. Imagination. But it's bad enough. That could be happening, right now. Because of me. They're being held by Smith somewhere out there. And my grand plan to save them is a total bust. It just got me stuck too, trapped again. A waste.

I sit up on the bed, twisting one of the pillows in my fist. Stare at Jones standing by the door. He's not watching me directly, but he might as well be. My own personal guard.

I'm not sure I'm going to be able to sleep at all. Hell, I may not even be able to close my eyes ever again.

I miss Rachel. She's the one who helps when I have nightmares, who knows what to say. Who kisses me and runs her fingers through my hair until I calm down. But she's a long way away, and thoroughly pissed off at me on top of it. I did just walk away from her. I wouldn't blame her if she was tired of the whole thing, chucked it all to take up normal life at school in Berkeley.

I may never see her again. And Mom and Myka? Who knows. I grit my teeth against a swell of bile. It's going to be a long night.

12

RACHEL

Salty Dog by Flogging Molly

"The Old Salty Dog?" the guy at the comics store says. "Yeah, there's two of them. Restaurant and bar, both. Which one do you want, Siesta Key or City Island?"

Ugh, I miss having a cell phone. Dedushka won't let them anywhere near us. He claims they're too easy to track. If I had my phone, I could've Googled "old salty dog," found the two bars, looked at them, and decided which one. And then had it mapped for me. Instead we had to find someone Dedushka thinks is acceptable and ask, while he complains about how there aren't pay phones and phone books anymore. He's ridiculously old school. It's taken us hours to find someone acceptable who has any idea. It's 5 o'clock now. This guy's about to close up.

I look the question at Dedushka. Why would Vladimir pick a place that had two locations? Better cover?

"Which is oldest?" he asks, his accent almost undetectable. He's trying not to stand out.

"Siesta Key," the guy answers. He's short, with dark hair and a straggling beard. He's been leering at me since the moment we stepped in the door. I almost wave to get him to look up at my face. "Been there almost 30 years or something." He smiles down at my breasts, and I want to punch him, right there under his chin. Pig. Dedushka does a hacking old-man cough until the guy turns to him.

Good distraction. I still want to punch him. Why do guys *do* that?

He gives us directions, and we get out of there. The bar is way out on an island, so thank God we have a car now. As long as the police aren't looking for it...but I doubt it. It's an ancient Volvo Dedushka took from a long-term parking lot at a bus station. We should have a couple days, fingers crossed.

Sometimes I step back and think how weird all this is. How quickly I got used to stealing cars and hiding out and sleeping rough. How quickly I got used to Jake being there all the time.

I miss him. There's a permanent ache in my chest, a Jake-sized emptiness. We got close in a short time, running away together. Even though I was mad at him for leaving, most of the mad has dissolved into worry and missing.

Dedushka misses him too—all of them, probably. He hasn't heard from Jake. He droops. We haven't been talking to each other much. With just us, almost-strangers, there's not much to say.

He drives west, over a bridge to an island. Once we're on the island, It's funny how we can barely see the ocean even though we're surrounded by it. From the road it's just all trees and houses, on and on and on. It smells like ocean, though. A saltiness in the air I'm not used to.

It makes me think of my dad, living his life in Hawaii now. Coward. I wonder how he'd like it, knowing what I've been doing. What I've experienced in the last couple months. I don't think he'd like it at all. Mom either.

Good.

He thinks I'm this sweet little girl, working at the library, getting ready for college. That I was fine, on-track, so he was free to go off on his glamorous dream life surfing or eating poi or whatever, and leave me with Mom.

I thought at least he felt bad, that he missed me terribly. He was the only one who knew what Mom was like with me. I imagined him wracked with guilt. Until Jake tunneled to him that first time, at Caitlyn Timmerman's party, and proved that Dad didn't miss me at all. All he was thinking about was waxing his surfboard and getting out on the waves. He was *happy*.

Yeah, he wouldn't be happy with me stealing cars and running all over the country. But I am. For now.

We see it at last, the parking lot almost full: The Old Salty Dog.

I try to figure out why Vladimir would've come here, picked this place out of all the bars and restaurants in Sarasota. It's nice, bright and airy, full of people who don't pay any attention to us. There's baseball on the TV. It smells like beer. But there's nothing Russian or spy-like or even that remarkable about it. I guess I was expecting a place like a TV show would use for a Russian spy, dark, with booths. I follow Dedushka and sit at the bar, keeping an eye on the exit. Just in case.

"I would like a beer," Dedushka says to the bartender, a big white guy with a crinkly bald head, both arms covered with full sleeves of tattoos. Dedushka lets his full accent out. "My friend Vladimir sent us here."

"Vladimir?" The bartender raises his almost-nonexistent eyebrows and points to the corner by the window. A woman sits there alone, a shot glass in front of her, staring morosely out the window. "I think you want a visit with Doreen. I'll bring your beer over." He looks at me in that judging way bartenders have. "You?"

"Coke, please." I don't feel like having a beer, even if he'd give me one. Which he clearly wouldn't.

"What kind?" he asks.

I laugh. "Um, Coke." I always forget that Deep South thing, where they call all soda Coke.

Dedushka is already almost to the table, so I scramble after. He walks fast. He stops in front of the woman, and waits until she looks up. "Vladimir sent me," he says, quietly.

The woman drops her head and starts to cry, big loud sobs, like he pushed a button and set her off. Dedushka takes a step back, frowning. His hand goes to his beard.

Because that's the best way to deal with tears.

I sit in the chair next to her and touch her hand. "It's okay," I say, my voice soft. "It'll be okay, Doreen. What's the matter?"

She cries for another couple minutes, while Dedushka brings up a chair and sits down, looking like he wants to be a thousand miles away. I rub her back and talk, low, soothing. She's a bit drunk, which isn't helping with the crying, but I have a lot of experience with sad drunks...Mom. Low and soothing works.

Doreen looks up, her face blotchy, when the bartender brings our drinks. She swipes at her cheeks.

She's pretty. Probably a little older than Mom, with thin gray streaks in her straight brown hair. But her skin is mostly clear and unlined, and her eyes are bright, if puffy right now.

"He's alive, then?" she says. Her accent is southern, soft and slow. "I thought he must be dead." She looks from Dedushka to me, and then her eyes change, and her mouth goes tight and hard. She must have seen it in our faces. "Oh. Oh no."

"I'm so sorry." I realize my hand is still on her back, and it suddenly feels awkward. I pull it away.

I expect her to cry again, but instead she nods, drunkenly, staring out towards the ocean. I wrap my hands around the cool Coke. It's warm in here, the doors open to the air, a big fan circling overhead. Of course it's warm everywhere here. That ocean tang blows in again, salt and seaweed.

"He said it might happen," she says, still looking out, far away from us. Then her gaze sharpens, and she turns to Dedushka. "Monday he said if he didn't call to say goodnight, I was supposed to head to this place the next day, and the next. For a week, and you might come any time. His friend, right?" She smiles, small, through tears. "He described you well." Her voice catches, but she pushes through. "I'm supposed to give you a message."

Vladimir was good at this trail-leaving thing.

"Da?" Dedushka asks. "He was a good friend."

He looks terribly sad sitting there, stroking his beard. Old. I wonder suddenly if he ever cries.

70

I want to cry for Vladimir, for Doreen.

Doreen rubs one finger around the rim of her shot glass, then licks it. She has a mole right in the corner of her mouth, like a movie star. "He said to tell you—and only you—to go to the place you love most, where you spend all your time. Go with Sara." She looks at me. "Are you Sara?" I shrug in answer, and she continues. "Number 56, he said." She rubs a hand across her eyes, and suddenly she looks old and tired too. "Does that make sense to you?"

"Da, of course," Dedushka says, his voice smooth. "That is all?"

She nods, sure.

He lifts the beer. "To Vladimir."

"To Vladimir," we echo, with our drinks.

He downs it in one go, though I've never seen him drink beer before, and wipes his mouth. "We must go, Sara and I. *Spasiba.*"

He holds out a hand, and Doreen takes it, squeezes. Her eyes fill up again.

I shake too. Her hand is warm, damp. "Thank you. You really helped us. I'm so sorry for...for your loss."

"He was a good person, wasn't he?" Her voice shakes.

"A great person," Dedushka answers. The faraway look again. "He will be missed."

She nods again, biting her lip, and we stand and go, leaving her alone. Dedushka leaves a twenty on the bar for our drinks, and hers. We don't speak until we're back in the car, side by side, looking out the window. I don't know what to say about her, about Vladimir. In the end I don't say anything. I don't think he'd like talking about it.

"Did that really make sense to you?" I ask. It didn't make any sense to me, but I figure it had to be some kind of code.

"No," he says, shortly. He sighs. "But it is the next step. We will have to unravel it, da?"

We will have to unravel it. Not as easy as I thought.

13

MYKA

Really Don't Care by Demi Lovato

Dad tried to prepare a bedroom for me.

I mean, it's not like a typical catalog bedroom with pink curtains and fluffy pillows and letters that spell M Y K A on the wall...and it's not like my own bedroom at home, blue and green with my big elements poster, and my signed picture of J.K. Rowling. But he tried. The room is tiny, about the size of a bathroom. But there's a twin bed with a real, blue-patterned comforter, a little white reading chair, and a bookshelf packed with Chemistry textbooks and fantasy novels, classic and new. He steps in and waves an arm around, grinning like he's done some amazing thing.

"Here it is, Myka! Your room!"

He actually says that. Like I'm still 9, or even 6, and I'm sulking about something., but I'll get over it because I'm so thrilled at my new space in an underground bunker.

I stay in the hall and grip Mom's arm. "I'm not going in there. I'm staying with Mom."

He frowns, and I can see all the emotions spill over his face, from confusion through hurt to irritation. "But this is your room," he says.

Mom puts her hand over mine. "She said she doesn't want it, John. She can stay with me."

He just frowns deeper.

"This isn't a family vacation," Mom says, sharp. "You kidnapped us. We're not going to be staying here." She looks down at me. "Myka is tired. We barely slept last night, handcuffed in the back of a van. I suggest you take us to whatever room you've prepared for me, and we can get some sleep."

I am tired, suddenly. We've been through a lot in the past two days. More than I want to handle. I wobble. Dad stands there for another second, but then he nods and leads the way down the hall, to the next door. It's an identical-sized room, but this one has a yellow comforter—Mom's favorite color is yellow—and a brown leather chair. There's a shelf with art supplies and a few books.

"Can we fit another bed in here?" she asks.

"Not tonight," he says. He slams the door behind him, leaving Mom and me alone. For the first time I see the electronic lock on the door, like in a hotel. Except in this room you need a card to get out. We look at each other. I can't decide if I want to cry or laugh.

She shakes her head. "What have our lives become?"

I sigh. "Unstable."

That's my only word for it. In chemistry, when something's unstable...there could be an explosion.

The door opens again, and a woman pokes her head in. She's not in military uniform like most of the people here—she's in nice pants and a white shirt, like Mom would wear to work. She has blonde hair pulled back in a ponytail, and a sharp nose.

"Hi." She smiles, a little awkwardly. "I'm Dr. Liesel Miller. I'm working with John now."

Mom moves forward like she's going to slam the door in her face, but Liesel comes in further, holding out a hand to stop her. "I know, Jake's told you the unpleasant side of

73

things. How I tricked him into working for DARPA, how I kept him a prisoner and made him work for me." She licks her lips. "I promise, it wasn't like that. I was honestly trying to do the best thing for everyone."

"The best thing for our family?" Mom asks quietly. "I thought my son was dead because of you. You *ruined* us."

I thought he was dead too, for a while. Though with Dedushka's help I put together the clues and figured it out after a few weeks, that he was just taken somewhere. Still. I don't like her either.

Liesel grimaces. "I'm sorry. I didn't mean for..." She stops, takes a breath. "I was looking at the bigger picture. I wanted to help him *help* people. We did some good, finding terrorists, kidnapped little girls..."

"*I'm* a kidnapped girl," I say, as bold as I can. "I don't want to be here. And you started everything. I was just wishing we could go back, before...you."

"Get out," Mom says. "Now."

Liesel's face falls, and for half a second I feel sorry for her. "But I have clothes, toiletries..."

"Leave them and go," Mom says.

Liesel nods, slowly. She goes back out into the hall and brings in two duffel bags. She sets them on the floor by the door. "Bathrooms are next door. Just knock when you want to go. I'm sorry," she says again, quietly.

She closes the door gently. This time Mom and I don't talk it over at all. We just silently get ready for bed.

14

JAKE

Allies by MUTEMATH

I stare at the ceiling. From the light, it seems like early morning. I finally fell asleep for a little while, though I still feel groggy. I hear something outside, patter and a low rumbling. A thunderstorm.

When Myk was little, she was afraid of thunderstorms—they were too loud, too unpredictable. But I sat her down when she was about four and told her she had to face her fears if she didn't want to be stuck in them all the time, something Dad told me once. She took it literally, like she did everything then. Ever since that day, at the first sign of a thunderstorm she runs outside, starts dancing in the raindrops. Laughing at the thundering sky. I used to go with her.

Mom thought it was pure insanity, like we were daring lightning to strike us. She always would stand in the doorway and beg us to come back in. But we did it just the same. It was better than cowering.

My stomach growls, loud. I stretch, look around. There's no Jones. He snuck out at some point in the night, and I didn't notice. I'm alone.

I have to tunnel to Dedushka, just to tell him I'm all right. I promised him that. With him, I don't need anything but memory and privacy. I just have to concentrate on him, his real self, and I can reach him.

I think of him. His warmth, his gruffness. The way he smells, like cigars and fish. I find him, and feel a burst of relief...but he's in the motel, asleep. I can't do anything when I tunnel to someone who's asleep. It's useless. I come back out again.

I push out of the comfy bed. I'm not going to lie here anymore. It's time to test the boundaries.

I turn the door handle, carefully. It's unlocked. I guess he knows I won't leave. But I do want to explore, while I have the chance. See if I can find clues to where Mom and Myka are.

I lean out, check the walls. I don't see any cameras in the hallway. Now...left or right? Right is the dining area we were in last night, and there was only one door along the way. Left is the red room, with the one mysterious door on the other side that's guarded.

There's probably stairs somewhere too. I go for right, for the door on the way to the dining room. I'm tempted to sneak along the walls like they do on TV, but I'm 99% sure it wouldn't do any good. If there are cameras, they see me. If there aren't, there's no point.

I think of Eric suddenly, in the graveyard warning me about satellites on the first day I worked for DARPA. God, I was so naive then. So much has changed, in such a short time.

I've changed.

There's no one else around, no one pounding after me. When I get to the door I put one hand against it, take a deep breath, and push it open.

It's not stairs. It's another bedroom, identical to mine except with a spectacular view east, towards the Arboretum and the Anacostia river, the rain streaming down the window. And Bunny, lying in the bed blinking, staring up at me like I'm not real.

I freeze, not sure how much trouble I'm in. It's like a standoff of silent staring. Just when I'm about to back out she jumps to her feet, and waves me in. This room is bare like mine, nothing personal in it. She's wearing men's pajamas that are too big for her. I don't think she lives here.

This isn't what I was aiming for with the exploration, but I should see what happens. I close the door behind me. She puts a finger to her lips, urgently.

I stand there, arms hanging at my sides, just inside the door. Awkward. If I can't talk, why am I here?

She grabs a notebook from the bedside table, and a pen. She sits cross-legged at the head of the bed, against the pillows, and writes. Passes it to me, watching me closely.

I look at the page, since it's obvious she wants me to. *This room is bugged*, it says at the top. *But there aren't any cameras in here. There are in some of the other rooms.*

Of course. I suppose I should be glad he doesn't video the bedrooms.

She gestures for the pad back, and writes again. She hands it to me. Her writing is ridiculously neat, rounded, like a grade-school girl's. *He's insane. I'm sorry about last night. I'm dying to get out of this, away from here. We can go together.*

I barely keep from rolling my eyes at her. "Come on. I'm supposed to believe *you*?"

She slams her finger against her lips.

I shrug my shoulders. This is probably all some elaborate trick of Smith's to catch me out in something. I'm too tired to try to figure out what.

She writes on the page again and flips it over to show me, her eyes big. *You have to trust me. Smith is out this afternoon, so we might have a chance to talk later. There's a safe place. Until then, go back to your room. Act normal.*

Great. This woman already betrayed me, over and over. She's still working for the man who stole my family. And I'm supposed to act normal? I trust her about as far as I can throw her off the balcony.

Which, considering how small she is, is actually pretty far. But still. Trust? No.

She shoos me out, and I go. I stare at the door to the red room, considering whether I should go there next.

I stop at the bathroom and piss. Splash water on my face, not looking in the mirror. I can feel my face sagging from tiredness, and the cloud of exhaustion is surging back into my brain again. Jesus, two days of this and I'm a mess. Smith is way worse than Liesel.

Does Bunny really want to escape from him? I could use that, if she does. I can't leave, not with him holding Mom and Myka. I have to get them out first. But I could use her to find out where they are, to rescue them.

Of course she doesn't want to leave. She's lying. I can't trust a thing she says. I can't make that mistake again.

Or should I?

One thing I shouldn't do...go mildly back to my room when no one is keeping an eye on me. I open the door to the red room. I'm going to see what's behind that other door.

15

JAKE

Surprise Surprise by Billy Talent

Time to try that door they guard. There's got to be something there. Maybe it's Mom and Myka.

I run across the red room as fast as I can and try the door. I half-expect it to be locked, but the knob turns in my hand. I know there are cameras in here for sure, so they've probably seen me. I'd better move. I push through and shut the door behind me.

It's another hallway, matching the one on the other side. There are two doors on the left, then a corner. I have probably ten seconds before Joneses come busting after me.

I keep going. I need to check out as many places as possible before they shut me down, see if there are any clues.

First door: bathroom. I leave it swinging, push on to the next. This door opens too. It's a study, crammed floor to ceiling with books, and two plush chairs that match the one in the other room.

There's a boy sitting in one, a few years younger than me, a book on his lap. Skinny, pale. Fourteen or so, maybe. His dark hair is in a military buzz cut. He looks up when I open the door, but he's not startled. Just resigned.

"Yeah?" he asks, bored. He's barefoot, like me, and taps his feet on the carpet. "Does Mr. Smith need me?"

I stand there uselessly for too long, staring, putting clues together. This isn't a Jones, or a guest. Not from the way he reacted. This is someone like me.

"Who *are* you?" I ask, the words hot in my mouth. Footsteps barrel down the hall.

Time's up.

He frowns. Then he seems to really see me, my rumpled clothes, my bare feet, my stubbled face, and his eyes widen. "I'm Lucas. Who are you?"

"Jake," I manage, before someone strong pins my arms behind my back, yanks me out of the room. The door falls shut. I struggle, but I'm outmuscled by a lot. I'm pushed towards the red room, firmly.

"You want to spend some time handcuffed?" he asks in my ear, and I recognize the voice from last night. The skinny Jones who escorted me back to my room.

I grit my teeth. "No. Come on. I was just exploring."

He lets go of my arms with one hand for a second to open the red room door, and I turn around just enough to see Lucas standing in the hall, holding his book, watching. His mouth is a little open. He must've not known I was here. Just like I didn't know he was.

Who *is* he? He thought Smith needed him. But he's a kid. Does he have a talent Smith is using? A power?

80

Jones shoves me through the door so hard I stumble, almost smack into another Jones standing there. The huge one. Bunny stands behind the sofa in her pajamas, arms folded over her chest, hunched.

"That's off-limits," the big one growls. "Got it? You stay on your own side."

The skinny Jones behind me makes a show of locking the door. "You do that again, you will be cuffed to your closet, standing. For days. You'll be starving, pissing yourself. Crying. None of us want that—you're no good to anyone like that. And I, for one, have no desire to be cleaning up puddles of your piss. So stay out of there."

I look at the door, imagining Lucas behind it. A whole story I know nothing about. I'll find out—I have to. But I'll have to come at it a different way.

"Got it," I say, straight-faced. "Nobody wants puddles of piss."

Jones smiles a little, I swear, even though his face hardly moves. "Go on, then. Back to your own room. We've got damage control to do now."

Damage control. Explaining to Lucas who I am, probably. I wonder what they'll say. Probably something that's nowhere near close to the truth. I look at Bunny, but she shrugs and points to the hall. I go, slowly.

Who the hell is Lucas?

16

RACHEL

Just a Girl by No Doubt

We slept in a fleabag motel—though I hardly slept at all, thinking of the thin door of the motel, and what happened to Vladimir even with a sturdy door. I keep picturing him there on the bed, so weirdly and finally still. Picturing poor Doreen crying for him.

I don't want to end up like Doreen. Or dead like Vladimir. Or taken like Myka and Abby and Jake. Man. Dedushka and I are the only ones left out here, still hanging out in the world. That's pretty bad odds, Dad would say.

I stare at the popcorn ceiling, imagining where everyone is—including Dad, and Mom. Where does Mom think I am? Was that cruel of me to leave her, after Dad did? Did I do the wrong thing?

I wonder if people ever feel sure they did the right thing. I don't. Except maybe applying to Berkeley. I was always pretty sure about that. And then I got in, and all I had to do was ride out the summer...

And I'm back to whether I did the right thing.

Dedushka rolls out of bed, glances over at me, and grunts at me to get ready. He seemed to sleep fine, snoring all night. He's got the constitution of a bull.

We have apples for breakfast, while he tells me his plan.

He wants to drive north towards Tampa, dump the car, do a bit of subterfuge, and then pick up another one. We don't know where to go today anyway. We can talk over the clue on the way, he says, and see what we can figure out together.

Seems all right. I don't have a better idea. Except…I'm tired of being passive and letting everyone else take the lead.

"I'd like to drive," I say, on the way out.

"No," Dedushka snaps, and slides into the driver's seat.

I stand there for a second, stunned. No? Just like that? He glances at me through the windshield—like he's going to give me one more minute before he drives away without me—and I get in on the passenger side. He takes off before I can even get my seatbelt on.

I feel the heat rising in my face. "Why not?"

He gives me the briefest of glances. "Why not drive? You do not know where to go."

"I could figure it out. I can follow signs. And you could tell me." I take a breath. "Do you realize I haven't driven since we met up with you? It's been you or Jake, the whole time. Even when we drove from New Mexico to Virginia. Why is that? Don't you trust me?"

He's silent, for too long. He navigates onto a freeway heading north, while I burn holes in his profile.

This is just like my dad, deciding he knows best for everyone. Like Jake.

"Well?" I say, once we're settled in a lane.

"You are a girl." He shrugs, not looking at me. "Girls are not good drivers."

I suck in my breath, hard. Wow, there it is. I didn't think he was actually that much of a Neanderthal. "I can't believe

83

anyone actually thinks things like that anymore, much less says them. Do you know how sexist that is?"

He grips the wheel tightly, his gnarled knuckles turning white. "I do not know this word."

"I bet," I mutter. I stare at those knuckles, at all the lines on his face. He's old, sure. And Russian. Do I let it go, this ridiculous old-man sexist opinion of me and what I can do, because he's old, and Jake's grandfather, and I'm supposed to be polite? Or do I challenge him?

I can't let it go.

"You won't know unless you try," I say.

He answers by raising his Groucho Marx eyebrows.

"Look, I don't know where you got your opinion," I say, letting the sarcasm drip through. "But I—an individual, not just a girl—am a great driver. Better than you, or at least better than Jake, who drives too fast. So maybe if you'd get your head out of...the 18th century, you'd see that."

He frowns, but I think I see a glimmer in his eyes. I look at the ocean flashing past him, past us. We're silent for a lot of miles, neither looking at the other. I stare outside at the green, flat landscape. Maybe he's mad, but I couldn't just be quiet. He's *wrong*. Wrong wrong wrong. I'm glad I said something. Let him be mad. More miles go by. I fold my arms and don't look at him.

But then I remember a sign we had on the wall in the library, near the customer complaints desk: 'It's better to be happy than right.' I never knew if it was for the librarians or the customers.

I'm still right. But I'm tired of being mad, and it's not helping anything. It might be time to make peace. I take a deep breath after we pass a sign for the airport. "Anyway. We need to solve the clue. What is 'the place you love most'? That Vladimir would know about?"

He's quiet for so long I think he's going to just freeze me out. I watch him for a while, completely still except for his beard moving with his breath, then turn back to the road, to my own thoughts. Maybe it is time to leave, if he won't work with me. If he has that little respect for me. What is this helping? How am I helping?

Maybe I really should go back home and face Mom. Stand up to her too.

"Da," he says, gruff. He still doesn't look at me. "I have been thinking of this. What I love most. There is home in Russia—but I did not love that, and Vlad knows. Home in Standish—da, I love this, but he could not get there. And we could not. It is too far."

"A place," I say. "Have you been here before? To Florida? Could it be somewhere around here?"

He shrugs. "I have. To see Vlad, once, twice, a long time ago. But no love of it, yes? It could not be this."

We go quiet again. I put my feet up on the dashboard, which just makes me realize I desperately need a new set of clothes, and shoes. My sneakers have a hole on the side. My shorts are scruffy and dirty. I should get some sandals anyway.

Except I'm on the run. I can't go buying shoes. It's strange, but sometimes I miss the mall, the normalcy of shopping with friends, somewhere I've been every year of my life. And the library even more, the familiar smell of books, the spaces I know so well I could walk through with my eyes closed.

"What if it's not a specific place?" I ask, suddenly. "What if it's a type of place you love? Something you always do, wherever you are?"

Dedushka thinks, taps the wheel for a while. Then he smiles, slow and warm. "Fishing. Vlad knows this very well."

Part of the tension in my chest loosens. "Okay, fishing. Good. Let's try that. There's a lot of fishing in Florida. So now we just have to figure out how you would go fishing with Sara, and what number 56 means."

"A boat slip, 56," he says, sounding completely certain. "But where, the Sara, we will have to find."

"Sarasota?" I say. "There's Sara in the name."

He glances at me, with another smile. This one feels like it's for me. Like he's pleased I'm here, finally. Like I'm really helping.

"Da," he says. "Maybe so."

I hug my arms to my chest and sit back, watch green Florida fly by. We don't talk about much until we get to Tampa, leave the car in a parking lot, take a cab to St. Petersburg, then take another car. This one, an old Honda, he starts with a mini-screwdriver. Once he has it started, he slides over, and points to the driver's seat.

"I will not know unless I try, *milaya*," he says.

I laugh, and drop into the driver's seat. Finally. "Hang on."

17

MYKA

Set Fire to the Rain by Adele

A woman with a fat, sleek bun, dressed in full uniform, comes and gets me after breakfast. She says Dad requested to see me, "to get to know each other again." Mom doesn't want to let me go, but I say it's all right.

I admit, I'm curious about him. Practically, what he did doesn't make sense. Why leave his family to come here? Why so dramatically, pretending to be dead? What does he want?

If I think about it like a puzzle, something I can solve, then it doesn't hurt as much. Maybe I can find the reason. Maybe I can reverse the reason.

I mean, I know it can't go back to the way it was before he left. Too much has happened. Too many bad things. Except...the Dad I remember was focused on his work, strict, even gone a lot of the time...but he also gave crushing hugs, and read to me at night, and listened to me even when I talked too much. He was the only one. And he was really good at asking questions to help me figure out whatever I was thinking about.

How did that Dad become *this* Dad, running a secret base?

But he's still trying to be that Dad, setting up a room the way he thinks I'd like it.

It's a puzzle.

So I follow the soldier-woman down a long hallway, then left, to a door at the end. She knocks briskly and waits for him to reply before opening the door and pointing me inside.

The office looks just the same as the one he had in the Pentagon, almost the same as the home offices he had at each base. A plain metal desk, with nothing on top except an open laptop and a phone. I know he keeps everything, carefully organized, in the drawers. Jake used to sneak in and mess things up on purpose. I never did. The entire back wall is metal bookshelves, almost full with reference books.

He looks up and smiles that thin, tired smile from last night, and waves me in.

I stand inside the door, uncertain. Seeing him, it feels like I shouldn't be here. Like it's a betrayal of Jake, of Mom. I stare at my feet.

"Come in, Myka," he says, his voice a little impatient. "Sit down. We need to talk."

I bite my lip, but I remember the puzzle, and I go sit in the chair. At first I keep my eyes on the desk, but after it's silent for a few minutes, I look up.

"There she is," he says.

My heart squeezes. He used to say that when I was little, whenever he came home from a trip. I don't say my line, which is "here I am."

"Why are you here?" I say instead.

He sighs, and runs a hand through his short hair. It's definitely grayer than it used to be. "I'm here because I'm heading a remarkable project that could change the world. For the better. I'm here because I'm the best possible person—some say the only person—who can do it. If we can isolate what makes Jake different from anyone else, if we can recreate it...the uses are mind-boggling."

"Super-soldiers," I whisper.

His eyes narrow. "Not just that. Jake was doing a lot of good too, with DARPA. He can help people. We could do that here as well. We could multiply it."

I frown. He's right...in theory. But he's also military. And he and the military are keeping this project secret for a reason. They kept the development of the atom bomb a secret too—so they could get it right before their enemies did. Jake, and possible copies, are weapons.

But that's not what I'm most interested in. I admit, I want to know *how* he's trying to replicate Jake's power. Is he manipulating DNA? Isolating some element in Jake's blood? I shouldn't care. I know that's not the point, not the puzzle I want to solve. I should be against him trying this at all, period.

"Do you even have Jake's blood, or his DNA, to work with?" I blurt, before I can stop myself. "You weren't involving him when you left. That's what he said."

Dad grins, and he looks more like I remember him. "There's my girl. Blood, DNA, and stem cells. Every time he went to the doctor, after I knew about his tunneling, there were a few extra tests." He looks proud. "Base doctors do what I like. Jake never asked why. But we're having some luck with the stem cells. Combined with...another source I found. I think we may actually have something, very soon."

I sit back, hard, in the chair. More people with powers under the control of the military. That's terrible news.

But it's interesting. Stem cells....

No. "Why did you pretend to be dead?" I ask, my voice sharp and accusing.

He sits back too, and is silent for a while, looking at me. I wonder if he's figuring out how to tell me or figuring out how to lie, or deflect.

"It was a mistake," he says.

I blink. "Really?"

"Really. I went along with the plan because I was told that was the only way to do the work. And I believe in the work. But in retrospect..." His gray eyes are steady. "It was wrong, to you, to your mother and Jake. I should've done it another way."

I take a few breaths, thinking. That doesn't make me feel better. I expected it to, but it doesn't.

Maybe the other puzzle will.

"Tell me more about the stem cells?" I ask.

He grins again. "How about I give you a tour?"

18

JAKE

Madhatter by Henry Ate

I guess somebody decides I stink, because they bring me new clothes. Nice-ish Jones hands me jeans and a white T-shirt, tells me to take a shower first *for God's sake* and shave, and then they'll give me some breakfast.

It's my first shower in a couple of days. I'm thrilled to scrub some of the muck off. The first few minutes feel like a miracle of sensation. And showers wake up the brain, make it easier to think. For once I'm don't worry about Mom or Myka or Rachel or Dedushka. I think about that boy in there, on the other side of a couple doors. Used to being here. Used to psychotic Smith needing him for something. He could be a genius, I guess, like Myk. Could have some special knowledge needed by a guy like Smith: technology, math. But Smith used to work in the program Dad ran, with Liesel, on using paranormal abilities. He's still so deeply entwined in it that he has Bunny spying for him.

The kid's got some kind of power, I'd bet on it. Not the same as mine, or he wouldn't need two of us. But what? And

91

how? I've never heard of anyone else with a power except Dedushka.

I shave, scraping thick stubble off. I was almost to beard level. I eye the razor, briefly, a generic blue one. They never let me have this kind in Montauk, for fear I'd use it as a weapon. But could I really do anything dangerous with a safety razor?

Not dangerous enough to be worth it.

When I step out I actually do feel refreshed, like a new person again. Exactly like Smith intended me to, for whatever sick reason he has. I read about manipulation of prisoners once in one of Dad's books. You withhold something for long enough, a normal human need or habit, and the prisoner is actually grateful to you when you give it back.

I'm grateful to be clean. And I'm about to be grateful for food. So I guess he wins that little battle.

I need to ask Bunny for information, whenever she arranges for us to go to her secret bug-less place. She knows about Lucas. Hell, she probably works with Lucas, with whatever he does. And somehow, I've got to get her to tell me. Trust that she really does want to get out of here, and not that she's manipulating me again for Smith, or herself somehow.

I have trouble trusting anyone. I wonder why.

Soon after I get dressed, there's a knock on my door and nice-ish Jones escorts me to the dining room. "Better," he says, and winks as he opens the door for me. He straightens his tie and stands there next to the dining room door, a tiny smile hanging on his face.

I go in. Bunny is in her place across the table, squinting up at me. Smith is sitting at the head again. He smiles. "Please, Mr. Lukin. Sit."

Crap. She said he wouldn't be here this afternoon—I was hoping he was already gone. I wasn't planning for a repeat performance of last night.

I sit carefully, like there might be snakes on my chair. Who knows, there might be. He'd probably have fun with that. And he's got to be majorly pissed off about me finding Lucas.

"You, Mr. Lukin, were not pleased to see me just now."

I swallow, look across at Bunny. Her face is pure blankness.

"Just surprise," I say. Which is dumb, because, what, I'm pretending I'm happy to see him?

"And I hear you've had an eventful morning. One impossible thing before breakfast: discovering one of my secrets."

Here it comes.

He shakes out a folded white napkin from his plate—they're all in shapes, like little hats—lays it across his lap with a flourish, and tsks. "I didn't think I actually needed to spell out to you that you ought to stay in the areas I've taken you. But I should have known better." He raises an eyebrow. "You always have been a troublemaker, haven't you? I still don't even know how you escaped from Montauk. Cecile here..." He points his big chin at her, and she flinches. "She wasn't able to tell me."

Cecile. That's new information. I shake my own napkin out, the linen heavy, and spread it on my lap. I'm suddenly reminded of Mom's State dinners, all those diplomats talking to each other over a table like this. Is it this tense, sometimes? At least I know all the rules, because of Mom. She used to make napkins like this for practice. Bishop's hats. I tried too, though I could never get them to sit up straight.

I can't forget that he has Mom. Has her hidden somewhere, with Myk, like he has me. And Lucas.

"Would you like to tell me how you escaped from Montauk?" Smith asks.

I twitch, involuntarily. That is absolutely the last thing I would like to tell him. He has no idea that I can take people over when I tunnel, if I want to. I didn't discover it myself until after I'd been in Montauk for a while, after the DARPA scientists kept pushing me. I can't imagine how he'd use that power if he knew about it. I'd probably be tunneling to people and shooting, left and right. Or signing checks, or contracts. "No," I say, grasping at calm. "I think I'd prefer to keep that a mystery."

"Ah." He nods, his eyes bright, like that's what he expected. "What if I told you who Lucas is? Would you tell me your secret in exchange?"

I swallow, then shake my head. If I could think of a good enough lie, and lie to him without him knowing, I would. If he offers Mom and Myka back, I'll probably try that. But I can never tell him the real reason, no matter what he offers.

"Oh, dear." His eyebrows curve. "It must be a good secret. I'll have to see what I can find out on my own."

Shit. I really hope he can't.

The door opens, and the blond Jones comes in with a bowl of scrambled eggs. I try to meet Bunny's eye as I scoop a spoonful, but she doesn't look at me. She stares at the wall behind me like a bunny trying to pretend it's invisible. The Jones serves Smith and Bunny, leaves the bowl on the table, and brings back a platter of bacon and buttered toast.

We eat silently for a while, which is a relief. Talking to Smith is like talking to the Red Queen in Alice in Wonderland. He might chop off your head at any second.

After Jones brings us coffee, though, I'm ready to try again.

"So what can Lucas do?" I ask.

94

Bunny startles, but Smith just eyes me appreciatively. "Perceptive *and* bold. Well, it's quite simple. Tell me yours, and I'll tell you mine."

"Tell me where my family is," I throw back. "There are lots of things I'll tell you then."

Bunny jerks and spills her glass of water, which cascades all over Smith's side. He jumps up, swearing, and calls for a Jones. Two run in from the kitchen and mop up the mess.

Smith brushes at the patches of wet on his pants, glaring at Bunny. "I think that's enough for you for the moment. You're clearly too nervous to eat with us. Mr. Lukin rattles something in you, doesn't he, Miss Milkovich?"

Bunny switches her cheek color to red, but doesn't answer. She just glances at me once, like she's trying to communicate something–I have no idea what–then walks around the table and heads out the door behind me. Smith moves to her place, since it's dry. As soon as the Joneses are done cleaning up, he tells them to bring more coffee, and eyes me curiously.

"So what happens to you when you take this medicine, again? That's another interesting twist."

"Tell me where my family is and I'll tell you," I say.

He laughs again, ugly. "No, that's not an equal trade at all. I'm just making conversation, Mr. Lukin."

He looks at my empty plate and pushes the bowl of eggs towards me. I take more, and more bacon. You never know when he'll kick me out too. You eat when you can, here.

"All right," I say, after a swallow. "Tell me what Lucas can do, and I'll tell you about the medicine."

He tilts his head. "Better. But still too valuable on my part. How about...you tell me about the medicine, and I'll tell you *who* Lucas is."

I think, take a bite of the bacon. God, it's good. Crispy, salty.

The man is a lunatic, but he has good taste in food.

I take a deep breath, swallow, and tell him about the hallucinations. I'm trading, so I'm fair about it. I give him details, tell him how they tried to hide it from me at Montauk. How the hallucinations got worse the more medicine I took. He asks questions, and I answer. I know I'm giving him ammunition against myself if he wanted to find more of those pills, stuff me full of them, drive me mad. But I suspect he wants to keep me sane, at least while I'm here. I'm more *useful* that way, like Bunny said. I'm working voluntarily.

I finish telling him just as I eat the last of my food. "Now you."

"Now me." He clears his throat, sets his napkin next to his empty, greasy plate. "Lucas Payne, my dear boy, is your half-brother."

I don't move. Don't even blink. I watch him, entranced, like he's a cobra. "I don't have a half-brother," I say, finally.

"No, that's not quite accurate." He pushes back from the table, stands. I stand too. My legs are shivery, and I grip the back of the chair. "You didn't *know* you had a half-brother. On your father's side, with a lovely lady he worked with on one of those bases. I...well. I ran across him, and I snapped him right up. The family resemblance is there, don't you think? In more ways than one."

I shake my head. It's not possible. I would've known. Somehow.

But my talent doesn't stretch to sensing other siblings. He did look like me a little, I guess. Like Dad. But that doesn't mean anything. Smith's got to be lying. He always lies.

"Isn't this a lovely revelation?" Smith smiles wide. "Two talented brothers, under one roof. Almost a full set."

Or he isn't lying, and Dad had another kid I never knew about. More lies. I feel like I've been punched in the gut by Dad, long-distance. Again.

"Almost?" I say, hollow. He has Myka too. He *has* a full set.

"Go," Smith says. He waves a hand. "Go on and get some rest. You look like you didn't sleep at all, and I need your brain later." He puts his hands on his hips, fake-stern. "And no going to visit your brother, now. You won't get in there again."

I stand there, lost in thought. One of the Joneses takes me by the arm and pulls me out, to the bathroom first, then back to the room. He locks the door behind me. "Don't try anything," he growls. "We're watching you."

I ignore him. I have a half-brother with a power?

If/when I do get out of here with my family, I'm going to have to take him with me.

19

JAKE

Everything Sux by Descendents

I decide even if they're "watching me," I'm still going to try to tunnel to Dedushka. I close my eyes, lie down on the bed, and focus. Dedushka. His yellowish smile, his bear hugs when I was little. His pipe-smell. I sense him. In Florida, in Sarasota...

The door slams open. "Be out in two minutes," the big Jones growls, and slams it shut again. I rub my eyes. It's always hard when I get jerked away suddenly from tunneling. Like when your alarm goes off at 3 am, in the middle of a vivid dream.

I feel like I'm never going to connect with Dedushka. Never going to find Mom and Myka. I wonder if they're even in this building. Are they nearby? Could I walk to them, if I left? If I only had something of theirs, I could tunnel straight to them and it wouldn't even be an issue.

Maybe Lucas can find them. Maybe his talent is different enough that I can use it, somehow.

Damn. Maybe I'm just like everyone else, wanting to use him for my own purposes before I've even met him properly.

I head out to the big room. Big Jones stands behind the sofa, Bunny sits on it. Smith is behind the desk. It's like a set for a play, a command performance. I almost say something smart-ass, but I skip it this morning, go straight to my spot on the sofa quietly. Smith's face looks dangerous.

"He wants proof that I know his secrets?" he mutters. "Very well, I'll give him proof."

Bunny clears her throat, glances at Smith, then passes over a girl's slipper, fuzzy and white, with tiny brown and black dogs all over it. I don't want to do it. I hate doing kids' stuff, in case it's bad. "Now?" I ask.

Smith's hands are folded on the desk, his bright eyes scary. "Why do you think I brought you here? Yes, *now.*"

I close my eyes, let the tingle come.

It's a girl, fourteen or fifteen. Dark hair matted, horror stamped on her face. She huddles in the corner of a wire dog cage, set in the middle of a vast, empty warehouse. Clearwater, Florida. The Clearwater 19 Commerce Center, number 22131. She's terrified–no, terrified doesn't begin to cover it. She's broken, little sobs coming from her chest. There's a man with her, standing above the cage staring down through the bars. He grins. He's small, muscles bulging grotesquely on his arms. Black, evil eyes.

"Are you ready to go to your new owners, puppy? It's almost time to move." His voice is deep, scratching. He leans over, his face close to the mesh of the cage. "I can't say you'll like it much, but at least you'll have a bed..."

She closes her eyes. She just wants to go back home.

I feel pressure on my shoulders, and I come out of it, open my eyes. Blink. Try to breathe. It feels like I forgot how.

"We have to get her," I whisper. "Right now. Send the cops in and free her."

"Get out of here," Smith snaps. His jaw twitches.

"But..." I start.

"GET OUT," he growls, spit flying. He frowns, puts his hand flat on the desk, and lowers his voice. "Miss Milkovich, take Mr. Lukin to his room, lock him in. Jones, I need..." he glances at me. "Bring me Lucas immediately."

Okay, I want to stay. *Need* to stay, to hide out behind the door or something so I can hear, so I can see what Lucas can do for him, what Smith's up to. How is Lucas going to help? Are they going to get that girl? Jesus. They have to save her, before it's too late, before that man moves her.

Maybe I can swipe something of Smith's, a pencil or anything, so I can tunnel to *him* and listen in.

But Bunny hustles me up and out, Smith's eagle eyes on us the whole time. I try to stop her once the door is shut behind us, but she keeps pulling, shaking her head.

"But that girl—" I say.

She presses her lips together. I could overpower her— she's so tiny—and listen anyway. But there are cameras. He'd check to make sure I'm not here. He'd send a Jones after us.

Damn.

I follow her back to my room, but she doesn't leave right away. She comes in with me, quiet, and writes on her notepad. She shows it to me, flashing it like a shield.

I have something for you to tunnel with, for us. We have to find some time to do it. This afternoon. On the balcony. There aren't cameras there.

100

I write back. *Do you have an object for Smith? Can I tunnel to him now?*

She shakes her head emphatically, her hair swinging.

I write. *We need to get that girl out.*

She holds the notebook tight against her chest. She looks so sad. Almost as broken as the girl.

There's a massive bang, and we spring to opposite sides of the room. Another. I think he's pounding on the wall. *He needs me*, she writes, her fingers shaking. *Later.*

She glances back at me once, then goes out. I hear the lock turn.

And I'm stuck in here again. Clueless, useless. Just when I really need to know what the hell is going on out there. When I need to *help*.

That little girl, younger than Myka. I don't know what Smith was trying to get—he said he needed proof of someone's secret. Is he going to even think of rescuing her, or is he just going to use whatever info he gets for blackmail?

I know the answer, like a stab in the heart. He's not going to save her.

What could Lucas possibly do that would help?

Thank God again that Smith doesn't know what I really can do. If he knew that, and he could combine me with whatever Lucas's talent is...fuck. He could practically rule the world.

But I don't want to rule the world. All I want, right now, is save that one girl.

I press my ear to the wall. I can hear voices, muffled. Smith's, and then a higher one. I'm guessing it's Lucas. Again I wish my power were something else, that I could hear through walls. But that kind of wishing never ends.

I know what I can do, right now, while everyone else is distracted. I can tunnel to Dedushka.

I get comfortable on the bed, squeeze my eyes shut, and think of him.

The sweet smell of his pipe. His full white beard, brushed even when we were at the cabin. His obsession with Russian novels he's probably read a thousand times. His cranky, prickly personality…stirred in with a good dose of love he tries not to show.

This heat, it is unbearable. How do these people stand this, day after day?

There he is. I dive in. He's at a small cafe in Sarasota, Florida (still!), chugging a glass of water. He wipes his beard with the back of his hand.

This place. Too much heat for this old man.

He's alone at the table, and my stomach clenches. Rachel's not there anymore. She left.

Dedushka, I say in his mind, in the way I only can with him and Myka.

Though I need an object for Myka, or this would all have been a lot easier.

It's Jake. I'm here, Dedushka.

Yakob? I feel the relief cascade through him. *The little voice. You are all right?*

I nudge him toward the pen and paper on the table in front of him, the check. It's easier to communicate with him that way. I fill him, use his hand to flip it over and write. Quickly. I don't want to stick, and I don't want another headache, after just tunneling.

I am fine. With Smith in D.C., though I will find a way out. I have allies.

102

I think of Bunny. That may be too strong a word, and she may be playing me. But I don't want him to worry and come try to rescue me, not yet.

Who is Lucas? I write. *Have you heard of him before? Smith has him.*

"I have heard this name," Dedushka says aloud, tugging fingers through his beard. "I do not know who."

"Are you talking to Jake? Is that Jake?"

Rachel. She's here after all. She drops into the other chair, staring into his face, tears in her eyes. "Is he okay?" she whispers.

Oh, Jesus, I missed her.

I lift Dedushka's hand, run it gently across her cheek. It feels different against his calloused fingers. "Are you all right?" I say in his voice.

She nods, grabs his hand. "You're okay? Where are you?"

"I'm okay," I say. "I'm in D.C. See you soon."

I pull away, breathing hard. I did it. They're fine, and together. That's all I needed to know.

20

RACHEL

The Dock of the Bay by Sara Bareilles

Jake's in D.C. That's not enough information to do anything with, so Dedushka and I decide to keep looking for the serum.

Thank God he's all right, though. If not safe, he's managing. I can breathe a little easier.

Dedushka and I stand on the dock of the Sara Bay Marina, peeking through the locked gate. You can see slip 56 from here, just around the corner.

Vladimir's clue wasn't too hard to figure out after all, once we looked at a directory of marinas after lunch.

It's a nice boat, a 28-foot Bayliner, though it looks like it's an old one. I used to go out on the water with my dad sometimes, in the summers. I wouldn't drive a boat in a race or anything, but I know where everything is, for the most part.

Which doesn't help us, since Vlad's boat is on the other side of this closed gate, with a passcode lock. I look to Dedushka for ideas. I don't know if the management people are even around. Does he want to bluff his way in? Wait for someone else to come out and slip through? He hasn't said so far. He just walked up, wrapped his fingers around the white iron gate, and stared at the water. He's still staring, the other hand combing his beard.

Of course we're both in a lot better mood than we were an hour ago. Jake's okay. That makes such a difference. My doubts about staying, or going back home, are wiped away. We do this, get the serum, meet up with Jake, and we're *done.*

I'm ready to be done. I feel like I've been running on adrenaline for weeks. I'm so tired.

"So..." I start. But it's like he's a toy and my voice activated him: he steps forward to the keypad and punches in six numbers. The gate opens with a click.

"Um. How did you *do* that?"

He snorts, but there's no pleasure in it. "Vlad I know. He would not send me here if it was not a code I knew." He swallows hard, and I see his eyes shining. He grunts. "I need a pipe."

He strides through the gate without looking back. I have to grab it before it slams shut in front of me, and follow.

I don't think Dedushka forgets Vladimir for a second. I do, a lot of the time. I can forget the larger picture of what's going on, and deal with what's in front of me. I've always been able to do that when things got tough. Dad could too. That's why we could live with Mom. Maybe it's a kind of survival technique.

But every once in a while, as Dad used to say, reality can come up and bite you in the ass. I think that just happened to Dedushka.

By the time I get to slip 56 Dedushka is already on the boat, like he's been here every day of his life.

"Cast off," he orders. "Then get on."

"I...we're going out on it? I thought we were just looking. How did you even get the keys?"

He turns and gives me his trademark glare, and I shrug and untie the bright yellow cord, then unwind it from the hook. There's no point arguing with him, not when he's like that. I've learned that much. There's a second tie in the front. I get it and jump on before the boat swings too far away, just as he fires up the engine. He adjusts a couple of things, then we move forward, slow and smooth. I sit on the back bench and let the salt breeze cool my face, ruffle my hair. I close my eyes. It feels like old times for a second, like Dad is up there at the wheel and Mom is making drinks, we're out on the lake for the day, and all I have to do is be the good daughter and relax.

No. Dad ran off to Hawaii, Mom lost her mind, and I took off with Jake because I couldn't deal with it, and other people's problems seemed easier. There's no point pretending otherwise. But I can sit here for a bit and enjoy the breeze, the motion that I remember. Go back to this moment I'm in, and not think of all the complications. I breathe deep, letting the ocean tang fill my lungs, feeling the sun beat down on my eyelids. Slow my heartbeat. Like meditation. Only the breath. Only here, now. This moment. I like this moment.

When I wake up we're anchored in a bay, rocking gently, and Dedushka is perched on a camp chair across from me, smoking a pipe. There's a big red umbrella over my head, giving me shade. He grunts when I sit up and rub my eyes.

"You needed this sleep," he says.

"And I got it, I guess." I look around, still a bit groggy. We're in shallow flats, with a sandy strip of land next to us crowded with bushes and grass. It's so dense I can't even see into it. I yawn. "Where are we?"

He scratches his jaw. "There was a GPS number in a drawer, and that is all. So I go there, on a try. Stump Pass State Park, the map says."

"Okay." I stand, shade my eyes. The sun is tilted toward the west—it must be close to two or so. If he hadn't put the umbrella over me, I'd be a lobster by now. I struggle to wake up, to think clearly. "We're on the GPS coordinates?"

"It is there—" He points with the stem of his pipe. "On the shore. I thought to wait until you wake. Every vegetable has its time."

I laugh so suddenly and loudly he jerks. "What? Every vegetable..."

He shrugs, his lips quirked up around the pipe. "A saying."

106

"I hope this doesn't mean you think I'm a vegetable," I say. I study the shore, the flat sand. "Do you think the serum is buried there? Like treasure?"

I can't squash the excitement that bubbles up in my chest. I know it's a vial of serum we're looking for, not a chest of gold coins. But I devoured Treasure Island and Blackbeard stories when I was a kid. I was a pirate for Halloween three years in a row. And we actually are on the Florida coast, where all that stuff happened. Ten-year-old me is *thrilled*.

He shrugs again, which is Dedushka for *We won't know until we look.*

He hands me a cup of water and a peanut butter and jelly sandwich. Vladimir must've stocked the boat with the same food that was in his house. I'm not really hungry, but I devour it—sometimes a PB&J tastes exactly right—then borrow an old-man fishing hat so I don't bake. We drop into the cool, shallow water for the hike in.

Even if we're not pirates searching for gold, I think Vladimir must've enjoyed setting this up. It's certainly more exciting than if the serum had been in the stadium locker in his shoe. And much more beautiful, with the too-blue sky, the clear water, the brilliant green of the head-high bushes on the shore.

I suddenly remember I'm in Florida, think about alligators, and move faster. That part I'm not so excited about. I don't know anything about them. What should I do if I see one?

Run, probably. Or maybe that's exactly the wrong thing to do. I wish I'd read about it sometime.

It takes longer to get to shore than I thought it would, pushing through the cool water, but I get there before Dedushka. He looks like Santa splashing through the surf, holding the GPS in one hand, his pants rolled up to his knees and still getting wet. Though he seems to be having fun too. He gives me a small grin when he reaches the shore, and I remember that the whole clue was that this was the place he most loved. Boats, the water.

"Better than a road trip?" I ask.

"*Idialnii*," he says, unrolling his pants. I guess that's good.

He checks the GPS again, and points into the brush. "We will be scratched." He eyes my shorts and t-shirt.

"That's okay," I say, breezily. After everything else, I'm not worried about a little scratching. He plunges in, and I follow.

Five feet in and I'm bleeding. There is zero room to move without evil little branches and rough-edged blades of grass attacking, no way to dodge. It seems like nothing and no one has been in here for a long time. I can't even see behind me, except for the slight trail we've made. There's no choice but to push through. The bushes are pungent, a sharp green smell.

We go on like that, making slight turns, for about ten minutes, and five hundred scratches, when he holds up a hand and stops. It looks exactly like every other part we've walked through, except there's a wide, flat rock at his feet.

"Under that?"

"Let us try," he says. "It is the GPS number."

We drop to our knees and dig in the sandy, thin soil with our hands. The sand keeps falling back in the hole after we dig it, and I violently wish for a shovel, or at least some water we could pour on it to make the digging easier. That's what I always did when I made sandcastles. I kind of hoped that the serum would be right there, just under the rock, but of course it isn't. Vladimir wouldn't have made it that easy.

We dig, and dig, the sun blazing on our backs. I don't know how long. Now I just want water to drink, a gallon of it. But at long last, I hit something solid. We look at each other and start to dig faster, more intensely, dirt flying in the air, like dogs. Until we uncover the box.

Dedushka reaches his gnarled hands in and lifts the box, sand trickling from it. It's dark wood, inlaid with a carving that's crusted with dirt. It has four round legs, like a jewelry box. He studies it, holding it at eye level, then hands it to me. It's heavy.

I rest it in my lap, and try to lift the lid. There's no latch or anything, though, and nothing happens. I try again. "It's stuck shut," I say. "Or locked."

Dedushka raises his eyebrows and smiles, lopsided. He looks like a deranged bear. "Is a Polish box. There is a trick. Hold it up?"

I raise it. In one quick motion he twists the front two legs forward, and the lid opens with a snap. I lower it to look. Nestled inside a red velvet interior is one glass vial, filled with a bright red liquid. It looks like blood.

Dedushka takes the box, runs a finger over the vial. "Red for stop," he says, soft. "Milena's idea."

I sit back on my heels. "Red for stop...for stopping the power?" After he nods, it hits me, like a slap in the face. "Wait. Please don't tell me if there was a red, there was a green. Green for go."

He looks guilty. "She made green first, to see how it worked, how they started powers. To understand how to make red." He closes the box and tucks it under his arm. "Vladimir destroyed it all, that one."

"God, I hope so. That's all Smith or Liesel or Jake's dad would need. A handy serum to make anyone like him."

Dedushka bites his lip. "If anyone asks, you do not know this, yes? There never was green serum."

"If anyone asks, I'm mute."

I fill in the hole while Dedushka stands and stretches like an old gray cat. We did it. We have the red serum. Now we can connect with Jake in D.C., he can take it, and hopefully this whole thing will be over.

I set the rock back over the hiding place. We just have to get Jake away from Smith.

Dedushka carries the box back out through the scratch-happy bushes, and I follow again, trying my best to hold them back. We're almost to shore when I come up hard against him, standing still. He raises a hand, and points. I peek around him and gasp.

There's a police boat tethered to ours.

21

MYKA

Bad Blood by Taylor Swift

Dad tours me around the base for a couple of hours at least. He's so proud of it, every inch. There are two full labs, with white-coated techs working with tissue samples and petri dishes in one, and chemical mixtures in another. I itch to go into that one, to see exactly what they're working on. To try out a few things myself. I wonder if I could help.

I'd definitely rather be there than in my fake bedroom.

We move on to a room where a scientist is testing a soldier, having him hold an object and try to tunnel. It doesn't work, but they keep trying. Then through a bunch of diagnostic machines—an MRI, a CT, an EEG. And then a whole lot of boring plain rooms: offices, housing, a big lunchroom. Dad suggests we have lunch here.

I'm hungry, but I don't want to have cafeteria food with Dad in front of a crowd of soldiers, everyone watching us. I think I'm ready to go back to Mom now, and eat with her. She's probably worried, with me gone this long. I shake my head. "I'd rather have lunch with Mom."

He looks a little hurt, but he shrugs. "Fine. I have one last thing to show you first. A big thing."

110

Back in his office, he sits in his chair, and tells me to sit. Then he pulls something out of one of his drawers and nudges it across the desk towards me. It's a wooden box, some dark wood. It has a crest of a bird carved in the top. I look up at Dad.

"Open it," he says. "We'll see how long it takes you."

I frown. Okay. It's a box. I try to open the lid, but it's stuck. No...I look at it closer. It's some kind of special lock. I turn it upside down, spin it around. I saw something like this once, at the museum store at the Smithsonian. It's a puzzle box. You have to do something to get it to open. But there isn't much to do. I look closer. No hidden panels. I press the carving, feel around the whole design. Not that. I push up on the legs, in case they're fake levers. No, but they wobble a little. I try to tip one of them, and it moves, but nothing happens. The back ones don't move at all. Interesting.

I tip the two front legs at the same time, and the top pops open.

Dad laughs. "45 seconds. Well done."

I laugh too, happy that I solved the puzzle. Then I actually look inside. It's all red velvet, with a special indentation in the middle, filled with a glass vial. It's half full of a bright green liquid.

"What's this?" I ask. "Where did you..."

I stop, realizing what this has to be. This is the serum Jake was going to get from Vladimir. Dad got it first.

I meet his eyes. "This is the serum that can stop Jake's power? Why did you take it? When?"

Dad's eyebrows crease for a second. "You thought it would stop his power? No. From our analysis, this seems to be a formula meant to *create* a power like Jake's. Except it doesn't work. Not so far. Though we've just started trying." He shakes his head. "I guess that old man was pretty reluctant to give it up, so he thought it worked."

111

I set the box down, carefully, on the desk. I don't feel like laughing at all anymore. I know the serum Jake was going to get was to stop his power. Were there two?

Why would Vladimir ever make one to start a power? And why would he give it to Dad, even "reluctantly"? Something in Dad's manner changed after he gave me the box. He twisted somehow, got creepy.

I stand. "I'd like to go back to Mom now."

"Sure, sure." But he leans back in his chair, and stares at the ceiling. "I wonder...if we can't get it to work in any of our subjects...because there's a genetic component. Maybe it has to go into someone with a certain DNA."

I go very, very still. I don't think he wanted me here to protect me at all. I think he wanted me here to experiment on me. Just like Jake.

"I want to go to Mom," I squeak.

"OKAY," he says, and sits up straight, slamming his feet on the floor. He pushes a button on the phone. "Take her back to her room."

"Yes, sir," a voice replies, and instantly the door opens.

"You can eat lunch with your mother," he says, his voice flat. "But then you are going to go to *your* room, and think about this serum. It could be a wonderful opportunity for someone. For you."

I swallow, hard. I've seen all the trouble Jake's power has caused him, first-hand. I don't want one. And more, I do not want to be Dad's guinea pig, stuck here forever while he tries out different things on me.

Right now I've just got to get out of here, while he lets me, and talk to Mom.

I turn and head out the door as fast as I can, like snakes are coming after me.

112

22

JAKE

The Monster by Eminem

I'm stuck in this room. I don't see anyone, can't hear anything. All freaking day. Except a Jones, once. The nice-ish one knocks about mid-day with some water, and tells me to take a bathroom break. He waits outside in the hallway, arms folded, until I'm done, then locks me back in the room.

What the hell is going on? I hate being in here. I start to get a touch of the claustrophobia that took me over after I got out of Montauk, that feeling that I'm going to scream if I can't step outside of walls, breathe fresh air. I couldn't handle being indoors at all for a while after I got out of there. I stare out the window, thinking, trying to keep from freaking out.

When there's another knock on the door, I nearly jump out of my skin. This time it's Bunny. She slips inside, leans against the door. In the dim room she almost glows, pale hair and white shirt. I expect her to write in her notebook, but she speaks instead.

"Mr. Smith has gone out, and you and I are going to eat lunch on the balcony," she says, breathlessly. "It's nice out."

You don't have to ask me twice. "Let's get the hell out of here."

The "safe place" Bunny was talking about—apparently free from cameras and bugs—is outside on the balcony. It is nice. More, it's outside. There's plates and stuff laid out on a table with one of those big striped umbrellas, and the smell of food. I'm hungry, but I don't even look at it yet. I stand there for a minute, breathing it in, the air warm, still damp from the rain this morning. A hint of wind. I take it all in. The view is amazing. We must be on the twentieth floor. Bunny touches my arm briefly, tentative.

"Thanks." My voice is low. "I needed to be out here."

She smiles, sadly. There's a whole conversation there, about how sorry she is that I'm back, about that terrible tunnel this morning, about helplessness. But the smile disappears, and she moves on. "I have something I think you should tunnel with. But we need to do it before anyone comes out or anything happens. Let's sit. It'll look like we're eating in case anyone peeks."

We sit under the umbrella. There's pizza in a takeout box, and breadsticks on our plates. I tear into one while Bunny rummages in her pocket. She tells me to hold out my hand and drops the object into it, watching me.

I know the feel of it the instant I rub my thumb over the surface. But I peer at it, just to make sure.

Jesus Christ, it is. It's Dad's tie tack. The one Myka hid in the library for me, ages ago. The one I was holding when I met Rachel again.

"Where did you...?" I start. But I remember. "Smith. He took it when he kidnapped us."

She nods. "Same time he got the medicine bottle. He took Dr. Miller's gun too, but he's put that somewhere else. I managed to get hold of this. I thought it might help to know where your dad is. It's not your mom and sister. But it's the only lead I have so far. And I think…" She bites her lip. "I think you should do it and see."

I nod, rubbing my thumb over and over the familiar shape, the Air Force logo. Can I deal with seeing Dad again? He's in a base somewhere, surely. Underground. Still trying to make people tunnel. It's not what I hoped for, but it would be good to see what he's up to, if he's looking for me.

I grip the tie tack tight, close my eyes. I go silently, just in case.

West Virginia. An underground facility hidden in the hills outside of Green Bank. The GPS coordinates flash through my head. Dad is in a small room, featureless, gray, just a table and two chairs. He's standing, leaning on the table with one hand, talking to someone. He looks the same as always, maybe a bit more tired. The other person has their back to him, and I can't see clearly.

He has to convince her. This isn't working, but it has to. He makes his voice calm, reasonable, even while he's pacing. "I don't see why you don't understand. It's for your own safety. For hers. If it hadn't been me, it would've been someone else. Someone worse."

The person turns, and I barely stay in the tunnel. It's MOM. Right there. Arms crossed, anger radiating out of her. "That's bullshit, John. I don't know why you really did it, but you have to let us go. This is intolerable. I need to find where Jake is, if he's okay. What does he think happened to us? Where does he think we are? You can't do this. I don't care what government branch you're part of."

115

He shakes his head. "I don't know why you refuse to understand, Abby. With the mess Jake's gotten himself in—gotten all of you in—it's the only safe place for you right now. Especially Myka."

She goes steely quiet, treacherous. He remembers that look. That look never bodes well for him. "You stay away from Myka. And none of this is Jake's fault. It's all you, John. Every bit of it is you."

I try to dip into him, gently, to see if I can control him. If I could have him send Mom and Myka away, when I'm closer. Rescue them like that. But the second I do, the second I start to expand, he lifts his head, sharply. It's like when I tunnel to Myk. I think he senses I'm there.

I back out of it as fast as I can, the tie tack biting into my fist, and stare, unfocused, at the table.

"You okay?" Bunny says softly, from my left. "What did you see?"

My lips feel numb, somehow. I feel numb. All this time I've been wrong.

Why am I always wrong when it comes to him? Why do I always underestimate how much he'll lie?

"He has my mother and sister," I whisper. "They're not here at all. They never were."

Smith didn't have them. Ever. I assumed he did, and threw myself at him, uselessly, to get them back. He just played along. And now I have to get myself out of it again, get to the real bastard who took them: Dad.

Christ, did he kill Vladimir too? Is he really that much of a monster?

116

"Did you know?" I ask her. "Is that why you gave me this?"

She grimaces. "I was pretty sure Smith didn't have them, so I wondered who did. It was a decent guess."

I grip the tie tack hard. The good news is I don't have any reason to stay here anymore. I can leave with Bunny—with her help, we can get out. Smith doesn't have a hold on me I can't break.

Shit. Except Lucas.

The headache slams into my brain with no warning this time, wipes me completely out with pain. I lose all awareness of everything around me. There's only the pain, the pounding in my head. I think I fall. I think I scream.

I pass out.

23

Me Against the World by Simple Plan

I come to still outside, on the balcony, with a view of something I can't figure out at first. Tubes, running together, and a big, round circle...oh, the table. I'm lying under the table.

"Jake? You okay?"

Not really. My head is still throbbing. I don't know how long I was out, but passing out doesn't get rid of the pain like the T-680 does. Just lets my body have a little break during the worst of it. It's still there, thrashing to get out. I look back over my shoulder—there's Bunny, sitting next to me—but that hurts, so I stop. Scowl. "Urgh."

"No one noticed," she says, then lowers her voice when I flinch. Every sound is magnified with the headache. "Even when you screamed, they didn't come. I think the glass must be soundproof. If you can get up soon, look normal, I think we'll be okay."

I groan again. I don't really care if anyone hears me at this point, if they're all standing around me in a circle watching. I can't move. It's excruciating.

But it would be bad if Smith found out I was tunneling with Bunny. It might make it a lot harder to get out of this place. And I want to get out *soon*.

I push myself up and bang my head on a chair. Swear. Have to lie down again.

Bunny tries not to laugh, and I brave the pain to turn and glare at her.

"Sorry." She muffles her mouth with her hand. "Nervous reaction. I do it whenever anyone hurts themselves." She giggles again. "It's not funny, I know. I can't help it."

I scoot out from under the table inch by inch and sit up, holding my head. "Not helping." I find the tie tack still curled in my other hand, shove it in my pocket. This I need to keep.

"I know. Sorry." She pats my leg. "Can you tell me more about what you saw? Your dad has your mom and sister?"

"Yeah." The shock comes roaring back, along with swirling anger. "I can't believe he did that. And I came here, thinking Smith had them..."

"I never thought he did," she says. I push myself slowly to my feet—ow—and she helps me. "The way he answered you—it was off. And I never heard anything about it. He doesn't hide Lucas at all. I would've known something. Or one of the Joneses would've said." She shrugs. "I didn't really know if your dad had them."

"I can't believe he took them." I shake my head. "The unmitigated jerk." I manage to sit at my place, though the food looks totally unappetizing now, and the cheese smell makes me feel sick. I can't eat with my head pounding like this. "I have to get them back."

"Where is he?" she asks. "In a lab?"

I sigh. "West Virginia. Green Bank. Another base."

She bites her lip, and stares out at the city for a couple minutes. "So...you're ready to leave with me then?"

I nod, wearily. "Ready to plan. Do you have a plan?"

"Oh." She smiles, and I see an evil glint in her eye that I like. "I have a plan. I've been here for a long time, long enough to figure out what needs to be done. It'll have to wait until I get a few things in place..."

"I have to bring Lucas with me. He doesn't have to like it, but I have to bring him along. I can't leave that kid with Smith one day longer than he has to be."

She tilts her head. "I knew you'd say that. I agree. And he won't know anything about it until it's too late for him to object. He's been here for a long time. I don't know how he'd react to leaving. To you." She sighs. "I'm sorry I didn't tell you about him sooner. I wanted to. There was no safe way, and it was too risky—"

"I get it." I drop my elbows on the table and rub my temples, hard. It doesn't help. I give up and flop back in the chair. "It must've been hell, being stuck with Smith all these years."

She covers her mouth with her hand and looks away, but I can see her fight off tears. She taps her hand once, twice, across her lips. "Yes" is all she says. "Now." She sniffs. "The plan."

It's pretty simple, considering. It involves the release of gas through the vents—with gas masks for us—Smith's master key, and using her car to get out of here. She has all the heavy lifting, and the knowledge of how we can dodge Smith after we're out of here. But it'll depend on opportunity, too, when

120

Smith and all the Joneses are in the right places. Smith being gone, hopefully.

She smiles, small. "One of the Joneses—his real name is Bradley—is a friend of mine. If something goes wrong, he might help."

"A real friend?" I ask. "Or a friend like I was to you at Montauk?"

Her mouth quirks up, but she doesn't answer.

I won't know when this escape is going to happen until it does. It could be tomorrow, or a week from now. She'll just come in and tell me it's time.

I'm really hoping for tomorrow.

24

RACHEL

Caught by Ari Gold

I'm praying that Vladimir didn't have drugs or spy stuff or anything else incriminating on this boat.

Dedushka and I sit together at the back, watching five Coast Guard agents comb the boat for "suspicious paraphernalia." Drug raid, they said—there's been some kind of drug activity in this cove. Which is kind of a relief, since both Dedushka and I assumed the boat had been reported stolen from the dock and we were being arrested straight off.

That may still come. One of the agents, a short one with a big belly, is running the registration on the boat. They'll run info on us too.

Who knows what Liesel or Jake's dad have put into the system. I know by now how tricky they are. I could be tagged as a runaway, or having a record. They could whisk us off to jail. To a CIA or DARPA cell. To an underground lab. We could be locked up by the end of the day.

I can't stop shaking. I'm not great at this part, the lying and keeping to a cover. I don't know how Jake—or Dedushka—can handle this obscene level of pressure. Of course you don't want to get good at it. If you're good at dealing with stuff like this, and it doesn't bother you, your life has gone wrong somewhere.

Dedushka is pissed off, at least on the surface. He's sitting there with his fists clenched, his face a volcano about to burst. "It is my friend's boat," he repeats again. "You will find this. We are hiding nothing."

And will they find that Vladimir is dead? Has that been reported yet? Then we might be held for murder too.

I shove my trembling hands under my legs.

At least we saw them before we strolled on board with that box—I'm sure they would've confiscated it. We abandoned the box itself behind a bush on shore, and Dedushka stuffed the vial in some sort of hidden inside pocket in his pants before they spotted us. Which is great, unless we get searched. A vial of bright red liquid won't be a trigger at all for drug agents.

I wanted to run when we saw them, or stay there on the shore and hide. But Dedushka said it wouldn't work. Said we had to bluff it out and take our chances.

I watch the short one, on the phone. He looks bored, standing there in his yellow vest, waiting. Like this isn't exciting enough for him. He has pale red hair, and a probably permanent sunburn. I bet he's married, with a belly like that. I bet he has little kids. I wonder if he's nice, in his regular life, or if he's always borderline hostile and bored.

His face changes as I watch. One of the other agents pushes past him, but he barely notices, focused on whatever he's listening to. "Yes, ma'am," he says, with a glance at us. There's excitement in his voice. "I understand." He whispers something to the agent near him, who immediately stops searching and turns around to face us, his hand on his gun.

Oh God.

"Sir," he shouts. He goes to the stairs below deck, shouts down. "Info on the boat came through. You'll want to hear this."

I look at Dedushka. I wonder if he has a back-up plan, a way to get out. He meets my eyes and frowns at me, small.

I breathe, too fast. Yeah. I don't have a back-up plan either.

The leader comes up on deck, a buff guy with an oddly flattened nose whose vest is straining on him. The two of them have a low conversation. Figuring out the best way to arrest us, probably. Which thing to arrest us for, out of their many choices. I bite the inside of my lip to keep my teeth from chattering. Not from cold, just nerves. I don't know what to do. What would Jake do? Punch someone and swim to shore, then run?

There has to be another way out of this.

The leader's phone rings, and he holds it to his ear. "Yes," he says, his voice amped up. "We have them right here. What did you get on—" He frowns. "Are you sure?" He turns his back and walks away. I can't make him out anymore. But he keeps talking. Arguing for a while, one arm flailing. Then he goes quiet for a long time, and comes towards us again. "Yes, sir. I understand."

He clicks off the phone and holds it for a moment, looking out to the ocean, before turning to his crew. "Pack it up!" he shouts. "There's nothing here."

I hold my breath.

"But sir—" the short one starts.

The leader shakes his head. "It doesn't matter. They've been cleared, the boat's clear. Time to go." He steps to us, inclines his head. "I apologize for the trouble. My people will get out, and you can be on your way."

I don't believe him, even a little. I don't trust them anymore. We haven't been cleared. They have something on the boat, on Vladimir. Whatever boss he just talked to wants to let us go for some other reason. Or was told to let us go.

Why? Who would have enough pull for that. DARPA? John?

Dedushka tilts his head, like royalty acknowledging a subject, and we watch them go. They're off the boat, speeding away, within three minutes.

I let my head drop between my knees, take deep breaths.

Dedushka strides to the wheel, scribbles something on the pad there, and hands it to me.

The words are in a thick scrawl. *We are probably bugged now. Do not speak.*

124

I nod, understanding flooding through. Maybe that's what he wanted, this mystery boss. To catch us on something bigger... the serum. Or follow us to Jake.

Will they follow us? I write.

He shrugs, and writes once more. *Not if we help it.* He starts the engine with steady hands. He brings the boat around in a wide curve and heads out of the bay, while I hold onto the seat as tight as I can. Spray splashes across my face. At least I have confidence he'll know how to deal with a tail. That's something Dedushka knows well.

I close my eyes in relief for a second. We didn't get arrested, at least for now. We made it through.

I want to throw up—adrenaline and Vladimir's sandwich sour in my stomach—but we made it through. We have the vial. Now we just have to get to Jake.

Now we just have to get rid of surveillance and tails, and get to Jake.

I have to believe we can do that, somehow.

25

MYKA

Piece by Piece by Kelly Clarkson

Dad is keeping me away from Mom.

I think he's just doing it to be cruel, because we want to be with each other instead of with him (ever). He let me eat lunch with her like he said, and then he had his soldiers push me over to "my room"…and that was it. I've been in here ever since.

I haven't cried, because even though I don't see any cameras, I think he's probably watching. But I want to. I think I heard Mom's door open a while ago, but nothing since. There are bottles of water on the shelf now, bags of snap pea crisps, and Oreos.

I pull the blue comforter off the bed, wrap it around me, and camp on the chair, staring at the door. For a long time—hours, I think—I don't do anything else. Then I have to take a few Oreos. I'm not looking at the books he got me, though. I'm not giving in.

I think it's night now.

I keep thinking about what Dad said about that formula, how it might have to have a genetic component.

It makes sense. Otherwise whatever they did to Dedushka back in Russia—it would've worked on a lot of people, right? And if it had worked on a lot of people, Russia would probably be using those powers all over the place. So it *didn't* work on a lot of people. It only worked on Dedushka, as far as I know. And then whatever it did to him, he passed on in his DNA to Jake.

Why not Dad? Why not me? If Dad got a power and I was the only one who didn't, I'd guess it was sex-linked to the Y chromosome. But neither of us got it...or got it so that it expressed. That probably means we just didn't get the gene.

But that doesn't necessarily mean that we *wouldn't* get a power if we had some of that formula like Dedushka did. It could trigger something, maybe. Without knowing how the gene works...and would stem cells from Jake affect anything?

Ugh. I don't know *anything* about how it works. I admit, I really wouldn't mind trying to figure it out, in the lab. If I even could. I bet even Mr. Pallon back at school, the head of Chemistry, would want to try to figure it out. But I'm 100% sure I don't want to be Dad's test subject.

It's weird enough having one freak in the family, with everyone after him. It'd be unbearable to have two.

A soldier comes in with a tray: a grilled cheese sandwich and tomato soup. My favorite dinner when I was five. Dad seems to think I stopped changing when I was five.

"I want to go to my Mom," I say. "Please let me go see my Mom."

He shakes his head and shuts the door behind him.

I eat the dinner even though it's stupid. Eventually I turn off the light and lie there in the chair, still wrapped in the comforter.

I cry a little when they can't see, before I fall asleep.

26

JAKE

Run Away (The Escape Song) by Oingo Boingo

When Bunny comes in my room the next morning, I'm awake, dressed, and sitting on the edge of the bed. I'm ready to get out of here, as fast as I can. I tried to tunnel to Dedushka late last night, to tell him about Dad, but I missed him again, asleep. If it's time to escape now, I'll just tunnel to him after, when we're out.

But it isn't time to escape. Smith wants me for a tunnel, she says. *Now.*

He's pacing the big room, prowling like an animal. Projecting so much tension the air crackles with it. I don't even really want to walk in. There are two Joneses, the big one guarding Lucas's door and the nice-ish one behind the sofa, his hands behind his back. Neither one looks at me.

I try to picture myself taking down even one of the Joneses, if that was our escape plan, and fail. I'd need to know karate, or at least be able to fight, to accomplish it. But that's not what I do.

128

"Sit," Smith growls. "I've been waiting for you."

I sit. He nods to Bunny and she rummages in her pocket, hands me the bag with a weird little thumb-size eagle figurine in it. I take it out, feel it in my fingers. Heavy, the wings rough.

"Okay already," Smith snaps. "Go. It's a judge, in his chambers. When you go, I want you to control him. You're going to make him sign something for me."

I clench the eagle against my palm, hard enough to hurt. "What?"

He frowns and leans back against the desk, hands braced on the edge. His eyes shine oddly in the light. "Lucas showed me what you can do. What you've been hiding from me *this whole time*. You can control people remotely. That's how you got out of Montauk, isn't it, Mr. Lukin? That's your big secret?"

I don't think I could move if I wanted to. I just sit there, staring up at him.

He'll never let me go. Even if we escape, he'll hunt me down and find me. Even if I do take the serum, he'll be pissed. If I don't...I'll never have another free day.

"So now you're going to make it up to me for *lying* and use your secret. Just a little one, to start. You're going to tunnel to this bastard, have him sign a document I've got ready on his desk. Got it? Good. It's almost time."

I swallow, though my throat feels full of dust. "I won't."

He bangs the desk with the flat of his hand, glares down his nose at me. "You will. Or I'll hurt your beloved little sister."

I've never been more grateful of timing. I know, as of yesterday, that he doesn't have her, that he can't touch her. I'm almost–almost–grateful to Dad for smuggling her away. Just for this moment.

No, I'm not. But I'm damn glad Smith doesn't have her.

"No," I say. I try to sound even, confident.

"No?" His voice goes high. "You'd sacrifice your sister?" There are lines on his forehead I don't usually see, a wildness in his eyes. He's lost whatever control he had. I can picture him smashing me in the face, laughing while he does it. "I'll do it, you know. Don't think I won't."

I press my lips together. I don't even know what document he wants me to sign, but I can't do it. He can't see me control someone for real. It's the edge of a precipice, and I can't take that step.

He studies me, his eyes narrow. Then his gaze shifts to Bunny, and he smiles. "Jones. Give me your gun." He stands and strolls around the desk, wiping his hands on his gray suit pants.

Nice-ish Jones behind the sofa hesitates, but hands a gun to Smith, butt out.

No.

I try to stand, but I don't make it far.

In one second flat Smith cocks the gun, drags Bunny off the sofa by her hair, and presses the muzzle to her head. She screams, her eyes huge. I struggle, but Jones grabs me, his hands on my shoulders pinning me relentlessly. I can't move an inch.

I have to stop Smith.

"Tunnel to the judge," Smith growls. "Or I swear to God I'll shoot her."

I stare at him, at Bunny. We've gone through so much together. I liked her even when I was in Montauk. I've always felt like I wanted to protect her. And now we're going to escape together. I *need* her.

I can't let him do this. Should I tunnel? Should I do what he wants?

He shoves the gun against her head and she twists, trying to wiggle away, but he holds her firm. A cat with a bird in its mouth. "Tunnel, Mr. Lukin. Now."

I still don't know, hovering at that edge. It's an impossible choice.

I can't. I can't let him see me control someone. But mostly I can't do what he wants. I can't make a judge sign anything, just because Smith is threatening me. It's too important. Who knows what else he'll make me do tonight, or tomorrow. For years.

Jesus Christ.

I make myself meet Bunny's eyes. I can't do it. I hope she understands. I see it sink in, that I'm not going to stop this. Her face falls. Her round blue eyes fill, drip down.

I am a terrible person. I feel like I'm frozen, unable to move either way.

I can't let her die. Maybe I'll do it this time, and find some other way to end it...

Then she takes a ragged breath and her expression hardens. She juts out her pointed chin.

"I was going to betray you anyway," she whispers. She stares at me, so intense it's like it's just us in the room. No Smith, no gun. No choices. I know, without a shred of doubt, that she's telling the truth. "So I could work with your father. That was my plan all along. I was going to take you to him and turn you in, and..." She gulps. "I'm sorry..."

"Oh, you are *useless*," Smith says. "I don't need you anymore." He pulls the trigger. Her head explodes in a bloody mess, and he lets her drop, lifeless, to the floor.

Time quits, for a while. It stretches and stretches and stretches and never ends, that moment. That horror.

I howl and shove against Jones, but he shoves me down, a heavy weight. Smith holds his bloody hands high, like he had nothing to do with any of it. "Your fault. I warned you. You're *worse* than useless. Let that be a warning. I will make you do the next tunnel, I swear to God." He points at the Jones by Lucas's door. "You. Go get someone to clean this up. I have to go do damage control with this judge." He nods at the Jones behind me. "Get him out of here."

He throws the gun on his desk and strolls away, out the door towards my room, and the other Jones follows him.

I can't breathe. I can't think. Bunny is crumpled on the floor, like trash he didn't need anymore, part of her head blown away. Dead. For no reason. Because of me.

It's worse than Eric. Maybe Bunny was going to betray me. I did believe her. But for her life to just be over—it doesn't make sense. None of it makes a drop of sense.

God, and now we can't escape, either. I can't do it on my own. Now I'll never get out of here with Lucas, I'll never see my mother or sister again...

Wait. The gun is lying there too, abandoned. Within easy reach. All the blood rushes out of my head, leaving that one point of focus. There's only one Jones. His hands are still on my shoulders, but just resting, light. He must've been surprised too. I have one chance.

I slide out from under his hands, scoop the gun off the desk and spin, cocking it as I go. I haven't pointed a gun since I was in Eric's body, but it works the same. It's heavy, I'm shaking like a goddamn leaf, and my vision is blurred, but I point it in the right direction.

132

I expect a fight, a shout, a tackle. But nice-ish Jones holds up his hands in surrender, his jaw clenched tight. "He told me to get you out of here," he says. His mouth crooks. "I'm following orders. Go. Fast. Take Lucas with you. Go down the far stairs. I liked Cecile." His voice softens as he looks down at Bunny. "I liked her a lot. She..." He swallows hard. "She didn't deserve that. And with my gun."

"Are you Bradley?" I ask.

He looks back up at me. "Get out of here."

I nod once and look at Bunny myself, one last time, what's left of her. Think of the first time I saw her, in her doctor's coat, buzzing around so excited about testing me. Her excitement about everything, always. She sure as hell didn't deserve that.

But there's no time. I take him at his word and run through the door towards Lucas. We've got to get out of this nightmare.

27

JAKE

Brothers by Penny & Sparrow

The door shuts behind me and I take a second to lock it, take stock of the hall. I need to get Lucas to come with me and then get the hell out, as soon as possible. Go down the stairs, he said. Bunny wanted us to leave that way too, take her car. Of course I don't have her keys. Or Smith's master key. I don't have Bunny with me to convince Lucas I'm okay, to bluff anyone who asks questions. Because Bunny's in there dead with her head splattered all over the floor.

I swallow bile.

She was going to betray me, she said. To Dad. Is that true?

I can't think of that now. I have minutes at most before someone finds out I got out of that room and hunts me down.

I go to the study door and open it, the gun at my side for now. It's the same scene as before. Lucas is in one of the big chairs, a book in his lap. This time as soon as he sees me he stands up, the book still clutched in his hand. "Jake?" he asks, cautiously. His gaze flicks to my face, then the gun in my hand.

"We've got to get out of here. We've got one chance, and this is it. Come on." I try to sound gruff, commanding, like Dad or Dedushka would.

I probably fail. He raises his eyebrows. "Get out? Away from Smith? We can't."

I wave the gun. "We have to. Now. I know he's using you. He's not going to use you anymore, or me. Do you have shoes?"

He shakes his head, wide-eyed. He's so tall, so skinny, it's ridiculous. Awkward, like a baby deer who might break if I pushed him too hard. "I heard a gunshot. How...?"

"No time." I wave him out into the hall with the gun hand, and I'm kind of surprised when he complies. I think he is too.

"He'll kill us when he catches us," he whispers as we start to move forward, quick, along the walls.

"He won't kill us," I say, confident about that truth at least. "He wants both of us alive." We keep moving all the way down the hall, around the corner. I see the stairwell Bunny and Jones promised, there at the end. No one between us and the door. I move faster, and Lucas keeps up with me. I stop at the door, gun up by my head like in video games, listening. I don't hear Joneses or anyone pounding up the stairs, so I open it, slowly. Clear.

My gut clenches. This is too easy. Security has got to be tighter than this, doesn't it? We don't even have a smoke alarm distraction. I guess the distraction is Bunny. Maybe they're all rattled. Or maybe nice-ish Jones is doing something to stall them.

I wonder if he loved Bunny.

135

I hold my finger to my lips and slip through, the stairs cold on my bare feet. It smells stale in here, like underground air, and I barely make myself move forward. But Lucas follows me, shutting the door quietly behind him. I breathe. Down. Deal with anything that comes up on the way.

We move slower here, trying to be quiet, taking one step at a time. I count the levels as we go. Twenty-four. Damn. My legs burn by the time we get to the bottom, and I'm panting. Out of shape. I stop again at the bottom door, wait for Lucas to catch up—he's not panting—and then open it, the gun ready.

It opens into a little lobby, with an elevator on our right and a door ahead of us into the parking garage. It's empty, clear. We step into it.

The elevator dings, loud in the small space, and the door slides open.

It's Smith, alone, another gun held loose in his hand. His eyes widen when he sees us.

Without a second thought I rush him, before he can even consider what to do. I crash into him in the elevator and he falls straight back, arms wheeling to try to catch himself, but there's no time. He smacks straight back against the wall, then slides to the floor. But he's not out. He blinks, stunned. I have to knock him out. We can't move fast enough to get away if he's conscious, aware of what's going on. He could call someone else for help. He could stop us too easily.

I glance back at Lucas, hovering by the wall, and then at Smith. He blinks again, his jaw twitching, and I see him gearing up the energy to move. Scream. Call for help. Fire his gun. The elevator doors start to close, then sense my foot in the way and open again.

I think of how many people he's hurt. How he lied to me about Mom and Myka, kept Lucas captive here for who knows how long.

136

Killed Bunny, just because.

I could kill him, right now. The threat would be gone.

Except I can't do that no matter what he did. Then I'd be just as bad as him.

I draw back and whack him in the temple with the butt of the gun, as hard as I can. There's a sick crack. He's instantly out, a line of blood trickling down his cheek.

I've never done that before. I've never actually hit somebody, certainly never hurt somebody like that. If you don't count Eric, but that was unintentional.

It's a rush, adrenaline surging through my veins. Powerful.

I don't like it.

I scramble off him, scooping up his gun. I dive out of the elevator doors before they close again, and grab Lucas's arm. He seems unsure, stunned. He probably saw, or heard, that hit. He has no idea who I am. He probably thinks I'm a lunatic.

I tuck the gun into my waistband, throw Smith's into the trash bin right there. It drops right to the bottom, hidden.

The parking garage smells greasy, like exhaust. I see Bunny's car right away, a pale blue VW Bug only a little ways from the door. But it's new, with a security system, and I don't have any tools. And I never was as good at breaking into cars as Dedushka is. I don't have time to figure it out.

I change plan and run with Lucas right alongside the barrier, out into the street. We'll be easy to spot, with our bare feet, but that way I don't have to navigate the car or the gate. We'll run until we find something else to steal, or some other way to get out of here with no money or ID. At least we're outside.

I see it as soon as we get on the street: a bus, just pulling up to the stop. I know DC buses—it's the 52, so north and west—and you can fake scanning your SmarTrip card, if you get in the back. It's risky, but I've seen people do it. I yank Lucas one more time, and we hop on as soon as the bus stops. I wave my empty, curled hand in front of the scanner, and Lucas does too. I sit down like I do it every day, squeezing in the space next to two old guys arguing about the Nationals. Lucas sits across from me, his eyes watching me close. It's hot, and smells like sweat, but the bus pulls away, and that's all I care about.

The lady next to Lucas, a short woman with tightly curled black hair, eyes his feet, then mine, then glances at the scanner. "You boys have a bad day?" she drawls, nice enough.

I shrug, as politely as I can. "A bet," I say. "At least it's summer."

She mmm-hmms and shakes her head. "All fun and games until you get glass in your feet."

Lucas fake-laughs, bad, and then stops. But afterwards he smiles at me, a hesitant but real smile.

We did it. We got out, the two of us. Part of my family is reunited, even if he has no idea we're family at all.

We only get off the bus when the line ends, at a place in Maryland called Friendship Station. I was hoping we'd be in some part of town that's a little rundown, sketchy...so two scruffy guys with no shoes and I-just-got-out-of-prison brand-new jeans and t-shirts—and a gun in my pocket I hope nobody can see—wouldn't stand out too much. No such luck. This stop is all wide streets and big-name stores, with women in heels and expensive sunglasses who glare at us to start their shopping day. We can't afford that kind of attention or that level of cameras. I casually walk down a side street toward the more business-ish district, Lucas following close behind.

We haven't talked yet. We stared at each other uncomfortably on the long bus ride, judging. Me, trying to see if he *is* my brother, if he looks like me or Dad, and guess what his power could be. What his history is. I don't know what he knows about me, except that he told Smith somehow about how I could control people. His stares are probably him trying to figure out how wacko I am.

After a pretty good stretch of walking, in which I barely avoided broken glass twice and dog shit once, we come across an old, beat-up apartment under construction. It's deserted—an empty Cat out front, cones and yellow tape and an industrial dumpster behind scaffolding. Some kind of complete reno, looks like.

Thing is, yellow tape and scaffolding are pretty easy to duck behind. I note the address and then we pop underneath it, down the alley alongside, and look for a way in. I find it around the back, a service door that's stuck open, and Lucas and I go inside.

This space, a storage area, has some portable work lights set up, but they're off, and the electricity to the building has been cut. There's only a thin strip of light from a window, enough to show the manic clouds of dust motes in the air. I don't know what the crew is doing in here that's making so much dust, but I can feel it smothering my lungs. I don't want to stay down here anyway. We need to hide here for a little while, if we can, and I don't want to be somewhere returning construction guys could find us right away when they come back.

"Let's find some stairs," I whisper. "Get up in one of the rooms and hide out."

"What are we going to do, stay here?" I can't really see his face, but I can feel his eyes on me in the dark. His voice is high.

"For a while. I'll ask Dedushka and Rachel to pick us up. It'd be tough to get anywhere like this, without money."

His invisible stare gets more intense—he has no idea who Dedushka and Rachel are, much less where we're going—but I ignore it and head across the back of the room, where I guess the stairs would be. I'm going to have to explain soon. I just don't know how much to explain.

"What about food?" he asks.

Ah, yeah. I've gotten pretty good at shoving down my body's need for food when I have to. But he's at the age where he needs to eat every couple hours, just to keep up with growth. I remember wanting to gnaw on my pencil in school, I was so hungry. I'll have to find him something. I open a door I think might be stairs, but it's a closet. Next one. Bingo. The stairs are solid dark, and smell faintly of piss, but we go in anyway. The door clangs behind us too loud.

"We'll forage," I say. "I think this is an apartment building. Let's try four flights. That should be enough."

After four flights of going up and around, the dark pressing in on me—way too much like being under the CIA hood in Montauk—I fumble for a door and push it open. There's light here. And air. I stop for a second, breathe. The window shows a long hallway. Definitely apartments. I head down to the last apartment and try the door. Locked. The next one in is broken, so I get in with a little jiggling. It's deserted, the only furniture a couple empty boxes and a metal bed frame, and everything's covered with that dust. A studio, all one room with a moldy bathroom and a tiny rectangle blocked off as a kitchen. It'll do fine. I cautiously look out the bent window blinds. There aren't any neighbors across, just a view of a brick wall and a pretty bare street below. It doesn't smell like pee or anything nasty, just dust. It'll do.

Lucas wipes a square of floor clean with a piece of plastic and drops down on the wood, pulling his knees up to his chest. "You want to tell me who you are now? And where we're going?"

I blow a breath. "In a minute. I've got to do something first."

I sit too, under the window, and close my eyes. First I've got to tunnel to Dedushka and ask him to come.

I try to slow my breath, relax. Think of Dedushka, his pipe smell, his wry sense of humor. How a hug from him is like holding a bear. It takes a few minutes of focusing, but I feel him. I get in.

He's in a car, heading north on I-95, around St. George, South Carolina. It's flat, with trees crowding the sides of the highway, clouds low overhead. A good day for fish. But he is not hunting that kind of fish, not today. He should see Yakob soon, he hopes. A better fish. He looks at Rachel, driving beside him, her hair flying in the wind from the open window. She is a good girl, that one. A smart girl. She smiles, humming to herself. She is happy to see him soon too.

I fill him, feel his recognition. Nudge him to the pad of paper and pencil waiting there on the dash.

"Yakob," he says aloud. "Hello, malchik. Yes, I will write for you."

Rachel inhales, sharp, but she keeps a tight hold on the wheel, staring straight ahead, as Dedushka gets the paper and holds the pencil ready.

I fill his fingers, feel the pencil scratch against the pad. OUT, I write. PICK US UP IN CHEVY CHASE, MARYLAND. 4568 WILLARD AVENUE. 4TH FLOOR. AS SOON AS YOU CAN.

"Us?" Dedushka asks. "Who is us? You have Abby and Myka with you?"

NOT YET. I consider. Then add BRING TWO PAIRS OF MEN'S SHOES.

There's a pause, but he doesn't question it. "We cannot go straight," he says, almost to himself. "Feds will follow us."

I hear paper rustling, a map. He stretches it over his knees, runs a finger over a route. "We will be there tomorrow," he says. "Morning. Soon, malchik."

I pull myself out of it. Message sent and received. The rest will come later. I breathe, deep.

But when I open my eyes, Lucas is watching me, unblinking. I guess the rest will come for him now.

"Okay, ask," I say. "What do you want to know first?"

"Where are we going to get food?" His stomach growls so loud I hear it across the room, and I laugh.

"That's the easiest question you could've asked. Let's try the kitchen first."

Several apartment kitchens later, we're back in our crash pad with a pack of dry ramen for Lucas—the water is off too—and some dusty crackers and wasabi peas for me. I also found a couple bottles of water that seem to be unopened sitting on the floor, so we should be good. Enough to stop the rumbling for a while. Maybe later tonight, after it's dark, we can go forage for something more substantial outside.

"So," I say, between bites. I don't want to ask, not really, but I should. "First question answered. Next?"

He stops shoveling the noodles in his mouth for a minute, long enough to give me a good stare-down, then takes a slug of water. "Who *are* you?"

I put down the crackers, brush off my hands. Take a deep breath. "Okay. Short version: my name is Jake Lukin. I have a special ability—which I guess you know about—that makes me useful for people like Smith, and the CIA, and DARPA, and any organization with initials. I was held in an underground facility for half of this year while they made me spy for them, until my Dedushka—grandfather—who you'll meet, helped me get out. I thought Smith had my mother and my little sister too, but it turns out..." I stop, clear my throat. I don't want to go into that yet. "Someone else has them instead, and now we're going to go get them."

He crunches on some more ramen, waiting. "Okay," he says finally, when he realizes that's all I'm going to say. He clenches one fist, unclenches, clenches. He looks so young...but all the same I can tell he's not totally shocked by what I said. He must've been through a lot of that hell too. "I get all that. I saw your ability. I know a little of what that's like. But...why did you take me too? Why would you risk it, for someone you don't know from a hole in the wall?"

"Well." I take another drink of water, trying to clear my mouth, hoping it'll make it easier to say. But it isn't. I just have to say it. "Apparently, you're my brother."

28

RACHEL

Car Chase by The Freebeez & Honey Horns

"Shoes?" I say, still looking at the road. My hands are warm, from the sun beating through the window. "Why two pairs of shoes?"

Dedushka does a big Russian shrug I don't even need to see to understand. *Who knows*, and *it is not important.* The goofy grin on his face tells the rest. I've never seen him grin like that.

I feel it too, a giddiness stretching all the way to my toes. We're going to him. He's fine. We'll see him tomorrow morning.

And we're going with the serum, victorious.

But he isn't with Abby and Myka. He's with someone, another man. Why would he leave with someone else? One of Smith's people who helped him escape, maybe? Then where are Abby and Myka?

Okay, I'm still curious even if Dedushka's not. But I guess we'll find out soon.

Some road signs come in view. "Which way?" I ask. "Do we stay on 95, or...?"

Dedushka bends over the map again, changing focus in a snap. "We could take this 95 all the way to him. But..." He looks in the Honda's scratched sideview mirror. "Are they still there? Can you see?"

I sigh. "I'm not sure. I think...two cars back, maybe? The same car. Will they really follow us all the way to Jake?"

"If we let them." He taps the map again. "We can go to west, divert, but we still need to lose them." He glances over at me, fuzzy caterpillar-brows raised. "You let me drive? I will do it."

"You'll lose them on a straight freeway?" I laugh. "I let you drive."

I squeeze the wheel, nervous. I'm getting used to a lot, but purposely trying to lose a tail? That's new. I shake my head to clear images of Dedushka trying to do a sharp turn in this old car and flipping us right over.

There isn't any chance to get off for a long time, but I finally exit at the crossroads for 178, a Wilco Travel Plaza. Like every other "travel plaza" in the south. Gas, a Dairy Queen, a Wendy's.

We go into Wendy's for cover...and to get sustenance. I was starving. I wipe my fry-greasy fingers on a napkin. When we get back in, Dedushka takes over, and I make sure the old seat belt is snapped in all the way, and hold on to the armrest.

Good thing. We fly out of that parking lot, west on 178. I see the tail car farther behind than usual. They weren't ready for that.

They're not ready for Dedushka's driving at all. I'm not either. I'd close my eyes, but that would be even scarier. He gets on the 95 onramp, still at ridiculous speed, and merges all the way to the left. I see the tail behind us, struggling in their sensible black car. He shoots along in the fast lane until there's a break in the fence of the divider, meant for emergency vehicles. The clearance is just big enough for one car.

He makes a funny little squeal, turns the car hard left, and plows through the grass of the divider, through the gap, and up to the southbound lanes, making a Jeep swerve and honk angrily at us. The tail is well past the gap before they realize what's going on. Dedushka whips back off the offramp at the 178, over the bridge, and back onto the 95 north again.

The tail is gone. I see them just making the turn onto the southbound lanes when we blow past them again, way too fast for them to catch up.

I don't think they'll call it in to local police, since they're trying to be stealthy and all. But they'll call it in to their people. We switch cars again at the next travel plaza, at the junction with 26. I'm pretty sure they lost us now.

I high-five Dedushka, even though he's awkward about it. I really wish I had a video of that whole thing, but the story will have to do.

Now we can head straight to Maryland. Home. It's only been about six weeks since I left, though it feels like a lifetime has happened already. Well, it feels like a lifetime since Jake left, and that's…what, three days?

We're going to be with Jake again. I'm not angry with him anymore. I just want to find out what happened, what he learned, and get Abby and Myka back. And then he can take this serum that's burning a hole in Dedushka's pocket, and we can…. .

I don't really know what we're going to do after that. I'm still registered for Berkeley in three weeks. But what happens with Jake?

I don't even know what I'm going to say when I see him.

I roll down the window and let the wind whip my hair, close my eyes. I guess I'll figure that out later. Right now, I'm going to enjoy the ride.

29

MYKA

Kill Em with Kindness by Selena Gomez

When I wake up I eat some more Oreos for breakfast—it's Dad's fault, since they're in here—and walk around the room a few times. It makes me feel a little better, but not much. I go look at the books on the shelf. Tempting. He got the new Dorothy Hodgkin biography. She's a British biochemist, who won the Nobel prize for Chemistry in the 60s. So he does know what I'm interested in, some.

The door opens, and I turn around, but it's not Mom. It's that doctor, Liesel Miller.

"Hello." She smiles, with big teeth.

"I want to see my Mom."

She sighs, and closes the door behind her. "I'm working on that." She points to the chair. "May I?"

I shrug, and she sits, and folds her hands in her lap. She's very neat., in a skirt and everything. Her pale hair is smooth, and her skin white. I'm all rumpled and messy.

"I thought we could have a talk."

I lean back against the bookshelf and rub my eyes. "I just want to be with my Mom, and then we can get out of here."

"I know. Believe me, I know. I am very against this isolation plan of John's. And his...other plans." She tilts her head. "Open your mouth for me?"

I frown, but open my mouth.

She laughs, which surprises me. "What is that...Oreos? Your teeth are solid black."

I shrug again, but it feels a little less awkward. Like maybe she's someone I can talk to. "You mean Dad's plans for me. With this formula."

"Yes. Exactly." She crosses her legs. "You know I worked with Jake, and I believed firmly in that. I still do, if managed properly. Jake can do a lot for the world, for his country, with the skill he was born with."

I roll my eyes. "You want to lock him up and use him."

She brushes at her skirt. "I want to use his talent, with his permission. I think it also might be acceptable to create such a power in new *volunteers*." She leans forward, dropping her voice. "I think it is completely unethical and unacceptable to try to use an untested serum on you, and I will continue to fight John on this."

My eyes fill with tears. I don't know if it's because she's being kind—and she wants to help me—or because Dad really wants to do that to me, and she's the one trying to protect me.

He wants to experiment on me. Like a lab rat. I think I hate him.

"Thank you," I say. "Do...you think Jake's coming here? Is that why Dad took us really?"

I don't want Jake caught up in this. But I miss him. And Dedushka. They could help, against Dad.

She tilts her head again. I think that's how she thinks. "Probably. But now that you're here and this serum has

148

come John's way...he's latched onto you as an opportunity. I'm sorry." She sighs. "Jake spoke of you so warmly, always. He will probably find a way to come." She stands. "I am fighting the larger war, so I may not push the smaller battle about you being with your mother at the moment. In the meantime, would you like to go to the bathroom? Clean up? Get some fresh clothes?"

I nod, and she smiles again. "I'll take care of it. Know that your mom is fine, and Jake is perfectly capable of taking care of himself. Yes?"

I nod again, and almost smile back.

She's not that bad.

30

JAKE

Oh Brother by The Fall

"You're my brother." I say it again, when Lucas doesn't react.

His head snaps up this time, his jaw clenched. "Don't fuck with me, okay?"

I have a stupid impulse to tell him not to swear, like he's Myka. Though he's probably 3 years older than Myka. And she probably swears too, when I'm not around. "I'm not, I promise. Smith told me. I...was surprised too."

"No. My dad was a soldier. Air Force. I only saw him a few times...." he trails off, his forehead puckered. "My mom said he was always on missions. But I did see him. He wasn't married. He said when things settled down he'd marry my mom one day."

I shake my head. Jesus. I never thought Dad was that big a straight-up, in-your-face liar. "Yeah, well, he's a flaming dick."

"Hey!" Lucas jumps to his feet, his hands flat against his sides like he's going to karate-chop me. His cheeks flush so dark I can see it in the dim light. "You don't know anything about it. My dad...it was complicated, but he wasn't...that. And he's dead, anyway."

"Yeah?" I swallow the reaction, try my best to sound curious instead of challenging. "When did he die?"

"Two and a half years ago," he says. "January—"

"28th. In a plane crash, right? In Colorado?"

He stops, bites his lip. Now his hands are in fists. "How did you know that?" His voice is thin, small.

I stand up too, tired of the imbalance, and rock back and forth on my heels. "Like I said, he's my dad too. John Lukin, when he was with us." I raise an eyebrow.

He swallows. "Luke Manchester. He said I was named for him."

"*Dick.*" It's all I can think to say, even if it makes his nostrils flare. "Sorry. Anyway, he isn't dead. That was a trick, one he pulled on us too. I found him a month or so ago." I skip a lot of the story, because he doesn't need absolutely everything piled on right now. "He's running an underground lab to try to create people like..." I wave between us. "You and me. And he took my mom and sister, right off the street. He's holding them to try to bring me back. Bait. To get me underground again, so he can use me."

Lucas leans back against the wall, arms crossed, like his will gave out and he couldn't stand up anymore.

"I promise," I say. "It's true, all of it."

We're silent for a while. Slowly he slides down the filthy wall and picks up the noodle bowl again. Absently crunches, staring into space.

"I don't think I believe you," he says to the noodles. He looks up. "No, maybe I do. But I don't want to."

There's a long silence. There's not much to say to that.

"You *are* named for him, I think," I add, at last. "But not his first name. Lucas...for Lukin."

His lips tighten, but he doesn't answer. I don't know him...and I can't read him. Is he taking this well, or not? Is there a way to take this well?

I didn't even know what reaction to hope for. It's not exactly a happy family reunion. Hi, I'm your brother—your dad is a terrible person and isn't dead.

I sit too, in my spot. Though whatever appetite I had is wiped out. I push away the rest of the peas.

"He'd use you too," I say. "I'm surprised he hasn't. Does he know you have a...an ability?"

He shakes his head, slow. "I never told anyone. Until he.... Until I thought he died."

"Sorry. Again." I shift, rub one hand over the thick, stiff jeans. I should've had Dedushka bring more clothes too. "And then?"

He swallows hard and coughs, chokes, so hard that I wonder if I'm going to have to give him the Heimlich or something, but eventually he gulps some water and stops. He wipes the streaming tears off his face, not looking at me. "Then I told my mom. Who was having a tiny drug problem at that point." His voice is small, only dots of sound. "Painkillers. I guess she told Smith, or someone who knew him? Anyway." He shrugs. "He offered to take me off her hands for some fair amount of cash, and she gratefully accepted." He half bows. "And here we are."

"Jesus." He looks so fragile suddenly, so thin and small and lost, that I want to give him a hug. I don't. I don't think he's ready for that. "That's messed up."

He nods, looking at his dirty, bare feet, but doesn't answer. I wonder if he's had shoes at all in those two and a half years. If he's left that god-forsaken apartment. Ripped out of school and his only family at 13, Myk's age, for that life I saw...I'm suddenly really glad I punched Smith. I should've done worse.

We're quiet again, long enough for the sun to slip down through the twisted blinds.

"You said you saw your dad, though?" I ask.

"Sometimes." He finishes the last of the ramen, scraping his fingers through the container for crumbs intently. "Five times. He'd swing by, bring me a whole bunch of presents—say they were for all the holidays and birthdays he missed—stay for a few days, and then take off again. I still remember him bringing me the red bike. How happy I was." He snorts. "Like I had a real dad, for that day."

My gut twists, foreboding. "A red bike?" I ask, carefully.

"Yeah. When I was five, I think. Red, with blue grips and cards stuck in the spokes. No training wheels."

My hatred for Dad bursts, seeping into my blood like poison, hardening me as it spreads. That was my bike. The one he taught me to ride on, up and down the street in Herndon. I put cards in the spokes so it would make just the right sound. Mom and I were going to give it to Myka, when she was ready, but we couldn't find it in the garage. We could never figure out where it went, and he said he didn't know.

He gave it to his other kid. The kid he hid from us, and treated like crap, like an afterthought. And it's not Lucas's fault at all. But still it burns in my veins. *My* bike.

I close my eyes, try to let the poison melt away before I talk to Lucas again. Before I take it out on him.

"You okay?" he asks, his voice high.

I breathe: one, two, three. Four. "Yeah." I open my eyes. He's still there, this little brother of mine. His eyes don't look like mine. They're dark, more rounded. But his nose does. And his ears, sticking out too far. I think he is my brother. God. I wish I could go back and take all this shit away from him. I wish we could've been a family or something, without Dad. Him and Mom and Myka and me.

Maybe we still can, kind of.

We talk about boring, non-personal stuff after that. Nothing that means anything for real. Sports—he used to play hockey, before everything. Tennis for me. Video games. TV shows. He was allowed to watch TV at Smith's, as much as he wanted. He goes on and on about *Supernatural*, which I've never seen. Two brothers fighting demons and angels together. He doesn't look at me or even pause when he says that, and I know it'll be a long time before we feel like brothers, if we ever do. We have our own demons to fight first.

I don't realize until after it's dark, and he's asleep sprawled out on a flattened box, that I never even asked him what his power was.

I wake up in the pitch dark and know instantly that something is wrong.

There's a little stream of yellow from the streetlights coming through the dusty blinds, but that's the way it was when I fell asleep. Lucas is still there, sleep-breathing, so it's not him. I must've heard a sound that woke me up.

I push up against the wall slowly, holding my breath, listening. It won't help much. I don't know this building, what it usually sounds like. It might just have been creaking in the wind. Or mice.

I would really not be surprised if it was mice. I close my eyes, half-expecting a squeak, or for one of the little freaks to run over my feet. I wait.

Nothing.

Nothing.

Nothing.

Then a scrape that is *not* shifting or a rodent. It's a step on the wooden floor. Another. Not close, but still.

Coming.

I get to my feet in one movement, shake Lucas awake the next. He's groggy, moaning at me, but I poke him hard, hold my finger to my lips until he understands.

"Someone's coming," I whisper.

There's a voice now, too far away to hear more than a murmur. Low, though. Male.

Christ, could Smith have found us? How? Did he install a tracking chip in Lucas? Or me?

I should've thought of that. The bastard is definitely smart enough for that. Something we ate or drank? Or injected with that shot? Something attached to our clothes?

Or it could be building security. At this point I'm hoping for that. I could handle being thrown outside, no problem. Or maybe they won't find us at all, sweep on past. Why would they, in a dark room on the fourth floor?

Unless there's a chip.

We move, glacially slow, towards the door. I want to hide behind it in case anyone opens it, looks in. It could give us a second of surprise.

I hope it wasn't stupid to bring Lucas here. That I didn't overlook something, and Smith is going to drag us back again, way more pissed and insane than he was before, if that's possible. I don't want to see that.

The stairwell door bangs shut, too loud. There are footsteps on our floor. Whoever it is isn't trying to be quiet. Two sets of footsteps, getting closer. They stop. The silence stretches long, so long, but it can't last...

"Yakob? Are you here?"

Oh my god. I almost collapse against the door in relief. It's Dedushka, early. And two sets of footsteps...Rachel.

I'm out of the room in a hot second. She's there, standing uncertain in the dark hallway, a flashlight in her hand. I can barely even see her.

I want to run and hug her, bowl her over right there, kiss her until I'm sure she's real and I'm real and we're both in the same place, together again.

But I stand in the hall, my feet chained to the floor, like a dumbass.

Dedushka doesn't have that problem. He takes the two steps and wraps his arms around me, and his familiar tobacco smell nearly kills me with happiness.

"We decide to take the faster way," he says, gruff. He doesn't say how glad he is to see me, but he doesn't have to. I know it in my bones.

When he lets go, Rachel's moved closer. "Hi," she says, soft.

"Hi," I answer.

Dedushka makes a disgusted noise and we laugh, and then I hug her. It feels like it's been months, years. She's soft, and her hug is fierce. She smells like ocean and car and Rachel. I drop my face into her neck, just for a second, and breathe her in. Her skin is warm.

"I'm mad at you," she says, her breath hot against my shoulder. She pulls away, tilting her face up towards me. I still can't see too well, but she's frowning. "I thought I wasn't anymore. But God, I'm mad at you. For leaving like that. For doing that."

"I'm that much of an idiot." I try to smile.

She punches me in the arm, hard.

It's not that easy, of course. It shouldn't be. I stop her, touch her hand. "Sorry. I was stupid. I should've stayed with you."

"Well. As long as you admit it." Her eyes shine wet, but she does smile, a little.

"Who's this?" Dedushka asks, more gentle than usual.

I'd almost forgotten, with everything. Lucas is in the hall, one foot still in the room like he's ready to dash back and slam the door if he has to. I don't blame him. He looks young, and skinny, and his hair is poking straight up like a brush.

"This is Lucas. Smith was holding him too, and he escaped with me. Lucas, this is Dedushka, my grandfather–" Dedushka growls at the word. "And Rachel. My..." Man, what do I say? I don't want to say 'girlfriend' since I just abandoned her and I don't know how we're going to just step over that. My girl? *No.* "My Rachel," I finish.

She laughs, and punches me in the arm again, then side-hugs, pulling close to me. I guess that was all right.

157

Lucas nods hello, and Dedushka shakes his hand. It's awkward, but not as awkward as it's going to be in a couple minutes.

"We think," I say, slowly, "that Lucas is also my half-brother."

Dedushka raises his eyebrows, but that's all. "We talk of that later. And Abby and Myka?"

I sigh. "That's the crappy part. They're with Dad. *Dad* took them. He's holding them at a base in Green Bank, West Virginia."

Rachel gasps. Dedushka drops his head and swears in Russian. "I did not think it could be so, that he would do this."

We all stand there, silent. Reflecting on how far Dad has gone.

Lucas's stomach growls again, and Dedushka grunts. "Yakob did not feed you, I see." He gives me a glare–though I know he doesn't mean it–and hustles Lucas down the hall, down the stairs, without another word. Rachel and I follow. We don't exactly hold hands, but our hands are near each other. Bumping, knuckle to knuckle.

"Your brother?" she whispers, when they're far enough ahead of us. "And Smith had him? Does that mean he…"

"Yeah," I whisper back, as low as I can. "He has a power too. Though I don't know what, yet. Dad would visit him every once in a while, but most of the time he just ignored him."

"Wow," she says. "Just…wow. That's crazy. Your dad is a piece of work."

"Wait." I stop her, at the top of the stairs. "I forgot to ask, before. Did you get the serum?"

There's a long pause. She looks down at her feet, and my hopes sink. It didn't work. I'm stuck running forever.

158

Then she looks up and grins. "It's us. Of course we got it."

Hope floats me down the rest of the stairs. I'd almost forgotten what it feels like.

31

JAKE

Meet Me in the Dark by Otherwise

We end up driving about half an hour away, out of the DC main area, and eating at a Denny's. It's not a typical Dedushka move, since there are security cameras, but I'm grateful. I practically drool over the pictures of the biggest breakfast imaginable, and Lucas excitedly orders a burger and fries. It's probably been years since he's been to a place like this.

If I close my eyes and listen to the talk of the other late-night customers and clink of plates, the smell of fried food and breakfast, it could be a normal Denny's outing from a year ago. With Chris and the theater gang, including Rachel, after a show.

Rachel's leg brushes against mine and I realize I'm happy, in this one moment. I'm missing the biggest piece—I still have to get Myka and Mom back—but half of my family and more is back together, we're safe for now, and we have the serum.

We have the serum. It may not work, but if it does…I could be normal. Safe forever. Not have to do any more tunnels like Smith made me do…and like he tried to make me do. That corrupt, dark world my power drags me into.

I have helped people with it, though. Sometimes.

Dedushka and Rachel tell us about their trip, a strange adventure with the Salty Dog bar and a boat and the police. A treasure hunt. I wish I'd been with them instead. I catch them up on what happened with me, all of it. Even Bunny. Lucas listens too. I don't know how much of that he knew.

Dedushka goes purple when I tell him about Smith shooting Bunny, and how he treated Lucas. He mutters to himself in Russian. That's always a bad sign.

"I hope that means we're going to stop Smith someday," I say, the words rough in my mouth. I couldn't let myself think of it until we got out, clear, but I can't let Bunny's death be avenged by one punch. There's got to be more to it than that. And holding Lucas like an animal. I should've done more when I had the chance.

"Da," Dedushka says. "Someday, I promise. But first we must deal with your–" He waves at both me and Lucas. "Your father. My son. Who also must pay."

"No argument there," I say.

"But what did he do?" Lucas asks. He flinches when all three of us turn to look at him, like a light is too bright. But he ducks his head, blinks, and goes on. "I…I've been thinking about it. He got your mom and sister out of Smith's way, right? Maybe he was smart to do that. Cautious. And he's running a lab, but is he forcing anyone? I mean, okay. It's not good. But he's not…evil, like Smith is."

Dedushka and I share a look. I get it. He just found out his dad isn't dead, like I did before, and doesn't want him to be the bad guy. Even though Dad threw him away, and would use him in an instant if he had control of him. Even though I remember with chills how Dad looked when he told me I was going to have to stay underground for the rest of my life, how I was going to 'help' him. But I guess I don't need to smash his image to pieces to Lucas. Not right away.

"Not evil," I say carefully. "That's true. But misguided. Making bad choices. You don't want to stay with him, Lucas."

"Listen. He is speaking truth," Dedushka says.

Lucas rubs his thumb over his fork, staring at the table. He sucks in his cheeks, in a weird way I saw him do yesterday. Like he just licked a lemon.

"I met him too," Rachel chimes in, soft. "He's...obsessed with the powers. I think he wants one for himself, and that's all he thinks about."

That. I know he does.

"You have a power too, yes?" Dedushka asks. He sets one hand on Lucas's arm. "What is it?"

Lucas shakes his head, still fork-focused.

"It's okay," Rachel says. "It's safe, with us."

Dedushka nods. "I had power also." He pulls at his beard, stops. "Long ago. I started this all. So tell me, boy, what did I do to you?"

Lucas rubs a hand, quick, through his hair—making it stick up even higher—and meets my gaze. "Do you have any personal things with you?"

"Of mine?" I ask. "Like an object?"

He nods solemnly.

"Do you use objects like I do?" I ask, low. "Can you do the same thing, see what people are seeing and hearing? See where they are?"

He shakes his head. "No. But I see something...feel something...when I touch a personal thing that was important to someone." He swallows, and bounces his knee. "I see the past."

Dedushka whistles through his teeth. "Death?"

Lucas frowns. "No. Not like that, at least most of the time. I see some event, or more than one event, that was significant to the person, that was linked to that object."

The waitress brings our food, and we abandon the conversation and attack it like wolves. Well, Lucas and I do. Dedushka looks amused, watching us, and Rachel slightly horrified. Once we've eaten half the food on the plate, I chug some coffee and look at Lucas.

"You saw me tunnel and control someone, for Smith." He nods, mouth full of fries. "What did you use? The green glass bottle?"

He nods again. I should've broken that thing when I left, or left it somewhere. It keeps causing heartache. Bunny...

"And the little girl?" I ask. "He brought you in after I couldn't tell him what he wanted to know."

He scowls. It changes his whole face, makes him older. "I saw what happened to her. When they took her off the street."

"You...saw?"

Lucas gives me the barest of nods. Dedushka glares at me, then claps him on the shoulder. "It is a hard seeing you have. I am sorry."

Rachel lays a hand on my knee under the table. It does sound rough. Probably most of the events he sees are

163

traumatic, or they wouldn't come through in an object, be stored that way. Not as bad as Dedushka's was, though, all death.

Wait. I turn to Rachel, whisper in her ear. "How much serum is there?"

She sighs. "I thought of that," she whispers back, her breath tickling my cheek. "It's not very much. Probably only one dose. We'll have to wait to make more, if you're both going to take it."

Crap crap crap. Which means we have to get Mom and Myka out first, and then find some way to make more, to duplicate whatever is in there, or either me or Lucas will be stuck forever with the power. Running forever. I was hoping to take it now and be able to waltz into Dad's lab, tell him I'm useless, and walk out with them. Now it's way more complicated.

She takes it out of her pocket and sets it on the table, a red vial. "You could still take it, here. Now. Get rid of your power. Leave a few drops..."

Dedushka and Lucas go silent, watching us. I touch it, this vial that could solve everything. I want to take it. I look at Dedushka, then Lucas.

I can't. Just in case.

I turn back to Rachel. "Better not," I say lightly. "I might still need tunneling to track them down, make sure they're okay." I curl a finger around the smooth glass. "Should I hang on to it, though? So if I need to—"

"You should keep," Dedushka says. "And if you need to, swallow it all."

There's silence for a while, while we all finish our food. Then Lucas clears his throat.

"Do you think...we could stop and get a book? Or two?" He sucks in his cheeks, lets it out again. "I'm kind of used to reading all the time. Or watching TV. It...um...calms me." He bounces his leg again, so much that it makes his whole body jiggle. "And I don't think we can get a TV."

Rachel, the ex-library aide, beams at him. "I think we can get you a book or two. And then we head to West Virginia."

32

RACHEL

And Then There Were Two (Magnificent Seven soundtrack)
by Elmer Bernstein

When we get close to Green Bank, West Virginia, we start seeing signs for the National Radio Astronomy Observatory. Then we see it, a huge white telescope that looms over everything. We pull over to read an information sign, to find out what we're dealing with.

"The Green Bank telescope is the world's largest steerable radio telescope," the sign says. The observatory builds telescopes for use around the world. It seems like the observatory is the focus of the town—that most of the people who live here have something to do with it. So... this whole place is full of scientists and government people. It's also something called a mandatory United States National Radio Quiet Zone: there are no cell phones or wi-fi allowed in the whole *town*, because they interfere with the radio signals they're monitoring. They check at the border, and ask you to shut phones and computers off until you leave. Extreme big government.

I rest my chin on Jake's shoulder as I read. "Ah. Smart."

It's not a coincidence that John put his new base here. Activity for the observatory means lots of cover for the activity of a secret government base, with the same type of people coming in and out. And security built-in, if you go through town.

"Right?" Jake says. "He's here on purpose. Cover. Plus I don't know if cell phones and wi-fi affect psychic activity—but I bet Dad thinks it would work better without interference."

I raise my eyebrows. "I don't know about that. It's a good thing we don't have cell phones, though."

"The Devil's tools," Dedushka says, and spits over his shoulder.

Well, then.

Lucas wanders off to look at the field in front of us, or maybe the mountains behind. There are a lot of mountains here, the famous Allegheny mountains, crouched all around the town. We drove through some too, windows down, cool air blowing in, the smell of pine filling the car. I wish we could've held onto that for a while, that moment of peace. But we're here now.

We don't have a plan. We know where the base is, because of the coordinates Jake saw, and Dedushka and I figured out on the map where that is. It's not in the town itself, so we don't actually *have* to go through the border checkpoint. But what does it look like? A metal shed? A trapdoor in the ground?

Jake suggested we lure John out of his hideout and make him give up Abby and Myka by force. Dedushka wants to present himself at the door and ask to talk to John. He thinks somehow he can negotiate with him and make him see how crazy he's being. I think they're both suicidal. I don't think we should see John at all, at least not at first. I think we should observe the base for a while. Watch how it works, who goes in and out, and see if we can sneak in and find Abby and Myka.

Okay, I have no idea how a secret base works, other than the one of John's I saw briefly before. I don't even know much about military bases in general. Maybe they're impossible to sneak into. But that's why I want to observe it first.

Lucas sat in the back of the car while we were discussing it all and bit on his thumb, staring out the window or reading his book while we argued it out. I feel terrible for him. He's been thrown into this bizarre situation, with people he doesn't know but is supposed to be related to.

167

At least we all have new clothes now, normal clothes we bought from Walmart, so Jake and Lucas don't look like jail escapees, and Dedushka and I aren't filthy.

I just wish I knew how to handle all of this. Any of this. Jake seems hard again, like he did when I first saw him after DARPA. Locking him up, and killing that woman in front of him, Bunny... it messed with him all over again. Sometimes I can barely remember what he was like before all this, before he went away. I mean, he was always intense. But there was confidence, a sense that he knew where he was going and he'd get there no matter what. I was drawn to that. He was easy to talk to, quick to flirt. I didn't see the anger that's always there now, simmering just under the surface. And the sadness.

I wish I could take it all away from him... but sometimes I wonder if he's just changed. If that's how he is now, or if it will lighten once we get his family back, and get rid of his power.

We went through all that search just to get hold of that vial. I want him to take it already and deal with everything from there.

Lucas loops back, and leans against the sign. He shuffles his feet in the dirt, looking down. "I thought of something."

He doesn't continue. After a couple seconds I nod, look at him encouragingly. "What did you think of?"

"Mr. Smith... he's my legal guardian." His face pinches. "He adopted me, when my mother gave me up."

"Jesus," Jake says.

I cringe. As a guardian, he's about the worst person I could think of. Unstable, terrifying, violent.

Lucas swallows, but doesn't answer. I don't think that's why he's telling us.

"Wait," Jake says. "So he has a legal right to chase you? To send cops after you, or us?"

He nods, an earnest bobbing. "That's why I thought of it. In case he can send the police."

"We could fight him, though," I say. "He's abusive. There's no way he's a good guardian..."

168

I drift off, looking at Jake, then Dedushka. Imagine it. A courtroom with Jake standing in it, trying to explain how he would be a good guardian. With the small fact that to most of the world, except a tiny branch of the government, he's legally dead. And that branch of the government wants to keep him in a cell. Dedushka's not much better—they were looking for him too, even before this. He's still standing by the car, leaning on the doorframe, his beard draped over it. Studying the observatory hanging over the town. I don't even know if he heard us.

There's Abby, the only normal one. But we can't even get to her. And I keep forgetting... Lucas isn't even hers.

"We'll just have to keep you away from him," Jake says. "And it's not like we're exactly legal anyway."

"While we're running, yeah." Lucas blinks, fast. "But if we do go with... meet with... John, would he turn me back over to Mr. Smith? He could." He swallows. "Mr. Smith would be so mad..."

"No," Jake says, firm. "There is no way John would ever give you back to Smith."

But I'm not sure John's better. "I don't think we should let John anywhere near him," I say. "Not now."

Dedushka's watching us now, his eyes sad.

"I won't let John take you either, okay?" Jake adds. "We'll find a way out of this, take the serum, and live normal lives. Together somewhere."

Lucas bites his lip. He has no reason to believe us over anyone else, to trust us. Does he even want to live with Jake? Does he want to be normal? He hasn't talked enough to know. "I'm hungry," he says, finally.

I laughs and ruffle his hair, though he shrinks away a little. "You're always hungry."

"I will go fetch food," Dedushka says. "You stay here, rest. I will go."

"Here? Why don't we all go?" I ask. "That way we can have a say in what we get. So you don't bring more of those horrible runza things."

169

I grin at him. Runza are Russian sandwiches, filled with ground beef, onion, and cabbage. He was so excited when we ran across a restaurant in Sarasota that served them. I was not quite as excited. I've teased him about them a couple of times, and normally I get a glare back.

Dedushka just turns away and drops into the driver's seat. He starts the car, lifts a hand to us, then backs up and drives off.

There's a long pause, when we all watch the dust fly up, then settle slowly down again. He left us standing at an information sign. There isn't even anywhere to sit.

Jake looks at me. "Wrongness?"

"Severe wrongness." I glare in the direction he went, shading my eyes. "Tell me that's not the way the base is."

He growls under his breath. "Of course that's the way the base is. And of course that's what he's doing. Going to confront Dad himself, just like he wanted. Leaving without a word. Idiot."

"Hey," I say, eyebrows raised. "It's the Lukin method. Runs in the family."

"At least I told you," Jake says, low. "I explained. I would never just…leave."

I touch his arm. That's true. He did explain…the second time.

"Are we going to follow him?" Lucas asks, eager. "To the base?"

Jake and I have a silent conversation. The risks, the chance of all of us ending up stuck with John…versus taking a look at the base, finding out what Dedushka's up to, and what happens when he gets there. It all ends up at the same answer. Like always, we don't really have a choice.

"Yeah," Jake says. "We're going to follow him. Just to see. Let's start walking."

Fortunately the base coordinates aren't ridiculously far from where we were, walking distance. It's on the fringe of town, a lonely spot in the hills. We see the car parked a ways out, so that's confirmed. Dedushka is here, heading to John on his own. To do what? Tell him how wrong he is? Convince him to let Myka and Mom go?

I just spent three days with him and I can't believe he'd do that. He's *smart*. He knows how these things work, all too well. So why would he give himself up?

Jake thinks it's because Dedushka hasn't seen John since all of this happened. Since John disappeared two and a half years ago. He hasn't witnessed the crazy firsthand. Maybe he really thinks he can talk sense into John?

Maybe it's just a Lukin male trait to do stupid things to save people.

At least Dedushka was on foot for a long stretch too, and we walk faster than he does. We shouldn't be *that* far behind him. Maybe we can stop him before he goes in there.

Maybe. I think of him in the surf, Santa with his pants rolled up, laughing, and I walk faster. My heart pounds like I'm running a marathon, even at a walk.

Lucas has been dead silent since Dedushka left. I have *no* idea what's going on in his head.

When Vladimir's GPS says we're near the right place, the three of us stop and check it out. There's a small valley between two hills, a dirt track winding through it that shows definite signs of traffic. Jake and I lie on our bellies and spy, carefully, from the top of one of the hills. I don't see anything on the ground, no trap doors like in John's desert base. No suspicious mounds.

I kind of expected there'd be wire fence and guards, honestly, and a big metal building. Not another actual *hidden* base. This is weird.

"There," Jake says. He points to another hill across from us, farther down. "Do you see a square shape in the side there? An outline?"

It's hard to tell—I squint—but I think I see it. A secret door in a hill. It's like we're in a book. I blink. Yep, it's still there.

"Dad couldn't have built that in the time he's had," Jake whispers. "It had to have been here before. Crazy-ass government agencies."

"How many of these do you think there—"

Suddenly I see movement. I grab Jake's arm, point. A dot, moving towards the door. A dot with hair glowing white in the sun.

"No," Jake whispers. "NO."

I just hold his arm, watching. Helpless. We can't stop him now. There's got to be surveillance by the door, probably in the whole valley, and he's smack in the middle of it.

It's too late.

He stands in front of the square door, arms crossed. No waving, or demands as far as I can tell. Just standing there, waiting.

"What's he doing?" I whisper.

And then Lucas is over the hill and in the valley too, sprinting towards the door, towards Dedushka. Jake lunges to stop him, but misses.

We weren't watching, either of us. We'd almost forgotten he was still standing there. And he's too fast. Too determined. We can't yell after him either, without giving ourselves away and getting us all stuck.

"He wants to get to John," I say, low. "Did you hear him, at Denny's? He just wants to see John again."

Jake drops his head in the dirt and swears, but I keep watching. I have to see.

After a couple seconds Jake lifts his head to watch too.

The white dot that is Dedushka turns and watches Lucas pelting towards him, unstoppable. I can imagine the defeat in him, even though I can't see it. No, I don't have to imagine it. I feel it, tears in my eyes as the door behind them slides up, revealing a dark tunnel into the hill. You could drive a truck through it, which is probably the point.

Two soldiers in desert fatigues with rifles come barreling out.

They bark orders we can't hear, and both Dedushka and Lucas sink to their knees, hands behind their heads. It takes ten seconds for them to be handcuffed, pulled to their feet, and dragged inside. Five seconds more and the door is shut again, sealing them inside the hill. Puffs of dust swirl around, the only evidence that anything happened.

"Now Dad has every single member of my family in there, captive," Jake says, slow.

I hiccup a sob. It's true. Just like that. Now we have no leverage left. The only one still out here is Jake. "I'm sorry," I say. Though it's useless.

He slumps against the hill, his back to it all. "I'm not giving myself up. Not again. Not this time."

"NO." I wipe my face and sit back too, next to him. I grab his hand like I can keep him here myself, by force. "You're not. I don't know what he—what they—were thinking. But you being in there too isn't going to help anyone."

"And then there were two," he says, bitter.

We started with five. Down to two, up to four. And now we're back to two. Me and Jake. That's all we have left.

33

MYKA

Family Portrait by P!nk

A soldier comes and gets me to have lunch with Dad. I'm happy. I'm past ready to talk to him, and tell him how upset I am. I need to see Mom. He needs to let us stay together. This isolation for days plan, whyever he's doing it, is dumb. It's not going to work.

I'm going to tell him that.

They take me to his office. He's got lunch all set up on his desk, places for two. Mac and cheese, and canned peaches. He smiles when I come in. "There she is!"

I drop into the seat and fold my arms. "I don't just eat cheese, you know."

"But you still *like* cheese. Don't pretend you don't. Eat."

"Dad. You can't keep me and Mom locked up separately like this. It's kidnapping. You're holding us against our will, and—"

"You're my *family*," he snaps. His voice rises. "That's ridiculous. You just need to understand."

I shake my head. "No. You need to let us go."

174

"EAT YOUR DAMN LUNCH." He shouts it, spit flying from his mouth, and I bite my lip to keep from screaming.

My hand shakes as I lift the fork and put a bite of mac and cheese in my mouth.

He really wasn't like this before. He never yelled at me. He just got quiet when he was mad. What happened? Why is he...

A horrible thought hits me, and I stop chewing, staring at Dad, while I think of it. Did he try some experimental medicine on himself? He's trying to affect the brain. If it went wrong, that would affect the brain too. That might make him crazy.

The macaroni sticks in my throat.

"Have you thought about the serum?" he says, casually. His voice is normal again, reasonable.

But now I don't know what to say. I don't want to set him off again. I take another bite and chew, slowly. It tastes like sand. "I...uh..." No, I can't pretend, or lie to him. I never could. "I'm not interested. I never will be. I don't want a power, and I don't want you to experiment on me."

His lips press all thin, and I'm afraid he's going to go off again.

"Dad," I say, as soft as I can. "I'm not a subject. I'm *Myka*. Your daughter. You don't want to—"

His phone beeps, and he snatches it up and holds it to his ear. At first he's irritated, but then he leans into the phone, interested. "I'll be right there," he says. His eyes lock on me. I can see the excitement in them. Something new is happening. "Isolate them. Don't talk to them until I get there."

Them? Who's them? My breath gets fast. Jake? I don't know if I want him to be here or not.

Dad hangs up the phone and grips the desk, staring at the wall.

"Is Jake here?" I ask. "Did he come to get us?"

He focuses again, smiles wide, and shakes his head. "Not yet. Soon. He slaps his leg. "But the next best thing. Two of the next best things." He points at the food. "Stay here and eat your lunch. When you're finished, one of my people will take you back to your room. I'll talk to you later. I may be...busy for the rest of the day."

He strides to the door.

"Dad! Wait!"

He pauses, and turns half-around, his hand on the door handle.

"Will you let me be with Mom? Especially if you're not going to be there..."

He doesn't even answer. He just goes out the door and pulls it shut behind him.

34

JAKE

Kiss by Prince

The two of us decide we should leave, get out of the area while we figure out what to do next. Dedushka left the keys in the car for us. We drive back out of town–the trees overhead flipping past the windshield in rhythm, flip, flip.

"Take the serum," Rachel says, low.

I hold onto the steering wheel tight, watching the trees. "I can't. Not now."

She scoots closer. She has dirt powdered in her hair, smeared on her cheek. "Take it. Before John has a chance to get hold of it. Before anyone–" she looks hard at me "–thinks of trading it. Or tricks you into going in there, to save them. Take it, stop your power, and all of this can be done. You can still walk in and ask him to let them go, once you don't have the ability anymore. Once he can't use you."

I touch my pocket, where the vial is hidden. Maybe that's what Dedushka wanted, leaving it with me. Down it, be done.

"But I can't," I say, barely out loud. "There's Lucas. What if he needs it? I can't take the only dose."

Rachel leans in, her eyes intense. "He didn't ask for it to stop. Your dad might not even know he has a power. He's not the one John wants."

"He'll know. If Lucas doesn't tell him, he'll figure it out. And then he can use Lucas too." I take a curve on the road, let myself consider the possibilities. "I shouldn't. In case..."

"Leave a little, then. For making more later. We'll hide it. But Jake. You don't need your power anymore to find them. You know where they are. You don't need it anymore at all." She breathes in, deep. "You need to use this—or we got it for no reason. You need to do this for everyone."

I pull over, in a little clearing off the side of the road. I take out the vial, look at it. It's cool against my fingers.

I think of the tunnels Smith made me do, that desperate little girl in a cage. The ones he wanted me to do, controlling people. He's still tracking me, I'm sure of it. I think of Dad right behind that door, waiting like a spider to bring me in, wring every last tunnel out of me. Of Liesel, making me hunt people. Of everyone, friends like Chris, thinking I'm dead.

I think of Mom and Myka and Dedushka and Lucas in there, all because of this power

I could do it.

But then I think more of that girl. If it wasn't Smith I was tunneling for, if it was Liesel or someone, we would've saved her. I have saved people. And yes, I don't need to know where my family is, but I can still use tunneling to control people.

"I can't," I say. "What if I need to control Dad? I have his tie tack. I could. I can't give up my only advantage right now, when I might still need it. We'll rescue them, and then I'll take it. And *then* I'll be done."

178

I tuck the vial back in my pocket. She nods, slowly.

Then she lunges across the seat and kisses me. Hard, demanding, nothing like the soft kisses we've had before. Nothing like ever before.

I like it. I kiss back, joining her frenzy. My hand slips to her neck, and I stop thinking. My brain explodes in a fire of kiss, of her. Of need. A while later she pulls away, her hand over her mouth. I try to follow—I can't do anything but follow—but she stops me, one hand on my leg.

"I wanted to do that for a long time," she says, a little breathless. She shakes her head, like she's clearing it. "Okay, you keep the power. But keep that in your pocket, as insurance. Let's go to Green Bank, get something to eat, and then we can plan what to do. Yeah?"

I don't even answer. I stare out, my thoughts on a loop now that I'm not kissing anymore. No power. Normal. Safe.

I wonder what that would be like.

We risk going through the border into Green Bank—though they don't even look at us, just ask about cell phones we don't have. There is nothing in Green Bank. It's very green, and very rural. Church, school, houses, giant telescope, smaller telescopes. Kind of a perfect place for a secret base.

We end up finding a General Store a little north in Arbovale, stock up on chips and beef jerky, crackers and water, and hole up in the car again parked off a dirt road. A huge blue water tower looms over us, the kind kids climb in movies and scrawl graffiti on, but this one's graffiti-free. I try to eat, but I don't want to. I want to do about five different things at once. I want to go rescue Mom, Myka, Dedushka, and Lucas from that damn base. I want to punch Dad, both for Mom and Myka and for how he treated Lucas.

Maybe more than punch him, but I won't let my mind drift that far.

I want to shake Lucas, and then Dedushka, and then Lucas again, for going in. And I want to kiss Rachel again. We're alone, and we haven't been alone very much at all, and she's close to me and her knee is touching mine. It's warm. I can feel the point of warmth through my whole body.

But I have to focus on the first one first. Rescue.

Rachel's reading a Washington Times she picked up at the store, devouring the political section before we settle in to plan. It helps her focus, she says. I forget sometimes she wants to be a poly sci major when all this is done. When—if—we go back to real lives. I pick up the front page she's discarded, scan the headlines.

A plane's gone missing. A whole plane, with 180 people, took off from China and vanished off the radar, somewhere over the ocean. They don't know if it went down, or landed somewhere, or was taken hostage. It's been missing for two days. I read the whole article. It's bizarre. They simply have no idea where any of those people are.

I run a hand over the page, my heart beating fast. I could solve it in two minutes, with any item from any one of those people. I could say whether they are dead or alive, where they landed, what they're seeing. There would be no mystery at all.

And if they are alive, stranded somewhere, I could maybe save 180 people without breaking a sweat.

I pull my hand back. That won't happen. I'm not going to do that anymore. Soon I won't be able to.

There's a rumble, and a car comes slowly into view behind us. I squint, trying to see better. It's a black car, a Buick, with a woman driving. In a suit, with her blonde hair pulled into a ponytail. She pulls over in front of our car, steps out, and leans against the door, her arms folded.

My blood freezes. "God. It's Liesel."

35

JAKE

Know Your Enemy by Green Day

I can barely think, my brain stuck playing a hundred remembered incidents. Liesel in my room at home telling me about DARPA that first time, and our deal. In my cell, once she got me to Montauk, trying to act like everything was fine. Livid after she found out I was tricking her, and busting her gut when she saw me escape using Eric's body.

Standing over Eric with her gun at her side, after she saved me by shooting him. That's the last time I saw her.

"What should we do?" Rachel asks. "Should we take off?"

I shake my head, slow. "She must be working with my dad. She wants to talk."

My heart thumps a drum solo, loud in my ears. I stare at Liesel staring at me.

"Stay here, get in the driver's seat. Turn the engine on. If I give you the high sign, *go*, okay?"

"No," she says, frowning. "You're not giving yourself up anymore. You just said…"

"I'm not giving myself up. If I tell you to go, it'll be because it's something bad, but it's not my plan." My voice is low. "I don't know what she wants."

She presses her lips together hard. "You have the serum now. You could be useless to her in a second. Remember that."

I nod, get out of the car. Liesel hasn't moved, arms still folded. She looks exactly the same. My hands start shaking just looking at her. But I make myself walk forward, step by step. The wind blows across my face, smelling of grass and cows, and I remember that I never have to follow this woman underground again. I can keep breezes and sun and places without walls.

I stop a few feet away, like she still might grab me.

"You're working with him now?" I ask, when I'm close enough to talk. "What happened to your own project?"

She shrugs. "I had no project without you. And your dad is continuing the work. It seemed natural."

I shake my head. "I wouldn't have thought it. How'd you find me, anyway?"

"Please." She laughs, her old laugh, and I fight the urge to shiver. "We have drones, Jacob. We followed you from the base. You had to be nearby, with your grandfather here. And this is a secured area. You went through a border."

I swallow hard. Drones. And spy satellites. I always forget to look up. "What do you want?"

"I *want* part of what your father wants: you working for us. Making a difference. Not vulnerable to people like Gareth Smith. I can't believe you were working for him."

I shift. I hate her voice. Soft, insistent, always with the judging.

"This Lucas told us already, about how he was with Gareth, how you were. Jacob. That is precisely what I was trying to avoid."

"Sorry to disappoint," I snap. "I thought he had my family."

She rubs a hand across her forehead, tiredly. Her ponytail swings. "No, *John* had your family. For safety. And he will, until they're not in danger anymore."

"You can't do that!" I shout. "Let them go!"

She doesn't answer, just looking at me. I know that look too well. Like a cat eyeing a mouse.

"Why are you working with him?" I ask. "You know he's insane. Unpredictable. He stole my family off the street. He probably killed someone."

She sighs. "It's complicated."

"I won't work for you." I say, short.

"Listen. The General, John, they don't know where you are, yet. I haven't told them. But they'll want to take you in by force. They think they can convince you once you're in custody." She smooths her hair, a gesture I remember. "Or force you. But I don't think so. I got to know you a little bit, didn't I, Jacob? You're one of the most stubborn people I've ever met. I don't think you will work under pressure. I think you'll be useless if they do that. And let's just say...I don't agree with everything they're doing."

"So?" I rub one hand against my leg, over and over, just to be doing something.

"So I'm talking to you on my own. Privately. In retrospect we were doing well in the field. Better than underground. I think that's how you need to work. I think we really could protect you, regardless of what John thinks, and we could get things done. Together. While you live your own life."

"I'm not working for you."

She raises her eyebrows. "No? Not even if it meant saving a plane full of people?"

My breath catches. Is she psychic? Does she have a psychic watching me?

She laughs again. "If you saw the news, you'd think of it. It was the first thing I thought of. We could save them, Jacob. I could get you an object."

I honestly don't know what to say. I do want to save those people. I ache to. It feels like exactly what I *should* be doing with tunneling. Finding lost people. Saving people. The best part—the only good part—of when I was working for Liesel.

"I want my family out. Free. All of them."

"Are you agreeing?" she asks.

I breathe in, slow, through my nose. "I'm not agreeing. I'm...listening."

"And Lucas?" She raises an eyebrow. I don't know if she knows yet that Lucas *is* my family.

"And Lucas." I swallow. She just watches me, and I know that's all she'll do until I say something else. "What do you want to do?"

She smiles, like the cat with a mouse in its belly. "Nothing, yet. I'm going to need to broach this with John, if you agree. He'll require some convincing. But for now, while you think about it, take this." She hands me an old-style pager. "This doesn't interfere with their satellite. If it buzzes, meet me back here as soon as you can. Under the trees, so the satellites don't catch us." She points at it. "There's a button on the side. Push that if you want to meet with me."

"It's a tracker," I say. "You're just planting a tracker on me."

She shakes her head. "I told you, I don't need to. Throw it out if you want. But I think this might be your best shot at getting everything. And mine."

She nods, slides into her car, and drives away.

I hold the pager in two fingers. That is not what I expected at all.

Rachel and I decide to sleep that night in the car. Neither of us wants to spend the bit of money we have left on a hotel, not when we know we're being watched anyway. Better to hunker down in one known place until we figure out our next move.

The old me wouldn't have even thought something like that. I'm getting more like Dedushka every day.

I do wonder, for a minute—a couple of minutes—what it would've been like to get a hotel room, just me and Rachel. We haven't been alone long enough to be together before, and if we got a hotel room with just us, with one bed...I think of the kiss, and I don't think we could've resisted.

But it feels like the wrong time for that. With everything.

Though I could be persuaded.

Instead we spend the time talking the situation over, up, down, sideways and inside out. More than we probably need to, considering there aren't really that many valid choices. Rachel's asleep, and I'm still going over them.

1. Go to the door like Dedushka did. Negotiate the release of my family. This is dumb, and neither of us wants to do it.

2. Page Liesel, enlist her help, and get everyone released first. Say I'll work with them if she does that. Then take the serum and tell Dad and Liesel, when Mom and Myk and Dedushka are safe, that I'm out of the game.

This is my play. I don't feel any particular urge to be honest and straight-up with Liesel. She never was with me. And if I can use her offer to leverage everyone out first, instead of trusting Dad's grace to do it...it feels like a stronger position.

And I can maybe even save the people on that plane.

The major weakness is Lucas. They know he has a power already, if they know he was with Smith. They won't just let him go, and I can't figure out a way to fix that problem. He leapt from one prison to another.

I'm going to have to figure that one out later. Mom and Myk first, and Dedushka.

But if I go with choice 2, that means I'm going to have to trust Liesel to let the rest of them out. That's the scariest part of all. I've been there before, too many times. Hell, I was just there with Smith. How can I trust any of them to do what they say they'll do?

I look back at Rachel, stretched out in the backseat. She looks somehow utterly comfortable, her head on her elbow, her hair curving around her face. Her lashes are long and dark, her cheeks that pink that made me notice her first. I've watched her sleep in so many strange places over the past weeks. In a rail yard, on Smith's plane, in Dad's other base. In the van so many nights. She's stayed with me through everything, though I still have no clue why. Why I got so lucky to have her with me, in this craziness.

I think I love her. That's the first time I've admitted it to myself. I liked her before—wanted her, even craved her—but it's different, now that I'm getting to know her for real. I can imagine being with her after this, now that I'm almost free of this thing. Figuring out a life together. Some version of what we originally wanted, her at Berkeley, me at Stanford, meeting in the middle....

I scramble over the seat, wanting to be near her, wanting to be romantic or something and wake her up, but she sits bolt upright with all the noise I make. I laugh over how smooth I am not, and she laughs too, startled. Her eyes bright, a little sleep-crease on the side of her cheek.

I kiss her, somewhere between that hard, passionate kiss and the usual soft exploratory ones. This one has the awareness of love in it, somehow. It's deeper, whole. We are whole together. I kiss her neck, her shoulder, she kisses my chest. Before I realize what is happening most of our clothes are off, unnecessary.

I could be persuaded.

No matter what else happens, for this little time, all is right with the world.

36

RACHEL

Love by Matt White

I wake up curled with Jake in the backseat of the car, using our discarded shirts as blankets. He's still asleep, one arm warm around me, his hair flopping over his face. We're together. For however long it lasts. Even if it was only once, I don't regret last night at all. I run one finger over his cheek. The stubble is getting long again, out here. I lean up and kiss it, prickly on my lips.

"Mmmm," he groans, his eyes fluttering.

"Sorry," I whisper. "We're safe from the satellites *here*, right?"

He opens his eyes, pulls me tighter, and kisses the top of my head, sleepily. "God, I hope so."

"I can just imagine some DARPA operative watching this scene closely." I grin. He kisses me again, his lips meeting mine. The warmth floods through me. This is what I need. Right here, for now. I reach for his arm, lose my balance, and fall off the seat onto the floor.

"Are you all right?" Jake asks, all worried, but I just laugh. Surprised, but not even really embarrassed.

"That seat isn't really meant for two people. Especially when one of them takes up as much room as you do." I sit up, find my clothes, and start to pull them on. "I don't think we have anywhere to be today, until we decide what to do or we hear from Liesel. Want to go for a walk?"

We end up walking along a little trail that winds through the trees over soft, pine-strewn ground. It's narrow, maybe more of a deer track than a trail, but most of the time wide enough for the two of us to walk together. Jake takes my hand to help me over a log, and doesn't let go. His hand is a little bit damp, but I don't mind. I feel connected, for the first time in a long time.

We come to a trickle of a stream and decide to sit on the bank, listening to the gentle burble of the water.

"It's so calming," I say, dipping my fingers in the cold water. "We always took beach vacations. I haven't been in the mountains much."

"I have." Jake pulls his knees to his chest. "With my dad. We did beach vacations too, depending on where we were living. But my favorite was the camping." He makes a circle in the dirt with one finger. "Did I ever tell you about Glue?"

I almost laugh, but I can tell he's serious. "Glue?"

He nods. "Not the school supply. It was a family ritual, something we did every time we moved to a new house. That was a lot, when we were little."

I dip my head and stay quiet, listening.

"The four of us—Mom, Dad, me, and Myka—would each say a line, and put our hands in together. 'We Lukins stick together like glue...together we can make it through...'" He looks up, his eyes hollow. "We're so cracked now. Nothing could ever put us together, no matter what Dad thinks. I need to save the pieces I can."

"You will. *We* will." I lay my hand on top of his. We stare at the water for a while. It drifts by, oblivious, without a care in the world. "I have an idea. Why don't we play a game?"

He groans, and I laugh. "Not like that. We pretend, just for a while, that none of this exists anymore. No power, no John or

190

Smith or Liesel or any of that. And we say one thing we'd like to happen in the future."

He raises his eyebrows.

"Fine," I say. "I'll start." I pull my hair up off my neck, and tie it in a knot. "In the future, I...will be a student at UC Berkeley, studying Poly Sci. I'll have lunch every day in the quad and listen to people talk about politics, and maybe even argue with them. And I'll win." I point at him. "Your turn."

He smiles, a little. "Okay. Same lines. In the future, I will be a student at Stanford, in public history. I'll...be normal." He leans back on his elbows. "Maybe not even a very good student. I don't care at this point."

"You'll be a good student," I say. "It's Stanford. In the future I...will see you on weekends. We'll meet at my apartment or yours, and not leave all day."

He grins at me. "I use my turn to second that."

We kiss, until I lose my breath. I pull away, lay on my back, and look at the sky. It's deep, sweet blue, the color of my grandma's china.

"In the future, my mom and I will make up and she'll come and visit every once in a while, but not too much. And it will be nice."

"In the future," Jake answers, "My mom and sister and grandfather will be safe, and free of all of this." He swallows. "Sorry, I think I broke the rules with that one."

"It's okay," I say, quiet. "I wish that too."

We stop the game there. But it worked, some. For a while we didn't focus on the bad stuff, the terrible situation, but what we wanted it to be.

It gives us something to work for.

37

MYKA

I Turn to You by Christina Aguilera

I finally give in and start reading the Dorothy Hodgkin biography. It doesn't hurt Dad if I don't read it, and it helps pass the time. So when the door opens I don't even pay attention. It's probably just food, or them telling me I can use the bathroom again.

Except this time it's Liesel. And...behind her...Mom.

I fly out of the chair and hug Mom as hard as I can. She hugs me too, rubbing my back, smoothing my hair. Until I finally let go, and look up at her. "You're okay?" I realize I'm crying. "You're really okay?"

"I'm fine, baby," she says. She touches my cheek. "I've been right next door the whole time. And you're okay too? They haven't...done anything to you?"

I shake my head. "Dad wants to." I gulp. "He won't listen to me..."

"I'm sorry," Liesel interrupts. "I really am. This isn't for too long. She can't stay. But I wanted to let you two see each other, and I wanted to give you some news."

Uh-oh. She doesn't sound like it's *good* news.

192

"News?" Mom asks, her voice shaky.

"Complicated news," Liesel says. "Go ahead and sit on the bed, and I'll tell you."

I won't let go of Mom, so we move to the bed together. "Is this about Jake?" I ask. "Dad got a call..."

"Jake and everyone else too." She takes a breath and sits in the chair, facing us. "I saw Jacob yesterday. He's fine—out in the area around the base with Rachel. I haven't told John I know where he is."

"He's not giving himself up again, for us," Mom says. "No."

"That's not the plan," Liesel says, her face stern, her tone a little sharp. She reminds me of one of my teachers. "Or the news. The news is that Grigory Lukin is here. He walked up to the base and turned himself in, so he could talk to John."

"Dedushka," I whisper, soft. He's here. I feel like I should've known that, should've felt him. I really want to ask if we can see him, but I still don't think she's done.

"He brought a boy with him, Lucas Payne." She looks at us strangely. "Do you know this boy?"

"No." We both answer at the same time. I clutch Mom's hand, lace my fingers through hers. I don't want them to take her away from me again.

"Why?" I ask.

"Jake was working with Gareth Smith, apparently, and brought Lucas back with him. Abby, I'm sorry to be blunt, but Lucas is John's son with someone else. He's 15. Myka, he's your half-brother."

I frown. That doesn't make sense. First, why was Jake with Crazy Smith? What the heck? Second, if I had a half-brother, why wouldn't I know about it? Mom's eyebrows are drawn tight together, her mouth pursed up.

"I'm sorry, Abby. But I wanted to let you know. I didn't want you to be blindsided when you see him."

"What is John doing with this boy?" Mom asks. "Taking him like Jake? Like Myka? Is he going to experiment on all of his children?"

I shift on the bed. I don't like this.

Mom lets go of me and stands, her hands clenched. She paces in a little circle. "He's a bastard. That's what he is. A complete and utter bastard. All this time...he had another *child*? Another family? When I was mourning him..."

"All right, Abby," Liesel says. "I understand this is difficult news." She glances up in the corner of the ceiling. There's probably a camera there. "I think you need to head back now."

"No!" I jump up. "I need her here. You can't—"

"I'll stay," Mom says, fierce. "We can stay here together."

"I'm sorry, Myka." Liesel takes Mom's arm. "Abby. I'm trying to play within John's rules as much as possible, while other things are in process. A final hug, and then I've got to get you back."

I hug Mom as tight as I ever have, burying my face in her shirt like when I was little. "I love you," I say. Will I ever get to say it again? I don't know anymore, or what will happen until I do.

"I love you too. So much." She pulls me even closer, tears dripping on my head.

"We've got to go," Liesel says.

"I'll tap on the wall, okay?" Mom whispers. "Twice means I love you."

I nod. I let her pull away even though I don't want to, and watch both of them go out the door. I'm alone again.

But Dedushka is here, in the base. Jake's nearby. And I have a half-brother I never knew about.

If I wasn't so upset that would be interesting.

38

JAKE

Decisions by Nathan Lanier (Halo 4 Soundtrack)

I stand alone at Liesel's meeting place, fidgeting. I made the choice. Door #2, and see where it leads.

Rachel really didn't want to leave me here by myself, but I insisted. If it's a trap, I want her far away from here. She's my safety, my back-up.

Besides, I just want her safe. I feel the bumpy top of her ring in my pocket. She insisted. In case I needed to reach her.

Of course if Liesel doesn't respond to the page button, I'm stuck here without a car for two hours, before Rachel swings by again to check.

At least I'm in the shade. It's stupidly hot now, in the middle of the day. Not quite as bad as Florida, but almost. A low roast instead of a broil. But it's cold underground. I shiver. No. I don't really have to go there. I just have to say that I'll work with them. That's different.

I don't feel good trusting Liesel again. Better her than Dad or Smith, but not much. But she hasn't called in the troops yet.

Besides, what's my safe play here? If they're tracking me now by satellite, they'll track me if I leave. Eventually they'll find me anyway, and drag me back here. No. Better to use what little advantage I have and try to get them free first.

I think I might throw up.

I hear it before I see it, a low rumble. Then another cloud of dirt, swirling. She's not coming slowly. I swallow my doubts. She's always wanted my talent so badly. But not like Dad does, for himself—she wants to use it for the world. She's the Big Picture Queen.

Which is worrying, when you're the little picture.

The car pulls up hard, and she flings open the door. I hesitate.

"Get in," she calls, over the engine.

I lean over the door. "I want to talk out here. Neutral territory."

She snorts. "Don't be ridiculous, Jacob. I'm not abducting you anywhere. But this is a lot more comfortable than standing in the heat, and I want to keep moving. Get in."

I take a look around to check—she's alone—and slide into the passenger seat, a wave of cold air washing over my face. As soon as the door shuts she jets forward. I guess it doesn't surprise me that she's an aggressive driver.

We don't say anything for a while. We're heading out of Green Bank, north. The way Rachel and I went before. Trees crowding in on the road. At least I know it's away from the base. It isn't a trick.

"I don't have an object for you yet, from the plane," she says. She doesn't turn, her profile sharp and serious. "It's only been a day. But you know that. What do you want?"

"How are my mother and sister?" I ask. "How are Dedushka and Lucas?"

"They're all fine," she says. "I promise. Well, if not happy. I just spoke with Abby and Myka this morning."

I take a breath. "Okay. I want to take your deal."

That makes her turn, her eyes stabbing at me. "What? Why? Why now?"

We drive past a little post office, and Liesel accelerates in front of a car waiting to pull out. I squeeze the edge of the seat. "I miss some of the work we were doing. It was the only time it was useful, this thing." I dare to meet her eyes. "But mostly I need to get them out of there. That needs to happen first."

She makes a small sound of victory, and I can't help thinking of the predator scenario again. "You'll really work with us? You'll agree?"

I clench my fists on my knees. "I'm not going underground. Ever again. It needs to be up here."

She nods once, considering. "I need to talk to John. He's...not exactly as rational as he used to be. I'll talk to him, feel him out and see if this can work."

I frown. "I thought you were promising it?"

She blows out hard. "With John, I can't quite promise. Stay out here, with your girl, and I'll talk to him. Though you need to know...there was an unverified report this morning that Gareth Smith is on the way here."

Jesus. "He killed Dr. Milkovich. Did you know that? Shot her point-blank in front of me, because I wouldn't do something for him."

Again the look, searing. "Dr. Milkovich? Why was she...?" She sighs, as she figures it out. "No. I didn't know that." She shakes her head. "Jacob. Sometimes I'm sorry I brought you into all of this."

"Sometimes?"

Her lips tighten again, and we fly around a corner. "Yes. Sometimes." She pulls onto a side road, bumping on the dirt track, barely slowing down. I hang onto the door handle. "I'll let you know after I talk to him."

She screeches to a halt. There across the road, parked in an unassuming spot next to a trailhead sign, is Rachel, in our car. I see her sitting behind the wheel, her face a white blur.

"I wanted to prove the point that you can't really run away," Liesel says, low. "We know where you are. He knows you're close. He could take you in any time if he wanted to force you again, now that you're near. He's waiting for you to decide to come." She rubs one hand across the steering wheel, slow. Her hands are rough, the nails short, neat. Unpainted. "I'm so glad you're willing to work with us. That's all he wants, Jacob. Even if he's bumbling it."

She meets my eyes. "I'm anxious to work with you too. That's *my* ultimate goal. It always has been." She smiles, a flash of white. "See, I'm being honest with you. It's a new leaf."

I snort. It definitely is.

And I'm...not being honest. I'm not going to work with her. I'm going to destroy the power just as soon as I can.

It almost makes me feel guilty, right now.

I slip out the door and across the road to Rachel. She starts the car—ready to run, I guess—but I go to her window instead. She rolls it down, her eyes wide and deep in the shadows. "How did she find me?" she asks.

I shrug. Lean through the window and kiss her, hard. It's not romantic. It's connection, a lifeline when you might be drowning. I pull away, rest my hand on the sill. "It's done. I agreed. We'll find out what he says."

39

Had a Dad by Jane's Addiction

When the pager goes off and we come back to the meeting spot that evening, Rachel *really* doesn't want to leave me there alone. We sit in the car, staring out at the trees.

She leans her head against the headrest. "They proved they know where we are anyway," she says. "There's no point. Besides...I want to see what's happening. What if your dad comes here? I've never even seen him."

I laugh, involuntarily. "When you see him, promise you won't kill him with your mind."

"If I could do that," she says lightly, one hand twisting her hair, "Don't you think I would've by now?"

"Point."

I wonder if I would, if that had been my power. Would I be able to kill my father, cold blood, after all he's done? I don't think so. I couldn't even kill Smith. I should have.

"Please," I say. "If anything goes wrong, I need you to be okay."

She shakes her head, touches her lips. They're red, still, from kissing. "I did this twice already. I don't need you to protect me while you go out into the danger. Like you're a knight and I'm the damsel."

"Not the reason." I cup her beautiful chin in my hand, kiss her again. Lean my forehead on hers. "They want me, is all. Want what I can do. Simple as that, even if they're wrong that I will help them. And if it all goes to crap, you're the only one left. You're our safety net. We may need you to rescue us."

She sighs, blowing my hair. "I hate it. But if anything happens…"

"I'm not going away. I'm right here. I'm just talking to her. But if they try something, I'll take the serum. Then they can't use me anymore. So they can't keep me."

"Oh God," she says, eyes on the mirror. "She's coming."

I pull away, hop out, and lean over the door. "Go now. Fast. Check back in an hour or two."

She nods and revs the engine. I slam the door and she jumps forward, Dedushka-style. I think maybe she picked up some of his driving.

Before I can take another breath two cars pull up, two black Buicks. One in front of me, blocking the way, and one behind. This feels wrong. She was supposed to be alone, like before.

I want to run, but there's no escape. Liesel steps out of the car behind, with two soldiers in desert camo, guns at their sides. Two more soldiers get out of the front car.

I get a hollow feeling in my gut. I know why there are soldiers, and it isn't good. I take the vial out of my pocket, and hold it in my hand.

Dad steps out of the passenger side of the front car. He looks the same as always, in casual military gear, his hair newly buzzed short. Eyes the same as mine. He stands there with his hand on the door handle and looks me up and down. I can see the disappointment from here.

"Liesel?" I say. "What's going on?"

"We're here to talk, Jake," she says. "To discuss the deal."

I watch Rachel's taillights go over a hill in the distance, swallow, and step forward.

"Dad."

He stares at me for a long time, his jaw clenching, then shakes his head. "No, Jake. I can't do it."

Liesel makes a noise behind me.

"No," he says. "I thought I could, maybe, but this—?" He waves at the trees, the road. The sky. "This is ridiculous spy stuff. I thought you would've outgrown this kind of thing. You want to work with me? You want Abby and Myka safe? That's what I want too. You be straightforward and come in and work with me."

"That's not the deal." Dammit, my voice is shaky. "You let them go, and then I'll work with you. From out here, not underground. Liesel said—"

"Liesel is not running this project!" He shouts it, and the silence after is complete for a full thirty seconds before the birdsong trickles back in.

"John." Liesel steps forward. "Don't be a fool. Listen."

"I'm done listening!" His cheeks are dark now. "You betrayed, me, Liesel. You were communicating with him behind my back." He half-growls. "Don't you see what you did, Jake? You set Gareth Smith after us. He's got some sort of tracker on that boy–he has to. He's heading this way. You think I'm going to let Abby and Myka, or that boy, or *you...*" He spits it. "...Out here with that lunatic stalking us? You've exposed two bases to him now, Jake. You're ruining me. And I'm done with it." He gestures to the soldiers, both sides. "Bring him in."

I hold up the vial, and pop the top off. "Stay back or I'll take this. It'll stop my power for good. Then what will you have?"

I hear Liesel gasp. Dad stops for a second. Then he shakes his head. "You won't. You can't live without your power."

I stand there for a heartbeat, deciding. But that's all it takes. I can live without it. I will. There's too much at stake.

I drain the red liquid in one gulp. It tastes like battery acid, searing my throat all the way down. Sweet battery acid.

There's a swarm of soldiers. I'm surrounded, pinned with my hands before my back, before I can speak or move again. I can fight, though. I'm tired of people forcing me. I shove, and kick. I resist with every inch.

And find myself face down in the dirt, handcuffs pinching my wrists. Dad's shoes in front of me. Hands haul me up again, and I stare straight at him. "I won't work for you now. Ever again. I won't ever be able to tunnel again."

He grunts. "We'll see about that. And in the meantime, Gareth Smith won't have you. I'll keep all of you safe, whether you appreciate it or not."

"This is wrong, John," Liesel says. Her arms are crossed, her face pale. "This is not the way. This is not what we agreed to. And if his power is gone..."

"Shut up, Dr. Miller. I will speak with you later." He gestures again and the soldiers wrangle me into the back seat of his car, one on each side of me. He gets in the front and another soldier drives, turning us around in the little space and heading back the other way. To the base. To underground and stale air and handcuffs. I swore to myself that I wouldn't let this happen, not ever again, but Smith and Dad—they keep taking choice away from me. Ripping rights away from me. No matter what I want my life to be, they can only see that one thing. Me as a pawn. The power. The tunneling.

Thank God I don't have that anymore. No matter what he thinks now, it'll change everything.

The base door creaks up slowly, way slower than it seemed when I watched it open for Dedushka. No armed soldiers rush out to take us. No need. I'm already trapped, pinned in the car between them. When the door snaps to the top we drive straight in and down a slope.

Inside is a vast room, not tall—restricted by the size of the hill, after all—but wide, and deep. There are lots of jeeps parked here, and even a tank and a helicopter on a flatbed truck.

This place has to be multi-use. There's no way Dad needs, or ever needed, a tank.

There are about ten soldiers, some at attention and some just eyeing us. All with guns, in desert fatigues. We pull to the side and park, and the soldiers open the door and yank me out. I taste the air. Stale, cool. Underground. My feet don't want to step away from the car. My hands twitch, an echo of the trembling they used to do underground.

It's temporary, I tell myself. They can't use me now, and they'll find that out soon. This is not for good, not ever again.

I want suddenly, desperately, to see Myka, to make sure she's really okay and he hasn't done anything to her. To hug her whether she wants it or not, even if she's mad at me for all this. To get her the *hell* out of here.

And Lucas, too. He deserves a real life.

I struggle every step of the way, while Dad watches. In the end the soldiers drag me down the hall, my hands still cuffed behind my back. Just like old times. I don't see Liesel anywhere now. I wonder if she did know he planned this all along, in spite of her protests, and she just delivered me. If she did, she's a fantastic liar.

Wait, I knew that.

Damn.

They throw me into an actual cell, with bars and everything. One of the soldiers looks side to side, to make sure no one is watching, before he kicks me, right in the ribs. He must not have liked it when I bit his hand, I guess. Dad's already gone.

I choke and double up on the floor as they slam the bars. Close my eyes to shut out the fluorescent lights, the white, bare walls.

I knew something like this might happen, true. I'm not as dumb as it seems right this second. But I thought at least if he decided to strong-arm me here, I'd be with my family. With Mom and Myka and Dedushka. And Lucas. And then I could figure out a way to get us ALL out of here, together. While Rachel was the back-up plan outside.

I never thought he'd throw me in a cell by myself. Like a real prisoner.

I wonder if that asshole soldier broke my ribs—it hurts like a mother—but after a while I move, sit up, and I can breathe okay.

I'm alive, I'm not shot, and my ribs aren't broken. These are the only things right now I have to be happy about.

There's plenty to worry about, though. Chief on my list right now is Dad's comment about Smith. If he's really got a tracker on Lucas, and he's close, we're in for a shitload of trouble. I'm not too worried about us here at the base, protected by a zillion soldiers.

But Rachel's out there on her own. And Smith has already used her to "encourage" me once. I know he'll do it again.

I've got to get me and everyone else out of here fast, and deal with Smith. He can't find Rachel when she's alone.

And then I collapse to the floor, suddenly *not* able to breathe.

"Help," I gasp. My chest is caving in, squeezing tighter and tighter, like one of those big snakes is around me. I sit forward, trying to get air. My head is fuzzy, blurred around the edges. I can't talk anymore. The serum. There's not enough oxygen. Not enough room, in this tiny pinprick I'm trying to pull air through. I panic, gasping, and my head explodes with pain, worse than all the headaches I've had before...

The fuzziness spreads, and all I can see is black.

40

RACHEL

Two Against One by Danger Mouse & Danielle Luppi

Jake's gone. I saw the two cars in my rearview mirror, instead of one. That had to be bad. And when I came back, nothing. He's been taken again.

I'm really kind of tired of this happening. So you know what? I'm going to stop this whole cycle.

It's not the best strategy anyone ever came up with. It's pretty simple. I prepare an account of everything that's happened—not Vlad or the serum, but all the things to do with DARPA and John—and I write it in emails and letters to a whole ton of news organizations. Then I wait. If I don't hear back from Jake in 2 days, I send them all at once.

It's the same idea, roughly, that Myka had to get Jake out of Montauk, if she needed to. But exposure is the only threat we have anymore. I'm out here on my own, with no way to fight against a big military organization except the only way military organizations are ever brought down: the press.

Some newspapers and TV stations will ignore it, I'm sure. It sounds crackpot. But hopefully some won't. It's got lots of intriguing tidbits, including secret bases and menacing military groups throwing their weight around. Someone will be interested. It'll be a big story.

The most important bit right now is that I stay hidden, waiting, so they can't come take me too. It was scary when Liesel knew where the car was, where I was.

This whole thing is terrifying, no lie. I always thought I wanted to be in government, since Social Studies in 8th grade: poly sci major at Berkeley, volunteering as a campaign aide, getting elected to the Senate...all that's in the long-range plan. But I never understood the power of the government before all this. The reach. Some days I think I should be an English major instead. Study Shakespeare. Or history, maybe. Something not dangerous or scary in any way. Stay far away from D.C. and all that I know happens there.

Some days I want to be elected President so I can stop at least a little of the bad stuff from happening.

Now: hiding. My thought is to stay near the car, but not in it, since they seem to be able to find it pretty easily. I found a nice piece of woods on the outskirts of town on the other side of the base, parked the car as far under the trees as I could, and then walked away from it. Far enough up the hill that no one who found the car would see me, not right away. But I can see the car. I sit on the leafy ground, my back against a cedar tree, my legs stretched out. The bark is itchy against my neck, but it smells fragrant, relaxing. It reminds me of the old cedar chest my grandmother had at the foot of her bed. Her hope chest, she said.

I have hopes too, but they're nothing like any my grandmother ever had.

I close my eyes, the sun dappling my face, and listen to the woods. Birds arguing, wind blowing through the tops. A creek trickling off to my right, somewhere. It's hot, the middle of the day. Thank God there aren't any ants. If I let my mind drift, I could almost imagine it's a normal peaceful summer afternoon, that maybe everything's going to be okay. It's hard to picture darkness and cold and underground from here.

But that's where they all are, the rest of them. My new family. I still don't know what Dedushka was thinking, giving himself up like that. Lucas. Myka and Abby.

Jake. I didn't actually see him taken this time, but I knew it was happening. I drove as fast as I could, far away. And then I pulled over and threw up in the bushes.

I rub my belly, still empty, still upset a little. I was crazy to get into this, and maybe I was crazy to stay. But I have no choice now—there's no running home. I'm the only one left in the sunlight, and I can't let them down.

The low sound of an engine cuts off the birds. I sit up, lean forward to see through the trees. Another car, a long blue one, pulls in behind ours—mine—and stops. The sudden silence when the engine is turned off is oppressive, pushing at my ears. I keep low, still watching as the door opens. It's a tall man in a suit, though I can't see his head. He stands aside, and someone else gets out. This suit is light gray. The new man leans on the car door, but I can still only see up to his arms.

"It is the right car. They must be nearby," he says slowly. "Search the woods. Find them."

A chill shudders through me from head to toe. I know that voice. It comes in my nightmares, along with the feel of a knife splitting my cheek.

Gareth Smith.

I stand, and run.

41

MYKA

Eyes Open by Taylor Swift

They're taking me for blood tests.

I know what that means. Dad's decided to give me his green formula, and start trying for powers.

Without Mom or Liesel or Dedushka to talk to, I don't know how I should handle this. Should I fight every step of the way, even if it's "just tests," because of what will happen next? Or do I let them do it, give them all the medical info they want about me, and try to find things out myself while I'm out of my room?

Do I try to talk to Dad again, if I see him? Do I try to slip away and escape?

I'm probably not going to be able to do that last one, especially without Mom. But I decide I'll keep my eyes open for escape *routes*, at least.

What I really want to do is go curl up somewhere and pretend this isn't happening, cry my eyes out, and have Mom tell me it'll all be okay.

The woman with the fat bun pushes me down the hall and past the lab I toured with Dad. People in lab coats are still working away, using beakers and Bunsen burners and microscopes. They look happy and oblivious. Do they even know what their work is used for? Do they care?

I wonder what Dorothy Hodgkin would do in this situation. I would never work there. Not now, after seeing Dad go crazy.

The soldier brings me into an office at the end of the lab, asks me to sit in the plastic chair, and tells me she'll be right back with medical staff.

I look at everything. There's got to be something here that will help me. It's pretty basic, though: two doors, a computer, filing cabinets, a long counter with a tray with syringes and lots of empty vials. There's a blood pressure cuff on the counter too, and an ear thermometer.

It's making me creeped out, actually. I hate doctors. You'd think I wouldn't mind them, since I want to be a scientist. But they make me feel helpless. Like a baby. Mom always has to drag me.

And I still don't see anything useful. I could steal a syringe, I guess. But what would I do, stab someone with it?

Then I hear something, on the other side of the far door. Someone talking, loud. Upset.

I slide off the chair and tiptoe to the door. I put my ear against it. Better, but I still can't understand any words. There are two people talking, the loud one—male, and young I think—and a woman, talking in soothing tones.

That's Liesel, I swear. And maybe Jake. I fling the door open wide, and they both look up at me, startled.

It is Liesel, standing in the middle of the room. But it's not Jake. It's a boy, a little older than me, skinny. With a huge Adam's apple and short hair, sitting on a chair that matches the one in the other room. He looks a little like Jake.

Oh my God. This must be Lucas.

"Myka!" Liesel says. "What are you..." Her eyes narrow. "Are they taking blood from you too?"

"Yes," I say, shortly. "I couldn't exactly stop them." I stand there for a minute, awkward, staring at Lucas while he stares at me. My brother from another mother, literally. Weird. Then I come in and offer my hand, because I don't know what else to do. "I'm Myka. Your sister, I guess."

He flushes, his whole face and neck going red. He shakes my hand. His is cool. "I'm Lucas."

I laugh, nervous. "I know."

We both go quiet, looking at Liesel. She shakes her head. "They're testing both of you, apparently. But there's more news." She sighs. "Jake's here, imprisoned. We were working on an arrangement, so you all would be let go and Jake would work with John from outside...but John reneged and brought Jake in. By force."

Anxiety fills my chest, sour. "Is he all right?" I say. "Where is he? Can I see him?"

"*I* can't even see him." She pulls out her ponytail suddenly and runs her fingers through her hair, letting it fall on her shoulders. It makes her look totally different. Almost pretty. "I'm not even supposed to see any of you. Only John and his 'loyal' staff."

The anxiety wall gets stronger, pushing my lungs. Maybe I don't trust Liesel, but I like her more than anyone else here. At least she's tried. "No," I say, small.

Liesel looks at me strangely, but then she nods. "Don't worry. I'm not going to let all this just happen. I'll help however I can."

"Excuse me? Miss?"

The medical staff is there for me, in the other room. Not happy I'm not there. A guy in a white coat busts through the door, takes one look, and grabs my arm. "You need to leave now." He raises his eyebrows at Liesel, but she doesn't say anything.

I get one last look at Lucas, his face still red, before I get shoved through the door.

They take a lot of blood, but I barely notice, my brain spinning out of control. Jake's here, in a cell or something. Dad is mad at Liesel, at Mom, at Jake, and probably me and Lucas too. But he's going ahead with his plan of testing us.

I wonder why he's doing that now, if he has Jake back?

42

Unreasonable Things by American Speedway

Dad leaves me alone in the cell for hours.

I don't know if he knows it, but it's probably the most effective way to mess with me...other than threatening something to Myka. It was the confinement that got to me in the end, in Montauk. My hands aren't trembling now, but only because my head hurts so badly that I can't focus on anything else. It feels like the garbage compactor scene in Star Wars, like the walls are squeezing my head so hard it might pop. I lie there sprawled on the cold bench and hold my head between my hands like it will help anything.

A while later, when I'm also hungry and have to piss, he finally comes.

He stands outside the cell and stares at me. I rise, slowly, to my feet, battling through the pain with every ounce of willpower. I don't want to be lying down when I talk to him.

"You okay?" He sounds like he really means it.

I don't answer.

He sighs. Then he drags a plastic chair from the corner and drops into it. He looks tired. "You're probably hungry. You'll get to eat soon."

"When?" My voice is raw. "After you make me do something for you? After you break me?"

"After we take a blood sample." His voice rises again, a little. "It's called fasting."

I pinch my lips together. "You're still desperate to make this serum to duplicate me. To make yourself a power."

"To solve this riddle," he snaps. Like he's mad at me for not getting it. "To figure out why you have this extraordinary gift, why my father did. It's my life's work, Jake. Can't you see that?"

"No, I can't see that. I'm trying to *escape* from that. From it. From you. That's why I took that serum. Why I don't have any power anymore."

There's a long silence. It's so still. I don't think a particle of air moves, for a long minute. Like I've frozen him with my words.

The veins stand out in his neck. "I don't understand why you did that. Are you insane?" he asks, quietly.

I don't answer.

"Why would you throw it away?" It gets steadily louder, each word. "Why would you get rid of the one thing that made you unique, that could *help the world*?" He's shouting now, his eyes burning with crazy, and I step back. He shakes his head. "You're a fool. You never knew how to use it right. What you could do."

He turns his back, and we're quiet for a long time.

I have to admit, I feel strange, knowing that I couldn't tunnel if I wanted to. That I can't reach Dedushka. That I can't ever save those people on the plane, or anyone else. It feels...empty. Blank.

But I had to.

"Is Smith really coming?" I ask. "Is that true?"

He sighs again. "Yes, Jake. Because of what you did, Smith is really coming. I think my people have disabled the tracker. But it's done enough damage. He's on his way."

"We can't leave Rachel to him." I don't want Rachel here, not at all. But I don't want her out there alone more. The image of Bunny comes again, bright red on the white carpet. Dead in bits because I wouldn't tunnel for him. He's a psychopath. If he really gets hold of Rachel, I can't even...

"*She* is not my family," Dad says, cold. "So she is not my concern. All I'm worried about is now in this facility. And you're the one who left her alone out there. So I'd say this is on you, right?" He paces, back and forth, in front of me. He looks wild, feral. Obsessed. "All you."

"Don't," I growl. "Don't go there." Anger flares before I can rein it in. "I'm not six and you didn't send me to my room for breaking a plate. I'm in a *cell* here. I nearly got a broken rib from your soldier kicking me."

He raises one eyebrow, which pisses me off more because it makes him look like Dedushka. "It's just a difference in scale. You took that stuff of Ivan's. Clearly you're not being reasonable."

"*I'm* not being reasonable?" I lunge for the bars closest to him, like that will do anything. "You stole Mom and Myka off the street. And now you kidnapped me." I think of Vladimir, my promise to him. "You...you killed an old man who didn't do anything to you, didn't do anything wrong, didn't you? You're way off the border of reasonable."

He flinches when I mention Vladimir. It was him. I don't know why, how he could go that far, but it was. He stands, turns his back, and walks towards the door. "I had nothing to do with the old man. My team went out of control, off orders..." He shakes his head. "Clearly you need more time."

Panic pounds on my chest. No, no more time. I take a breath, grip the bars. "And shall we talk about Lucas? How you had another family you didn't tell us about?"

He whips around. "Lucas is none of your business. You shouldn't have brought him here. And this serum of yours? We will overcome this hiccup. I happen to have a drug that I think will work, this time. That will induce power like it did with Ivan. I'll use it on you, after some tests, and see whether it works. Whether it restores your power, or gives you a different one. I even wonder if it will erase this headache you're trying to hide from me. A side effect of your little red serum, yes?" He stares at me like I'm vomit on the sidewalk. "I think I might try my activation serum on Myka first."

"No," I say. Desperation strangles me. "NO."

"She's smarter. Younger. And once she gets over her initial qualms, I think she'll make a more willing subject. Lucas too, since he's here." I see the crazy again, stamped in his face. "Yes, I like this plan. We're doing blood tests first, of course. Make sure we have everything lined up. But don't worry, Jake. I'll keep you down here, as back-up. I'll want to trigger you too, eventually. Then I can have all three of you working at once."

"You can't!" I shout, hoping he'll listen. Hoping it will go through to the Dad that I remember, instead of this madman. "You can't experiment on Myka!"

He shakes his head again, slow. "You just gave her your spot on the team."

He slides the chair into the corner, straightens it so it's perfectly neat. "My people will be here in a minute to draw your blood. It would be really smart if you don't resist them, Jake. Then I'll let you have some food, and something to drink. That's all you get for now. I'm sorry, but your time has come and gone. I hold all the cards. I tried not to involve you at all, but you were too stupid and foolhardy to stay out of it. Then you wouldn't stay safely with me. Worse, you endangered them, Abby and Myka, and I had to bring them here to be safe from that maniac, from other people after you. And now you laid in bed with Smith, and Rachel's going to pay the price for it, and Myka's going to get her own power. All of this, every bit of it, is on you. And right now you'd better start listening to me, and do as I say."

He turns, and walks out the door. The lock clicks behind him.

I sink to the ground, tears sliding down my face. Taking the serum didn't help at all. All that work to find it. Somehow, in trying to be free, I made it all worse.

I didn't think it could get worse. But this is my nightmare.

43

JAKE

Grandfather by Afficionado

A little while after Dad leaves, two new people come in. Both are wearing lab coats and carrying medical bags, as if that's going to make them any less threatening to me. One's a white woman with a tiny red bun and freckles, and one's a Hispanic man, small. Smaller than her. They stop outside the cell and peer nervously in at me.

I stare at them. My head pounds in steady rhythm.

"Mr. Lukin, if you could go sit on the bench, please," the woman says, in a polite-to-patient voice. "We need to take a blood sample."

"And if I refuse?" I ask, my hands clenched.

"Then we go get more people to hold you down," the man says, blunt. "As many as we need." He meets my eyes straight-on, challenging.

I don't have enough energy to fight this, these people. I'm not even sure it would do any good. They've got a shit-ton of my blood from when I was in Montauk anyway. It's not going to matter if I let them have more now.

I sigh, back up to the bench, and sit on it, cold on my butt.

The man pushes some buttons and the door slides open with a clang. They both come in carefully, like I'm a tiger or something, and approach me.

"Stay still," the woman says. "You don't need to do anything."

I briefly consider shoving her into the bars, punching the man like I did Smith. Bolting out of here. But the outside door is still shut, presumably locked. It would give me a couple minutes of feeling better, strong, but that's all.

And how far would I get, with my head like this? I'm judging everything—every light, sound, breath—by whether it makes the headache less or better. I kind of wish for T-680.

She kneels next to me, stretches out my arm, and squeezes my hand between her knees. She takes a syringe he hands her. I look away when she pinches my skin with a needle, when the blood starts flowing into capsule after capsule. Five, I count. I don't move until they're done.

They pack up, labeling the vials of blood, putting everything away neatly. Slowly. Giving me time, I realize. To make sure I don't pass out.

"All done," she says at last, and stands, looking down at me. She's entirely too cheerful. Almost pretty, with dark eyes like Rachel. When she holds out a hand to me I'm almost not sure what to do.

"You'll get food soon. But Dr. Miller gave us an order too," she says, low. "We're to take you to another room now."

I frown—I still trust Liesel as much as I trust a snake—but I take the woman's hand, let her pull me up. Wobble a little. She navigates me gently by the arm: out the cell, out the door, down three doors to the left in the hallway, and then through another door.

Dedushka looks up when we come in, from a metal chair in the middle of a plain metal room. His grin, yellow through the familiar white beard, makes me hope again. Lucas is there too, sitting awkwardly next to him, his hands hanging between his legs.

I'm to Dedushka, wrapped in a big bear hug, in seconds. He doesn't smell like cigars anymore, or even fish-just stale, lifeless air. I probably do too.

It doesn't matter.

"*Why* did you do that?" I ask, squeezing his arms. I pull back. "Why did you turn yourself in?" I look at Lucas. "And you. Both of you."

Dedushka looks ashamed, a little. Then he shrugs. "I thought it worth a try, to not involve you. Not all my plans work, *malchik.*"

"Mine either." I sigh, and we share a look.

"I wanted to see him," Lucas says, quietly. "I thought maybe you were keeping me from him, that he'd want to see me..."

He looks up, his eyes dark.

I pull over another chair and sit across from them, quiet.

"How did he react to seeing you?" I ask.

He shrugs, and it's so full of helplessness, sadness, that I want to scoop him up and take him out of here right now. "He was excited to find out I had a power. Really excited. But then he tested me, and he told me I was practically useless. 'Who wants to know the past?' he said. 'I want to know the present. And the future.'"

Dedushka lays a hand on his knee. "He is wrong."

221

"He's a raging prick," I say. "I told you."

Lucas laughs, a bark. "You did. That's true." He sighs, long and loud, then sucks in his cheeks. "So what now?"

I kick my heels against the metal chair. Lean in. "I took the serum," I say. "My power is gone." I don't tell them about the headache. Maybe it will go away on its own.

Dedushka's eyebrows crawl up high. "Thanks to God." He grins, wide. I smile myself—I can't help it—before it falls off my face, and I have to tell him the rest.

"But he says he has an activation serum to counter it, and it's ready. And now he's going to test it on Myka. She's a 'better candidate' anyway, he says." I gesture between me and Lucas. "I guess we're the B team now. He's all focused on her."

"That's true," Lucas says. "I met her. He was testing her blood."

The lines in Dedushka's face multiply. "He is a devil."

I nod. "We have to stop it. Also, he said Smith has some sort of tracking device on Lucas. He's headed this way."

"No!" Lucas stands up, and starts pacing around the room. "No. He can find me anywhere?" He bangs his fists against his legs. "I told you we'd never escape him. Not really. That he'd come after me."

I lean over to Dedushka. "Rachel—" my voice breaks. "She's out there alone."

Dedushka is quiet for a bit, tugging on his beard. Hard. "*Milaya* will be all right. She is smart, da? She will hide from him."

I don't know whether he believes it, but I'm grateful to him for saying it. For caring, unlike Dad with his 'she's not my family.' She's *my* family. And Dedushka's. He's frowning again.

"It'll be okay," I say to Lucas. "We'll get out of this, somehow."

"I do not understand why he would let you both in here with me, now," Dedushka says, under his breath. "Isolation makes more sense for him. It is strange."

"He didn't," I say. "Liesel did." I lean in close again, whisper. "I'm not sure they're exactly on the same side anymore. She was trying to make a deal for me to work above ground. Like before. And then Dad took over and dragged me underground again. It seemed like she wasn't happy about it."

He does one of his big Russian shrugs, which can mean anything, and lays a hand on my knee. "We must first stop this activation of Myka. This is first priority."

I look at him, really look, for a second. He looks old, beat-down. Sick, almost. He did swear he'd never be underground again, and here he is. Here we all are.

Lucas circles back to us and sits, his eyes wild. "We have to get away from John *and* Smith," he says, low.

"Agreed," I say. "But the big question: how?"

I keep expecting any minute that Dad or his groupies will bust in here and separate me and Dedushka and Lucas again, yell at us, kick us in the ribs. The doctor woman brings us some food, eggs and toast. And then nothing happens. Long enough that we let the lights go off and try to sleep, Dedushka on the cot, me and Lucas on the floor. Long enough that I wonder if we really are the discarded ones now. The ones no one will care about.

That would be fine with me, if it didn't mean Myka is the primary target. That's unbearable.

It's a joke to call it "sleep," really. I lie on the floor, staring into the dark, pondering impossible questions. My head is getting worse, not better. I can barely look at any lights, and sounds make me cringe. If I had Dad's medicine in front of me right now, would I take it?

If it was between me and Myka, hell yes. I'd take all of it. I'd down it all so fast it'd make his head spin. Every drop, so there was none left. And then I'd send them out of here.

But I'd throw myself in front of a train for Myka, so it's not like it's much of a question. And it doesn't work that way.

I let myself picture Dad or Liesel making Myka tunnel. All the shit she'd have to see, do. Life lived underground in captivity.

I sit up, the lights snap on, and I moan. Dedushka sits up, stares blearily at me, then lies down again. Soon enough I hear him snoring. He can sleep anywhere. Lucas is asleep too, curled up in a ball.

I can't sleep ever again.

Myka's supposed to have a brilliant future. In a lab, sure, if she wants, but in one that she's running. Working out new chemicals. Saving the world and getting a Nobel Prize. Not this. Not ever this.

We've tried to escape this room. There are no other exits, no air ducts except on the ceiling, no handy trap doors or wires I can use to pick an electronic look that's unpickable anyway. I pound my fist on the floor, but it just hurts my fist. I'm stuck. Dad really has outwitted me, and we're all stuck, except Rachel, who may or may not be hunted by Smith the Insane.

The door clicks open, and I jump, flinch at the light. Wait for Dad's asshole soldiers to come barging in.

After a second or two it opens, slow, while I hold my breath.

Liesel pokes her head inside, all stealthy, and gestures for me to come out in the hall with her.

I'm there in a heartbeat, with one look back at Dedushka still peacefully sleeping away. I close the door, as quiet as possible. Liesel looks worn, with circles under her eyes I've never seen—though she's still dressed perfectly in a suit, hair in a neat ponytail like always. She puts a finger to her lips and gestures for me to follow her.

Not a problem. I'm out of that room. I'll follow her almost anywhere.

We go down the hall only a couple doors before she chooses one. Oddly enough, it's a shower. Deserted now, but there are five stalls all lined up, gray concrete, with white curtains pushed to the side. It smells like the ghost of old shampoos, and bleach. She sits on a wooden bench along the front wall, pats the bench next to her. I sit. "No bugs in here?"

"One of the only places in this whole blasted facility." She folds her hands in her lap and turns to me. "I have the item, from the plane. Can you do it here? Or did that stuff really work?"

She takes a tiny china cat, one of those ones that wave their arms when they're in the sun, out of her pocket and hands it to me. I turn it, the china slick under my fingers. For the first time I feel guilty about taking the serum. To whoever this belongs to, someone I could possibly save if they're still alive. To their family, who I could help just by telling them for sure *what happened*. To Liesel, a little. Sometimes she does seem to want the best for me, for all of us. She looks at me expectantly, her pale eyes intent on my face.

Well, I haven't tried. I close my eyes, take in a long whiff of bleach smell, and focus on the object.

Nothing, except the headache sends little worms of pain down my neck. I don't get any sense of the object at all.

225

I shake my head and hand it back to her. I stare at the floor, the big circular drain in the middle. "It worked. I can't do it anymore."

It hits her hard, like I punched her in the face. No, like I took her puppy out to the alley and kicked it dead. She sets the china cat down, a ways down the bench. Maybe she's afraid she'll break it.

"You could help us escape," I say. "All of us, the way we are now. We could run."

"And he'd catch you again in a day. Or you'd run into Smith. It wouldn't work, Jacob. You're going to have to leave with our protection, one way or the other. Running on your own is over."

I don't know if I accept that, exactly. But I admit I do keep ending up here, or somewhere like here, no matter how I try.

"This serum," she says suddenly. "Is it reversible?"

I snort. "You never give up. I don't know. I guess Dad's concoction, whatever it is, might work on me? I don't know. I'm not taking it."

"Right." She walks away a few steps, one hand pounding on her leg, then spins. "Even if it kept him from injecting Myka?"

"I'd do almost anything to stop that. Though I'm not sure one would stop the other." I narrow my eyes. "Do you have a plan? Are you against him using Myka?"

"With every fiber of my being." She picks up the china cat again and flips its arm, so it waves insanely at her. "This is from a little girl. Fourteen years old. I personally got it from her grandparents. They're frantic. They may have lost their whole family, but they don't know. Can't know." She turns it so it's waving at me. "I need you, Jacob. You and your natural gift, however we get it back. I have never agreed with impressing

226

the gift on other people. Especially not someone unwilling. Especially not someone underage. Ever." She brings the cat up close to her face, like she's inspecting it, and I see the sudden shine of tears in her eyes. "And I like Myka very much. She doesn't belong here."

"And I do?" I can't help it.

There's a long pause, and then she sighs. "No. I admitted that I was wrong about that. That John is wrong about that. You belong out in the world, protected. Working, but getting properly rewarded for it." She slips the cat back into her pocket, and I feel that guilt again. Selfish, like I chose my own life over that little girl's. I'd find her right now, if I could. I swear I would.

"Will you take John's medicine, if I can make that stop him using it on Myka? If I can get you out of here working above ground?" She steps closer, so she's right above me. Threatening, almost, until she puts out a hand and pulls me up. Her hand is cold. Or maybe I'm hot. "Will you work with me for real?"

I press my tongue against my teeth hard. I just got rid of tunneling. For a reason. Dedushka and Mom and Myka and Rachel and Lucas, all of them. They'll be disappointed in me if I throw that away, start again. Disappointed isn't a strong enough word.

But they're still not safe. And I have to admit...I miss it. I feel hollow, empty without the ability that's been mine my whole life. I can't even check on Myk if I want to, or connect to Dedushka. I can't keep tabs on Rachel from in here and make sure she's safe. I'm blind—but I blinded myself.

"Okay," I start, but the headache explodes behind my brain. I could manage it before, keep functioning, but this....

I moan, hold my head, and sink to the cold floor, my eyes pressed shut. I feel Liesel there, her hands on my forehead.

"What's wrong?" she asks, frantic, but her voice just hurts, driving the ice pick further into my brain.

I moan again. "Side effect..." I whisper. "I can't...."

The ice pick splits, shatters into tiny pieces of pain, and I gasp, wishing I could pass out. Wishing I could just die.

And then my body gets fire-on-the-sun hot, and I start seeing things.

Dad blowing a heater on my face, laughing.

Bugs crawling up the inside of my veins, wriggling out the ends of my fingers. Bright blue bugs, with green wings.

Liesel poking me with needles, everywhere. Over and over. Even the soles of my feet. I thrash to try to get away from her.

Mom doing some sort of strange, wild dance around the room, in a suit dress. Rachel kissing me on the forehead, soft and gentle. Dedushka leaning over me, tickling me with his beard. Staring owlishly at me.

I throw up on the floor, retching. My eyelids are too heavy and hot to keep open anymore.

"Oh God," Liesel says, through the fog. "I'm going to have to call John."

44

RACHEL

Fight Song by Rachel Platten

I can't believe this is really happening. Every few minutes my mind takes a step back, realizes I'm in a bizarre horror movie, and tries to convince me to turn it off. Because yes, there are bad guys in the woods with guns. For real. And I'm hiding in a mound of *rocks,* trying really hard not to move or breathe or...I don't know, smell like anything. For all I know Smith has someone with the superpowers of a bloodhound, and they'll find me that way.

I've been hiding for hours. It'll be dark soon, and harder to see. Now I understand why prey animals like the dark. Maybe I can outlast them, and they'll give up and go away.

I can hear them again, not terribly far away. Two men, I think, searching separately. The only hope I have is that they're looking for two people, not one. And maybe they won't look that hard?

Right. They will. They've come all the way here from D.C., fueled by Smith's rage, just looking for us and Lucas. They know the car's here, and they'll assume I—we—are here somewhere. Smith wants Jake *bad.* He'd probably find a use for me too, like he did before. As *incentive.* As bait.

I barely keep myself from moaning. I'm wedged in a tiny horizontal space between two giant slabs of granite in this mound, as far back as I could slide in without getting stuck. I hope. I'm trying not to think about snakes, which love spaces just like this. Or rats. Or spiders.

God, spiders. I hate spiders. I breathe in the musty dirt all around me and close my eyes. Concentrate on listening. I can only hear one set of footsteps now. Good. They split up.

Bad: They're a little closer. A voice swears, and I bite my lip to keep from making any noise.

How did I get here? How did choosing to follow Jake out of the library lead me *here*?

I'm definitely not staying in poly sci. If I get out of this, I'm majoring in English. Or Library Science. I'll become a librarian and never leave those doors again. I'll move to Hawaii with Dad and surf all day. I'll live with Mom. Anything but this.

He's close. In the rocks, I think. I hold my breath until I can't anymore, let it out in a long, silent stream. Hold it again. I open my eyes, but I can't see anything except the rock an inch from my nose, a tiny speck of mica. A sprinkling of dirt falls on my cheeks.

I hear him thumping, scratching. Banging on stone. My hope now has shifted: that he won't look in this crevice. He'll see it, think it's way too small for a person—Jake wouldn't fit, no way—and move on past. I wonder how long I'd have to stay here if he passed by to make sure they were gone. An hour, maybe. Two. For safety. He'll pass by. He has to.

The feet shuffle to a stop right outside the crevice. The mica above me shines, suddenly bright, surrounded by sister flecks all around I couldn't see before. A flashlight.

He found me.

He doesn't even say anything. He just grabs me by the arm and yanks me out, scraping my knees and elbows on the sharp rock, out into the sun. I don't cry out, though. It's like if I don't talk to him I can pretend that it didn't happen. That I'm not caught.

My knees are bleeding.

The guy is, unbelievably, dressed in a suit, navy blue, with a bright blue tie. Buttoned and everything. He's built like the Hulk, his muscles already popped but his suit just holding him in. He keeps one beefy hand on my arm, stares me down, and punches a button on a cell with his other hand. I flail my free arm to stop him, but I can't reach. "I've got one," he says. "The girl."

'The' girl, not 'a' girl. That's bad. That means they know who I am.

Duh, Rachel. You were hiding in a crack in the rock. They know who you are, and that you know who they are. You're toast.

Damn.

"Yes, sir," he says. "Coming now."

That's all. He doesn't say a word to me. He yanks with his ridiculous grip, and I have to follow him down the hill, back the way I ran. I can kind of see my frantic path through the woods in the leaves and broken branches. I guess I wasn't that hard to find after all.

At the road the big guy opens the back of the blue car and shoves me in. The locks click behind me.

Gareth Smith is sitting there, cool and neat, exactly the same as the last time I saw him on his plane. Except even more pissed off, his jaw clenching. And there's a massive purple bruise on his cheekbone. I stare at it, my chin high. Jake did that.

"Ah," he says, his voice low and dangerous. "The sweetheart. And tell me, dear, where our beloved Jake is?"

I swallow hard and shake my head. No words. It will be smarter if I don't answer at all, right?

I don't see the fist coming until it smacks me in the mouth, snapping my head to the side.

I don't even know how to react. I've never been hit before. I've been cut—by his man—but never punched. The pain and shock fill my head. Slowly I turn back to him, my hand cradling my lips, already puffing up.

"Don't you mess with me," he says. Growls. "I've had enough of that already. I am very tired of all of this by now."

We do a standoff, staring each other down.

231

"Where is he?" he repeats.

"I'm not going to tell you anything." I lift my chin. This is the only thing I can do.

He sighs. "Why can't any of you JUST MAKE THIS EASY?" The last he shouts, leaning in my face, spit flying all over me. I flinch, but I don't move. After a minute he sits back. Then the fist comes again, on the other side of my mouth. At least I'm not as shocked this time. It still hurts just as much, though. Blood drips from my lips, onto my bare legs, onto my bleeding knees. I glare at him.

"We can do this all day," he says, calm. "Jake is mine. Lucas is *mine*. And I will get them back, both of them. You should not doubt it for a second." He smiles like the Joker, and I shiver. "Now where is he?"

I don't answer. He hits me in the cheek, the same place he has his bruise, and my head flies back, smacks into the door. Black creeps in around the world, the edges, spreading across Smith's face....

"Lovely," he says, his voice heavy with disgust. "You're a fainter. We're going to have to move this somewhere more convenient."

Everything is black.

It's not a very nice hotel room. I'm sure it's the best he could swing here, considering who he is, but it's still dingy and cheap, and smells like dust and old, stale sweat.

We've moved on from the car. Smith needed someplace he could get more rage-y, have more room to swing. I'm sitting in a terrible pastel 80s chair, my arms held back by one of his beefy guys. My face hurts.

"Hurts" is not a strong enough word.

My belly hurts, where he decided to kick it when they were moving me here. My fingers are radiating pain in a way I've never felt before. He has hold of my pinkie and is stretching it back. He says he'll snap it if I don't talk. Then the rest of my

232

fingers, one by one, until I tell him exactly where Jake and Lucas are.

I believe him. I'm so afraid I can't last much longer. Of course I don't know what would happen if Smith went marching into John's lair. I don't know who would win. But I know I don't want to give Smith anything more than he has already. Not with Jake there. Trapped. Helpless.

"Don't you know already?" I ask, trying to stall him. My breath is coming in little gasps. "Don't you have a tracker or some—"

He pushes it farther, leaning across to glare at me with his manic blue eyes. "Where?" he asks, so low I can barely hear it. I gasp. It can't go much further... it can't....

The bone snaps, with a volcano of pain that takes me over entirely, every particle focused on that one little finger. I scream, loud and high, until someone slaps a hand over my mouth, and I inhale fresh sweat, feel the meaty hands on my skin. The intense pain recedes a little. Enough that I can think again, see anything but red. Smith comes slowly back into focus. He lets go of my hand and stares at me, sulky. He looks like a little boy whose treat was taken away.

He sighs. "You are being difficult." A smile, predatory, flicks on and off across his face. "And I'm being so nice, just breaking them and not cutting them off. But give me a couple more finger bones and you'll talk. And yes, I had a tracker on Lucas. *Someone* disabled it before I could narrow it down. Where are they, Rachel?"

I drop my head and stare at my feet. They look so strange in this context, so normal in their sneakers. They should be bloody or something. They should be on fire. This whole room should be on fire, and everyone should see what's happening here. My hand throbs, and I can't imagine having that happen again. Two fingers. Three. Five.

I think I may have to tell him.

He grabs the pinkie he just snapped, full force, and yanks it back and forth viciously. I scream, and scream and scream.

233

45

MYKA

Brother by NEEDTOBREATHE

I think Jake might be dying.

They came and got me and Mom a while ago. They didn't tell us anything at first, of course—so we were just happy to see each other. I didn't let go of her hand all the way through the hallways. Then I started to get a bubble of hope that maybe Jake had done something, since he's here, and they were going to let us out. Why else would they come get us like this and bring us somewhere together? That must be what's happening. We're going to walk right out the doors into those pine trees.

And then they opened a door, and Jake was in a hospital bed, moaning and thrashing around. His face was bright red, and there was sweat rolling off him. The bed was wet with it.

And Dad was standing there in the corner, his fist to his mouth, staring at Jake. His eyes wild. "Abby," he said, soft. "It's that damn serum of Grigory's he took. We can't get his fever down."

Mom made a little noise and jumped to the bed. She wiped off his face, barked at Dad that they needed to get a

234

nurse in to change the sheets, and then started interrogating him about what had been done already.

But it's been two hours, and he's still not any better.

Mom and Dad are fighting in the corner, low, while I hold Jake's hand. He's not thrashing right now, but he's not sleeping either. He keeps saying crazy stuff about bugs and walls closing in. My tears drip onto his hand, and I'm surprised they don't make steam, he's so hot.

I don't want him to die.

Ever since I can remember, it's been the two of us, together. He always protected me, took care of me. And when I needed it, when I was upset about something, he'd tunnel to me. I always knew it was him, this voice in my head that told me it would be okay. It took a long time before I realized all brothers didn't do that.

Jake is in all of my first memories. Playing with me in the yard of one of our houses, balancing me on his knees. Watching endless cartoons with me on Saturday mornings. Dancing with me in thunderstorms.

I lay my head on our hands, tears coming faster. I didn't accept it when they told us he was dead last time. I'd know, I thought. If he was dead, I'd *know*. Part of me would be gone. But if he dies here, now, I will know. And what will I do? I wish Dedushka and Rachel hadn't even found that serum. Maybe it stopped something important. Maybe Jake's body needs the tunneling, to keep it working.

I lift my head, look at Jake closely. It could be true. It could work.

"Give him the green serum," I say, hoarse.

"What?" Mom says. "No! You're not messing with him any—"

But Dad holds up a hand, his eyes fixed on me. "Why?"

"He needs it. The other one, it stopped the tunneling, but the tunneling was part of him." I talk fast, trying to keep up with my thoughts. "It hurt him when it got taken away. You said you had a version of this other serum using Jake's

235

stem cells, right? Who would it work on better than him? And he needs it." I clasp his hand. "I think he needs it to stay alive."

Mom stares at me, her hand over her mouth. Dad nods, once. "I'll get it. I'll do it myself."

When he leaves, Mom comes slowly to the bed. She brushes Jake's hair back, gently. "Are you sure?"

"No. It's just a guess. But he's going to die without it," I say, my voice breaking. "It's worth trying."

Still. I wonder if Jake's going to kill me if it works. When he wakes up, and he has his power back.

46

JAKE

Back Against the Wall by Cage the Elephant

I open my eyes, blink. Blink again, and there's Myka. She looks a little bedraggled, but okay. We're alone, the room cleared out, the one door shut.

I must be hallucinating again.

Myka smiles, a sweet smile like she used to give me when she was little, and I smile back even though it's not really her. Then she pinches my arm, hard, and I slap at it. "Ow!"

She smiles again. "I keep telling you I'm real. Are you really awake this time, Goofy?"

Oh my God, she's really here.

I grab her hand like she's going to slip away again. My hand feels strange—there's an IV in it, taped to the back. I'm in a hospital gown. What the hell?

Myka squeezes hard, and touches my cheek with her other hand.

237

"Are you all right? How long have I been in here? Out of it?"

"In or out?" Myk snorts. Gently she lets go of my hand and leans on the bed. "I'm fine. And I don't know. They let me and Mom come in about four hours ago, but I bet you were sick a while before that." She squints. "You had a terrible reaction to the serum you took. Your fever was 104. You were going to die."

"But I didn't." I tap one finger against the back of her hand. I don't feel hot, and I'm not seeing things anymore. "I'm fine."

"You didn't." She takes a deep breath, looks away, then back. "Because I told Dad to give you his activation serum. It worked right away."

I inhale, sharp. *No.* The whole point was to be without the power, to make everyone safe. I was only without it for what, two days?

"You can't live without it," she says. She lets go of my hand. "I know you didn't want it anymore, and I don't know why it's like that. But it was killing you not to have it."

I shake my head. I'm stuck with it? For the rest of my life? "It'll never end now. They'll be after me forever."

"Well," she says, eyebrows raised. "We don't know that. It made you better. But does it work? Can you tunnel?"

I frown. "Are my clothes still in here somewhere?"

"Fortunately," she says drily, "yes."

"Okay. Find my jeans. There should be a ring in the coin pocket."

"*Find* your jeans? I told you your clothes were here. It doesn't take a lot...okay." She rummages in the corner. "Got it."

"Put it in my hand?"

238

I close my hand around it as soon as I feel it. I waste no time. I close my eyes, feel the familiar warmth tingle down my hands, and try.

It works, instantly. Stronger than before. Sharper. Like I upgraded to HD.

Rachel's in a hotel room in Green Bank. She's staring down at her shoes, her whole body flaring with pain. Her hand...she looks up, just as Smith bends her finger back, so far and so cruelly it's going to snap. Just like the one flopping at an odd angle next to it. She's crying, tears and blood streaming down her swollen face.

Blood. He hit her. He's breaking her fingers to tell her where I am. My Rachel.

I come out of it, so furious I can barely form words. "He's got her. Smith. He's...torturing her."

"Rachel?" Myka squeaks.

I start breathing fast, clutching the ring. I have to do something. I have to stop it. "To find out where I am."

"Then tell him," Myka says.

I don't even answer. I just give her that blank stare she's probably used to.

She sighs, then leans in close again. "The only way we're all going to get out of here is with a distraction, right? And he's hurting Rachel to find out where you are. So you tell him, through her. And then he leaves Rachel alone, and comes here and makes a big distraction. The biggest."

"God," I say slowly. "You're right."

"I know," she says, victorious. "We'll have to get out past him, but it's better than him hurting her out there while we're stuck in here."

I nod, go back in without another thought of weighing risk or Smith or anything. I have to stop him hurting Rachel, *now*.

I fill her completely, and snap my head up. "Stop," I say, firm. "This is Jake."

He stops. He doesn't let go, but he loosens his grip, tilts his head. "Jacob? Is it really you?"

"It's really me, you bastard," I say, in Rachel's voice. "You need to let her go, leave her out of this. She doesn't know where I am. But I'll tell you, if you leave her alone, safe."

He lets go, and Rachel's hand drops painfully back into her lap. I cringe at the strength of the pain. I don't know how she can stand it.

"I'm listening."

"Agree," I say, "or no more. I know you and your deals."

"Very well," he sighs. He brushes a piece of dirt off his sleeve. "I agree."

"I'm with my father. But I don't want to be. He's far worse than you. But I can't get out. You can come and get me."

He snorts. "While I don't believe you for an instant, Mr. Lukin, please do tell me where you are anyway. I'll do my best."

I don't feel like I'm sticking. It's been so long since I tunneled, and I haven't done controlling in a long time. It takes practice to push past the suffocating feeling that their skin is closing in on me. But there's no sense of that, no panic.

I tell him the location of the base, tell him to come tonight, 1 am, when their guard will be down.

I tell him to leave Rachel at the hotel with a phone, so she can get help. And that I'll check on her.

"And if I don't?" he says, smiling wickedly.

"I thought you were a man of your word." I make Rachel smile, which must look grisly with all the blood. *"But if you don't, you'll pay for the rest of your life. I swear to that."*

"Very well," he says. *"She's useless anyway except for this. I'll see you again tonight, Mr. Lukin."*

I stay just a second longer, to whisper something only to Rachel, and then I'm gone.

When I come out of it again, Dad is standing in the doorway, watching me.

47

JAKE

Glue by Nina Nesbitt

I curl the ring in my hand so he won't see it—but I think I'm too late. From the expression on his face, he already saw way more than I wanted.

Myka stands, and his thundercloud expression shifts to her.

"What in hell are you still doing in here? They were supposed to send you back to your room."

She steps toward him. "I begged, and they let me stay. I didn't want to leave him alone."

"They let you?" Dad says, dangerous. "I'll deal with them. And what were you doing, Jacob Benjamin?"

Middle name. I'm thrown right back to school, whenever I'd broken Dad's rules. Didn't make my bed the right way. Didn't finish my chores. Got in trouble for mouthing off at school. Made Myka join me in some illicit adventure.

I push up, fight a wave of dizziness. I'm weak, wobbly. I guess that kind of fever takes it out of you. But I'll be damned if I'll let him see it. "Nothing," I say innocently.

He shuts the door behind him. He looks at me, and I see it in his eyes again, the hunger. "You were tunneling. It worked."

I swallow. "I told you I can't do that anymore."

"And you were telling the truth. But not anymore." He waves at me. "You were doing it." He strides over to me, touches my arm, eager. "How is it? You have to tell me. Is it the same as before?"

"I don't have to tell you, actually." I sit back, which is good since my muscles weren't going to hold me up much longer. "I didn't tunnel."

His hands go into fists. "You TELL ME!"

"Stop it!" Myka yells. "Just stop!"

There's a moment of silence. Each one of us is breathing hard, furious. For different reasons.

"Give me the object," Dad says. "I only want you tunneling when I can see you."

He doesn't know I can tunnel to Dedushka without one. But I shake my head. I need the ring. It's my only connection to Rachel, to make sure she's safe.

Myk moves closer, on my other side, like she's protecting me. She squeezes my arm, silent support.

"I'll tell you whatever you want," I say, calm, still holding the ring. "I'll even see if I can tunnel for you. If you let the rest of them go. Now. Give them a car and get them out of here."

"*Jake*," Myka says. That's not the plan, her eyes say. Smith. Distraction.

243

But if it works, isn't it a better plan? mine say back. Leave me here to slip out while Dad and Smith fight over me. Less chance of failure, and less casualties if it does fail.

Her eyes narrow.

"Absolutely not," Dad says. "Smith is out there, if you've forgotten. I'm not sending them outside when it isn't safe. Besides..." He looks at Myka. He doesn't finish the sentence, but we know what he means. "And Lucas. I'm not letting any of you go."

Myka and I exchange another glance. We'll just have to leave you on our own, then.

"Let us stay together," I try. "All of us. Please. If we're going to be kept here, let us at least be a family."

So we can escape together.

He had his mouth open to say 'no,' but that word stops him. *Family* still holds some power. He taps one finger on the bed, then impatiently runs his hand through his hair. He looks like Lucas. "Dr. Miller already started that, I discovered, putting some of you together. I still need to talk to her about that. And...other things. Fine. The rest of them can stay together. You..." His mouth tightens. "You will tell me everything. And we will start some tests. And give me the object. Now."

Myka gives me a tiny nod, which means she'll take care of the rest of them. When the distraction comes, 1 am, they'll be ready. I won't be able to tunnel to Rachel, but I guess I'll just have to trust that she'll be okay, now that Smith is going to leave her alone. I'm pretty confident he'll keep his word.

"You know how I love tests," I say. I'm losing steam, still wiped out from everything, but I reluctantly drop the ring in his hand. "But right now I need to rest. If you test me now I'll just fail spectacularly. Or get sick again." I hold my head, for emphasis. "Nobody wants to see that."

244

"I don't want to see that," Myka says, a smile in her voice.

I smile at her, for real. "Love you, dorkus."

"I know." She beams. Star Wars reference accomplished. She trips to the bed and throws her arms around me, an awkward half-hug. I hug her back as well as I can.

"That's enough," Dad takes out a walkie-talkie and speaks into it. "I need an escort, Room 532. And Dr. Miller, please see me in my office immediately."

In seconds the door opens and a soldier comes in, one of the bulky guys. He salutes Dad. It turns my stomach.

"Take her to the main common room," Dad says. "And bring the other guests there as well. Give them whatever they need to be comfortable."

"See you later, Jake," Myk says, her voice only a little shaky.

"In a while, crocodile," I say back. She gives me one more smile before she goes.

"You," Dad says. "Rest, fine. I will be back to talk to you."

"You'd think you'd be happy," I snap. "You've got me back. I'm your guinea pig again."

He tilts his chin, considers me. "Oh, I'm very happy, Jacob." It gives me chills, the way he says it. "Very happy indeed."

It isn't until long after he's gone that I hear a crackle, and find something hidden under the sleeve of my hospital gown. I pull it out carefully, then turn and lean over it, hopefully hiding it from any cameras.

It's a small square of paper, neatly creased and folded. I open it carefully.

245

A drawing, quickly sketched, of a bottle of glue. Folded inside, a curl of dark brown hair.

Myka. She left an object for me, under Dad's nose. So I could tunnel to them when the time comes. So they really can get out of here.

And maybe, me too.

I rip out the IV, get up, and put the rest of my clothes on, and stuff Myka's paper far down in my pocket. Even if I'm going to rest, I'm not going to be a patient anymore.

48

RACHEL

Setup by Via Audio

I think I passed out with the pain, or at least went to some happier place. When I come back to consciousness I'm alone, laid out on the lumpy bed, my mangled hand wrapped loosely in a shirt. A cell phone sits on the bedside table next to keys and a note that says "Your car is in the lot. You're welcome."

It takes me a long time to figure out where I am, what's going on.

Then I remember Jake speaking through me. Telling Smith where he was, and to leave me alone.

Damn it, Jake. I was resisting *torture* to not tell Smith that information. And then you just pop into my body and tell him? I don't get it. Now they're just going to go straight to John's base, and...do what? Have a gunfight? Have a tug of war over Jake? Play chess to decide who gets him?

No. With Smith and John involved, both desperate to use him, it's going to be bloody. Brutal.

I can't really remember anything else from when he was speaking through me, except the general sense of helplessness, of being shoved aside in my own body. Though it seems like there was something I was supposed to remember. Something at the end. A message, I think. I try to grasp it, but it flits away like a butterfly. It was important, but I can't access it. I was in too much pain, shock. What with people breaking my fingers. I try to move them, a little wiggle, but the pain of it sucks away my breath. Okay, whatever I'm going to do next, I'm not going to want to move my fingers.

At least I'm away from that lunatic. Jake accomplished that, and I'm sure that was most of his goal. I'm still here. I'm okay.

Mostly. I hurt, and I don't know if I'll ever get over Smith treating me like that. That feeling of the total loss of control.

How can that happen? How can one person take all choice from another like that? And *enjoy* it. Gareth Smith definitely enjoys it. Something in him is broken. What if something in me is broken now too?

Maybe I should be a psychology major instead. I take a sobbing breath, and then laugh. Now is probably not the time to figure that out.

I know what might help a little: taking control back. Deciding what I'm going to do, instead of hiding here. Taking action.

I'll follow him, to John's base. I don't know if I can help, but I've got to try. Be there, at least, with everyone else. See what's happening. I can still send my press releases if it all looks bad.

But first I have to do something better with my hand. I'm not going to be able to drive anywhere like this, with one finger completely cracked and the other one not quite broken but spitting pain like fire.

I cradle my hand, trying to figure out how to wrap it better without touching it. Quickly, so I'm not too far behind Smith. I think maybe I can make a sling out of one of the hotel towels, so it won't bounce everywhere. At least the car is an automatic. I think I can drive it with one hand.

I have one moment, trying to wrap my crushed hand in a hotel towel, when I wonder how insane I really am to even think of going near Smith, and John, and all of it again. If I was smart,

248

or had one scrap of self-preservation, I'd probably take the car and run the other way.

But I can't. I'm not useless, and they need me. I'm coming to join the party, Jake. Thanks for trying to leave me out of it—really—but I'm still in it, with everyone else. Really everyone else. For once every single person will be converging on the same point, tonight.

I figure out the sling, and get up to clean my bloody face so I don't scare any small children I come across.

It's time for the next act, and I will be there.

It's then the message comes to me, dropped in my head like a gift.

I love you, Jake said. *Remember that.*

That's the first time he said he loved me.

I think I love him too. Well, I love all of them as my family—Dedushka and Abby and Myka, and I like Lucas. I'm doing this for them as much as him.

But I think I love him too.

49

MYKA

Roar by Katy Perry

I can't believe we're all together! Except for Jake, and Rachel. But they'll be with us later. This is going to work. I have a good feeling, for the first time in a long time.

For now me and Mom and Lucas and Dedushka are all in the big lounge, together. They moved cots in, and a sofa, so we can actually all sit, and sleep. Like a weird slumber party.

Except everyone is pretty emotional at the moment. Mom hugged me, and then Dedushka, and then Lucas. I hugged everybody, and cried. Especially Mom. Lucas held really still when I hugged him. He's so bony it's like holding a plank.

I feel sorry for Lucas the most. This must be so confusing. He grew up with Mr. Smith, and then he tried to run to Dad and that didn't work out well. Mostly he looks muddled, and sad.

I hope I can make him feel better after we get out of here. Like a real family. He needs more hugs. Or tickling. I tickle Jake all the time. I wonder if Lucas has ever been tickled.

I told them all about what happened with Jake after Dad sent Mom away, and then—in a whisper so no bugs can hear, if there are any—what we did with Mr. Smith, telling him where we are. That he's coming at 1 am.

Mom and Dedushka weren't happy with that part at all. I...didn't tell them it was my idea. But at least something will happen, tonight, and we can really use it to break out of here. I am so tired of being in here, of all of this. When I think of school starting soon at Nysmith, seventh grade, I ache. Seventh grade is when we get to do oceanography, and paleontology. I have to get back before it starts and I have to explain to everyone where I was. As if I could.

I just have to get back. We all do. Or...maybe if we can't really go back, we have to go forward, I guess. Out of here.

I also tell them about Rachel. Mom goes pale when she hears about the fingers, the blood. Lucas stands up, clenching his fists over and over, and stalks to the kitchen. Dedushka grunts, and tugs on his beard hard. He looks boiling mad. If he runs into Mr. Smith, I bet he's not going to let it go. I think Dedushka really likes Rachel.

I follow Lucas. He stands in the middle of the kitchen, still with the fists, staring at nothing. I slide next to him, and lean back against the counter. I don't say anything for a while, just looking at him. His nose that looks like Dad's. His big hands that remind me of Jake's. Finally he acknowledges I'm there, with a quick glance.

"Hey," I say.

"Hey," he echoes, quieter.

"You okay?" He shrugs. "Are you freaked out about Mr. Smith?"

He swallows so hard I can see his Adam's apple bounce. "He's coming here," he says, flat, low. "To get me. He's going to take me back with him."

"No!" I scoot in front of him, so he has to look at me. "He's not." I remember to keep my voice to a whisper. "That's the point. We're just going to use him as a

251

distraction, and get out while they're busy with each other. Dr. Miller can help us..." I stop. "Except I haven't seen her for a while. I wonder where she is."

He raises his eyebrows. I dive forward and try to tickle him, on his side where it always works with Jake, but he just jumps away, frowning. "What are you doing? Stop!"

Okay, then. We need to work on the brother/sister stuff another time. "Sorry. But it'll be okay. Wait and see."

He bites his lip hard, but he lifts a hand, and meets my eyes for a second. We'll get there.

I bolt over to the intercom on the wall and push the button. "Hi. This is...Myka." I let go. Ugh, I hate these things. It's like the phone. I never know what to say. I push again. "I'd like to see Dr. Miller if I could. Please." The intercom crackles, and I let go.

A male voice comes on. It takes me a second before I realize it's Dad's. "Dr. Miller is busy on a project for the next few days and unavailable. Do you need anything?"

I lick my lips, then push the button. "No." I push it again. "Thanks."

That's bad. How are we going to even get out of this room when Smith's here, without Dr. Miller's help?

Lucas makes a low noise, and turns his back. I narrow my eyes.

No, I'm not giving up, even if he is. With the four of us, we'll think of something.

50

JAKE

Dangerous by Big Data (featuring Joywave)

Dad didn't leave me alone very long this time—a few hours, I think. Enough to get some sleep. But now he's back: by himself, intense, with several ziplock bags in his hands.

Perfect.

I move the bed as far upright as it'll go, since there's only one chair and he's in it. He spreads out his bags, picks one, and for-real smiles at me. Like it's old times and nothing's happened, and we're going to play CLUE together. I look away. It hurts more to see him smile like that than when he's yelling.

"Let's try this one," he says, all excited.

I take the bag, and examine the object inside. It's an earring. But I think I recognize it. I think it's one that Liesel was wearing, when she came to see me in the woods. Dangly with a green stone.

"Why would I be tunneling to Dr. Miller?" I ask, forcing lightness.

He shrugs, but I don't like the look on his face. "Go and see. See where your new friend is."

Uh oh. I slide it into my hand with dread, but there's only one way to find out. I close my eyes and go.

The base, room 603. A prison cell. It looks like the same one I was in when we first came here. She's sitting on a bench inside the cell, her hands cuffed behind her back. She looks forlorn, defeated, her hair slipping out of the ponytail.

"Out loud," Dad says, sharp. I startle out of it, blink, then go back in, this time narrating out loud. Skipping the forlorn part.

The base, room 603. A prison cell. She's sitting on a bench inside the cell, her hands cuffed behind her back. She breathes slowly, in, out, like she's doing yoga. She didn't want to hurt John, she thinks. Or even mess anything up. She only wants to help. To do what's right. To use Jake's power—and Lucas's—in the best way. God, and Myka! How could he even think—

"That's enough," he snaps. "Give it back to me."

I drop the earring in the bag, seal it, and hand it to him. "You locked her *up*? What the hell, Dad?"

He wrinkles his nose. "She has been disobeying me all along. Trying to take this project—take you—for herself. I won't have it." He throws the bag on the floor, like he's throwing her away with it. "I'm in charge here, and I'm going to stay in charge."

"She really was trying to help," I say, but I stop when I see his look. *Batshit crazy*, I think. I don't say anything.

He lifts another bag, hands it off. "Less interesting."

254

It's far from less interesting. I know this object well. It's Dedushka's ring, the big silver one with the eagle stamped on it. Liesel must've brought it with her when she came here. She'd tried to get me to tunnel with it, back in Montauk.

That seems like a lifetime ago.

"This is Dedushka."

"Just go," he says, waving his hand. "Aloud. Let's see what the old man is up to."

I take the ring, rub my thumb over it like I used to. Feel a rush of affection that has nothing to do with tunneling. Then close my eyes, and dive in. I really hope he's not doing anything interesting.

The base, room 532. A strange big room with a corner that's a kitchen, beds along the walls, chairs and a sofa in the middle. Dedushka is leaning over the table, drawing something. It's cold, this underground air pinching at his bones. The flat air clogging his lungs.

"What is he drawing?" Dad asks.

I blink out of it, disoriented. "What?"

"What is he drawing?"

"I don't know. I couldn't see it."

I know perfectly well. He was drawing a map of the compound, Myka leaning over his shoulder helping him puzzle it out. Lucas and Mom were helping too. Planning their escape.

No way in hell I'm going to say that.

"I don't believe you," Dad says evenly. "Go back in and tell me."

I stall, flipping the ring over in my hand. Usually I can't lie when I tunnel. I just relate what I see. But I think there's

255

something different now that I have Dad's serum in me. I feel stronger, more in control. I hadn't told Dad what Dedushka was drawing in the first place, consciously.

Can I go in and lie, omit things? Or do I need to not go and just totally make it up?

"Jacob," Dad says, warning.

I have to assume he has cameras on them, can double-check what I say. I'd better go, and see if I can lie.

The base, room 532. Dedushka is leaning over the table, drawing...

I pause. I feel the strong urge to say the truth, say what I see, the map. Like in a dream, where you have no control. But I do have control. I can. I can be aware, not just a conduit...

He's drawing a cartoon, a strange monkey with ears almost as big as his head...

I know Dad will recognize this monkey. It's an old Russian cartoon, simple to draw. Dedushka used to draw it for me and Myka when we were little.

Cheburashka. It's Cheburashka. Myka is watching him, and Lucas is laughing.

I open my eyes. It's close enough to what they're actually doing that video probably won't catch me, if they cover the map. Dad squints, but he doesn't say anything. He holds out his hand, and I give the ring back. I sigh with relief. That was close.

"Now for the *pièce de resistánce*," Dad says, stone-faced. He hands me a bag with a gold cuff link in it.

Oh no. I think I know who this is. I only know one person who wears cuff links. One person I don't want to see, especially now.

But there's no point putting it off. I bite my lip, take the cuff link in my hand, and go.

A hill outside the base, just in sight of the dusty valley. I say the GPS coordinates. It's a man, tall, salt and pepper hair and a prominent chin. Gareth Smith. It's hot, so he's removed his suit jacket, but he's still wearing a long sleeve button-down shirt, with no tie. He's got his arms folded, peering down towards the base entrance.

Oh, I've got to be ready to lie again. If he says anything about me telling him where the base is...

"It's there? You're sure?"

One of his suits looks at a GPS reader, nods. "That's what..."

He says "That's what he said." I say *"That's what it says."* instead.

I want to pull away, but I know Dad won't be happy with that. He'll want to know what's going on.

"Interesting," Smith says. "Only one exit, is there? Well, we'll pin him down, then. Tonight. Those boys are mine. And if I destroy John in the process, who's going to mind?"

I come out of it. Dad is standing, pounding one fist into the other. Damn it. It's not going to be much of a distraction if he knows it's coming. He may lock us all down out of the way by the time Smith moves.

"Smith is really here," I say, feigning shock. "Crap. What are you going to do?"

"Do?" Dad frowns, but not at me. It's like I'm not really even there, and he's seeing Smith. "I'm going to kill the bastard dead, and end this once and for all."

He strides out, without another word. I jump off the bed before the door can shut, wedge it open with my discarded gown. He doesn't even look back.

He left me alone with the objects.

I only have a few minutes if I want to get out before someone notices the door. I grab the ring and tunnel to Dedushka first, throw myself into him like I used to—it's easier, everything's easier—and fill his hand.

"We've got to go," I write on the map. "It's happening now, not tonight. I'm coming for you."

I hear Myk exclaim something, but I can't stay. I have to redirect this, or it's going to be a slaughter of Smith in the valley, and that won't help anyone. But we can get out of here. I saw something on Dedushka's map.

I enter Smith, in that full way I haven't done with many people. Where I can feel the real him, control him if I need to.

I don't like being in him. It feels jarring, broken. But I open his mouth.

"This is Jacob Lukin," I bark, to his man. "With an urgent message. John Lukin knows you're here and is on his way."

I come out before I see any reaction. Next up is Liesel. I grab the earring from the floor.

I tunneled to her several times before, in Montauk, so it's familiar. I don't waste any time, though. I fill her, make her hands move in the cuffs. There's no way to write a message, so I give that up. I'll have to speak, like I did with Smith. Make her sound like the crazy one for once.

"This is Jake," I whisper aloud. "Smith is coming, right now. John is expecting him. I need you to get out of here, now. Help however you can. We're getting the hell out while everyone is distracted, the back exit." I pause, wondering if she'll be able to escape. She's pretty helpless at the moment. I could keep controlling her, help her...

Nah. This is Liesel. She'll figure it out. I have my own work to do. I have to get to my family.

I pull away. That should do it, for now. My last tunnels underground, if everything works out the way I want.

The start of many, if it doesn't.

I stuff all three bags in my pocket. I should feel woozy, after doing three controlling tunnels in a row. I should probably get a headache. But so far, I feel fine. Maybe I won't get headaches anymore—and there was a good purpose behind taking both those serums. Maybe it cured me of my side effect.

I hate that Dad improved it. That he succeeded in what he's been trying to do this whole time, even if I had to use Dedushka's serum, and nearly die, to find that out.

I'm not thinking about that. I open the door carefully, peek into the quiet hall, and step out. I just need to remember the map.

51

JAKE

Come with Me Now by Kongos

I head down one hallway for a really long time, then branch off to the right, straight, left, straight, right...trying to follow that map Dedushka was making, in my head.

God help me, it reminds me of Montauk, except there were stairs up and down, and they made me wear that awful hood. At least now I can see and hear. I have a hope of reacting if we run into someone.

How strange that this is my life, that I can actually compare secret bases.

So far there were only two soldiers, running down the hall towards the front entrance. I ducked into a closet and hid until they passed by.

My instincts are all screaming at me to run myself, as fast as possible, but I keep it to a fast walk. I know the soldiers are busy, distracted, but I don't want to give anyone reason to notice me at this point.

Room 525, 526...I'm close. A few more doors. When I get to 530 I stand outside it for one breath, astonished that it looks like any normal door. It holds almost everyone I love.

It opens no problem–there's no security from the outside. They're all there. Still all around the sofa, talking.

Dedushka is the first to stand when I come in. He grins, his teeth bright through his beard, and I can barely restrain myself from running to him. Then Myk's in my arms, and Mom, and I'm struggling to hold the door open while hugging. I nod to Lucas, over Myk's head. He nods back.

"Everyone okay?" I ask, breathless. "We've got to go now."

"There's a back exit, with a ladder," Myk says, in my ear.

"I know, I saw it on your map. It's perfect. Dad and Smith are both headed the other way. We should have a few minutes while no one cares what else is happening."

Lucas runs his hands through his hair, his eyes huge. "They'll get us," he whispers. "Smith will always take me back." I pat his arm, trying to be comforting. I want to protect him so badly. All of them.

"He won't," I say. "We'll do it."

"It is time," Dedushka says. "Let us go."

We go, a little line of escapees. Dedushka and Myka lead, then Mom and Lucas. I take the rear. We hug the walls, ready to duck into rooms if we see anyone. With all of us together, even the densest soldier is going to know we aren't where we're supposed to be. We twist and turn, following a course I'm glad I didn't have to figure out myself. It seems like ages. Everything tonight feels stretched, like time isn't following the usual rules.

There are footsteps behind us.

"Someone's coming!" I whisper. I try a door, peek in. It's a sleeping room, a soldier's, with soldier's gear hanging neatly on a rack, the bed made up. Not locked from the outside. "Everyone in here." I usher them in as fast as I can, but there's no time for me....

I let the door close just as Liesel comes around the corner. We both stop, staring at each other. Then she crosses in two steps and gives me a quick hug. I stand perfectly still. Liesel's never hugged me before. Ever. It's bizarre.

"You're okay?" she asks. She steps back. "We need to go get your family."

"I've got them safe." I don't tell her where, yet. I never know just how far to trust her. "How'd you get out?"

She laughs. "Persuasion. I heard a call to the front entrance...so Smith is here? Now?"

"Yeah. He and Dad are going to battle it out."

"Good God. I haven't seen Gareth Smith in a long time."

The door behind me opens, and Myka pokes her head out. "Oh, it's you. We need to go, Dedushka says."

Liesel tilts her head. "You're going out the hatch?"

I nod. There's supposedly an escape hatch in the roof and a ladder right around the corner from us, like the one we went up in Dad's last base.

"All right then," she says. "It's just up here."

She starts walking, her always-brisk pace, and we all fall in behind. I can hardly believe that she's helping us escape, when she's the one I was escaping from before. But she's not cautious enough. She's not creeping, like we were. She's barreling like she's in charge.

"Slow down," I say, panic suddenly shooting into my veins. "We have to look..."

262

She turns the corner and runs straight into one of Smith's men, a Jones. There's the ladder, pulled down in the middle of the corridor in front of us, but they must've known about it too. There's this Jones—he grabs Liesel's arm—and one at the bottom, looking up.

And I'm too close. He sees me too. So much for that brilliant plan. Lucas was right.

All right, it was never a brilliant plan. It was a hope and a prayer, and if Liesel hadn't been charging ahead, we might have done it.

I turn. Myk and Mom and Dedushka and Lucas stop short, still hidden, their eyes shining with naked fear. "Go!" I say, hoarse. "Find somewhere to hide!"

Before they take two steps the Jones comes around the corner, holding a gun high. "Freeze! All of you, get over here." There's a pause, where you can see each of them decide if they have any choice. Then they shuffle over, staying by the wall. I move too. Lucas looks like he's trying to blend into the wall. Myka stays behind me.

Smith himself drops down to the floor, brushes off his suit, and eyes us. "How perfect! Here you all are, wrapped up and ready like Christmas presents."

My nightmare begins again.

52

RACHEL

I Won't Give Up by Jason Mraz

I park the car in a lot not too far from the base with a bunch of other cars. Big, nondescript. Probably every single one of them government vehicles. This junky old car will stand out, but it doesn't matter. Hopefully we'll be gone by then.

I shut off the engine and let the silence fill in. Stare out the window at the dark hills around me, while I figure out what I should do now.

Do I want to follow Smith *into* the base? And then have to find my way out again, or be stuck in there as leverage or bait?

I cradle my broken hand, relive the moment when Smith snapped it. I close my eyes and shudder. It would be brave to do that, I guess. It would be adventurous. But I'm not going to go that far unless I have to. It's not smart, not this time.

Discretion is the better part of valor. Falstaff said that in Henry the Fourth part 2, and people mocked him for it, for being a coward. I wrote a paper about it, sophomore year. But I get it now. It doesn't make sense for everyone to jump into the fire. Someone has to be the safe one, the one to pull everyone else out.

I wish I could see what was going on in there, that I had a power like Jake's. But I put a brake on that thought right there. Not after what I've seen, what I've been through. What all of us have been through. Even if someone offered me an amazing power like invisibility or instant travel, right now, with no side effects and no strings attached, I wouldn't take it. I'm perfectly happy to be the normal one, thanks.

Jake still has his power, since he tunneled to me. I thought I saw him take the serum, when they took him in. Either I was wrong or it didn't work.

That makes me a bit sad, after all we did to find it. After Vladimir's death. What was it good for?

What was any of it good for, except trying to keep Jake—and then all of us—free and safe? No, there's more than that. We need to keep power out of evil hands. If Jake's power, or Lucas's, is out there, and the solution isn't taking a serum to get rid of it, then we need to make sure it's only used for good purposes.

I don't have a power. I'm barely functioning, after hiding in the woods, after being tortured by Smith and his men. But I can still do something. I'll be the witness, and the getaway. I'll watch the entrance and see them when they come out (not if). Then I'll bring them all up here somehow, Abby and Myk and Jake and Dedushka and Lucas, cram them in this car, and drive the hell out of here, no matter what we leave behind.

I can do that. I will.

53

MYKA

Break Free by Ariana Grande

Mom gasps, loud, and Lucas makes a sound like an animal. Gareth Smith, here. I can't believe it. I've heard so much about him—and seen Lucas's reactions to just the idea of him coming. But I've never seen him before.

Jake jumps in front of me, his arms spread wide like a shield. I can still see Mr. Smith, though, under his arm.

He looks tired, like he hasn't slept for a while, and he has a big purple bruise on his cheek. He's neat, though. He's in a suit, all perfectly pressed, clean-shaven and with his hair slicked back. Like he wasn't just torturing Rachel hours ago. The way Jake described him in the tunnel, breaking her finger...I stare at him. He must be a psychopath. Unfortunately, once a psychopath is fixated on something, it's really hard to get him to move to something else. And the way he's looking at Jake...he's definitely fixated. He stops in front of Jake, and his men, four of them now, surround him.

Jake lifts his chin, and Mr. Smith laughs. It's creepy, low and intense. "Same old Jake. Honestly, when will you learn that you're my property, and you can never escape that?" His voice is low, almost soothing. He reaches out and strokes Jake's jaw, with one finger. I tense. Now? I run a finger over the stun gun in my pocket. I found it in that last room we were in, the soldier's, recharging on his desk. I think I know how to use it. I turned it on. All I have to do is push the button.

"Liesel," Smith says, nodding. "Lovely to see you again."

She frowns, but doesn't say anything.

Smith turns to Lucas. "My boy." His voice softens more. Lucas cowers back against the wall, like he's trying to burrow into it. "How could you leave me? I know, it was his fault. He convinced you. We were fine, you and I, weren't we?"

I think Lucas is going to cry. I would too. But then he turns and lifts his chin too, like Jake. "I'm not your boy," he says, loud. "No one owns me."

Smith laughs again, like he's pleased. Wow, he's insane.

"I'm not going back," Lucas says. "Never."

Jake steps forward. "Let them go. You and I can talk. Let the rest of them go up the hatch. Now. They need to get out of here."

No. He can't do that again.

Smith leans in, his eyes glittering. "You've used that gambit before. Too many times—it's old. They stay, every last one of them, until I'm done, and then all of you come with me. You may have the skills, but I'm smarter than you. I always will be. And you're mine." He turns back to tell his men to do something—grab us all, probably.

Now.

"You're not smarter than me," I say. I duck under Jake's arm, the stun gun in my hand. My breath coming fast. I shove it up into Smith's side, and jam down on the button. It buzzes, and his body dances for half a second, but it doesn't last long. One of the big guys yanks me away and drags me off to the side, twisting my arm behind my

267

back. It hurts, bad. He pushes it up, up, until I drop the stun gun on the floor and cry out.

I look at Mom, Jake, Dedushka, Lucas, lined up on the far wall. They're all staring at me, open-mouthed.

But it didn't even help. Smith just seems more mad now, unfocused, like a wasp whose nest has been smashed. Or a bull, enraged. He turns to me, rears back—I try to cringe away, but the big guy holds me tight—and slams his fist into my face.

There's an explosion of pain on my cheek, so bad I wonder if he smashed it. Then he fades. Everything fades. The last thing I see is Smith's face leaning over me, pure rage, as I crumple to the floor.

54

JAKE

I Bet My Life by Imagine Dragons

"You stay AWAY from her!" I howl. Mom screams, and Dedushka growls behind me. But two big guys pin my arms behind my back, and another one slams Dedushka into the wall.

"Gareth. Listen to him," Liesel says, quiet. "You don't want to hurt them." She steps forward, so she's close to Smith. "You don't want to—"

"Shut up!" he snaps. "You don't know what I want. And you don't get to tell me what to do anymore."

I strain against the arms holding me, but can't move. Mom braves it and goes to Myka on the floor, pulling her into her lap. No one stops her. Myka's still out. You can already see the bruise blooming on her cheek. It's the same place as the one on Smith's, where I hit him. I bet he did that on purpose.

I'm going to kill him. Rip him in tiny, painful pieces. And then I'm going to find some place for Myka to hide so no one can hurt her again.

Smith laughs. "I told you I'm smart. Smart enough to figure out your little plan, and circumvent it. Why would you invite me here? Hmmm, distraction? Maybe? Find another entrance then. Find where you were going out."

I scowl, still tugging uselessly.

"Tell me, then," Liesel says, still low. "What do you want here? Surely it's not your grand plan to be hitting little girls."

"Him." His voice is oddly high, breathless, as he points at me. And Lucas. "And him. You can't have them. I know what they can do, both of them, and they're mine. I'll take that one—" He points at Myka's still form. "As part of the bargain."

I yank again, feeling stupid tears welling in my chest. "That's *not* going to happen."

Liesel stands very still, a foot away from Smith. "If that's truly what you want, you can let the rest of them go, can't you? There's no reason to keep them here. Let them escape while they can."

"No one is leaving."

Dad. Because this wasn't bad enough. He stands in the hallway, feet apart and fists down like he's ready for a brawl. About twenty soldiers are lined up behind him, guns pointed at Smith.

Smith smiles, unbelievably. It even looks real. "John! How lovely to see you again. How long has it been? Five years?"

Dad clenches his jaw, but doesn't reply. I swear he's so absorbed in looking at Smith—all of them are—that we could just sneak out past them.

But not really. I move, and Dad's attention snaps straight back to me.

"What were you trying, Jake?" he asks softly. He has the gall to sound hurt. Like I've betrayed him by trying to get my family away.

Myka moans, her head still on Mom's lap. "Let them out of here," I try again, desperate. "Mom, Myk, Dedushka, even Lucas. You don't really need them, either of you. Let them go, right now."

Lucas, still and silent until now, steps forward. His chin is trembling. "I'll stay too. Let the rest of them go." He looks young, rumpled. But unbelievably brave. I know how scared of Smith he is.

I still don't know him—I simply haven't had enough time with him. But I'm proud he's my brother.

"I told you," Dad says. "NO ONE is leaving."

"You're wrong there," Smith says. "He is." He nods to the guys holding me, and one of them flips out a gun before the soldiers can react. I hear the click, feel the hard barrel press against my temple. I close my eyes. My hands start shaking. The last time this happened I was in Eric's body, pretending to hold a gun on myself. This is real.

"Any move toward me or mine, I will kill him," Smith says, almost gleeful. "Well, Jones here will. That beautiful brain, destroyed forever. And none of us want that, do we?"

"He will," I whisper. "He killed Dr. Milkovich, for no reason."

I open my eyes. I can't look at Mom, staring up at me from the floor. Or Dedushka next to me, though I feel both their gazes, as heavy as if they're touching me. But I look at Liesel, watching carefully. Then at Dad, his face slack with horror.

I guess Dad does care. Now that I have my powers back, at least.

"Orders, sir?" the soldier at Dad's elbow asks, gruff. They still have their guns raised, but that one shifts, so it's pointing at the guy holding me, instead of at Smith.

271

Dad doesn't answer. He shifts his feet, staring at me, then Smith. Who's staring back at him. It's like he truly doesn't know what to do.

Smith smiles again, slow. "Jacob and I are going to go back up now, up to the fresh air. And you, Lucas, my boy. And the girl. And then you're going to let us out of this place." He looks around, dismissively. "Fine. You can have the rest of them. Consider it a parting gift."

"Sir?" the soldier repeats. But Dad seems frozen, unable to move.

"It was nice doing business with you," Smith goes on. "And I'm not going to sell him back to you, not this time. Now that I know how very valuable he really is." He laughs. "He can *control* people, did you know that? Think what I can do with that!"

Smith moves backward, toward the ladder. The two holding me drag me forward, stumbling, the gun still pressed to my head. Another one grabs Lucas.

I look at their faces, each of them. Mom, her eyes big and scared. Myk, eyes still closed, sprawled on the floor. Dedushka, too quiet. What is Dedushka thinking?

Dad looks like he's having his heart ripped out. But he also looks helpless. Small. "Stand down," he says, low. His soldiers stand up straight and lower their guns. Smith's guys drag me farther.

But they're busy dragging me, not paying attention. I stuff my hand in my pocket.

"Stop," Liesel commands. Oddly, the guys—even Smith—stop. She steps across, looks me in the eye. "I can't let you go like this, Jacob. We've been through too much together. It was you and me from the beginning, wasn't it?"

The gun presses tighter against my head. I think it's making a mark. He's getting nervous.

She steps in front of me, to Smith. "I can go with you, if you're willing. I know how he works now. I can help."

I have a moment of thinking she's gone completely insane, but realize she's distracting him. So I can feel in my pocket. So I can awkwardly poke the right ziplock bag open, and pull a cuff link into my hand.

I close my eyes and dive into him as fast as I can.

I hear something going on around me, some disturbance, but I can't stop to see what it is. I have to keep going.

Smith. I skip past the location, fill him as quickly as I can. *He's bubbling with nerves. I can feel it thrumming in his blood, all the way to his fingers. I focus, really look at what's going on. The goons are still tugging me and Lucas. Dad is watching, still quiet. Mom and Myk are on the floor. Mom's crying, though Myk is starting to stir. Liesel is watching me, Smith.*

And Dedushka is wobbling, blood trickling from a hole in his shoulder.

I almost come out of it right there, with the shock. I feel Smith's exhilaration, and I almost can't stand it. What happened, in those seconds I was tunneling? What did Dedushka do?

But I know, right? He provided distraction. He knew what was going on too—he would see right through Liesel, and me—and decided to help, so Smith couldn't stop me.

And got himself shot.

I want to run to him, make sure he's okay, that he doesn't go into shock. I want to help him, to stop the bleeding.

273

But I can't.

I have to be Smith.

I take control of Smith's arms and legs, his voice. "That's it," I say, like he would. Sounding tired and annoyed. "You've messed everything up, old man. Now I want all of them."

Mom gasps, but Liesel and Dad are both blank-faced. Dedushka smiles. He was right. He knows it's me.

"Come on," I snap. "You're slow. Get the little one up. You–" I point at Liesel. "Get the old man. They're all coming with me, the whole family." I meet Dad's eyes. "Except you. You can stay here and rot, John. You can imagine your whole family, somewhere else, working without you."

I mean that. Except the working part. I don't want Myka or Lucas working for anyone.

"Send your soldiers away, right now. I'm tired of looking at them. You don't need them anymore."

I can feel Smith inside, like I could Eric. Shifting, protesting. He's livid, of course. I'm going to have to leave his body unconscious or something, or he'll kill me as soon as he's back in control.

I think Dad's lost it, with everything that's happened. He's still motionless. But then he waves a hand, says a word, and the soldiers all back away. Down the hall, out of sight.

I can't believe he'd give in that easily. He'd really let Smith have all of us, without a fight?

No, that's what I want.

I breathe easier. The goon has my body almost at the bottom of the ladder now. It looks like I passed out, and I hope they all think that's what it is. Lucas is almost there too. Liesel

274

has her arm around Dedushka, and Myka is up, blinking, standing dazedly with Mom.

We'll get out. We're going to do it.

"What are you going to do, Jake?" Dad says, staring straight at me—at Smith. "You're not going to be able to stay in him long enough."

I take a deep breath, shocked, and Smith pushes back somehow. He almost shoves me out.

"Let's go," I say, in a strangled voice. "I'm sick of this place. Get out now."

Dad folds his arms. "He's strong, isn't he? He's not like the others you've taken over: weak or confused. He knows what you're doing, and he doesn't like it."

The goon with my body pauses, looks at me questioningly.

"Put the gun away and get him up there," I say, for all the world like Smith would. "I've got this." I shakily pull Smith's gun out, point it at Dad. "Don't follow us. I'll kill Jake. You know I will."

The goon throws my body over his shoulder and steps onto the ladder. The hatch is open now, and I can see stars through it. I stare at them, in case they're the only stars I see again. No. Only a little bit farther.

Dad takes a step forward. "I know very well that you won't."

Mom and Myk are almost to the ladder. Mom has guessed what's going on—I can tell by the set of her shoulders. But she keeps going. They have to take advantage of this chance. Myk's still groggy. She probably doesn't even really know where she is.

275

Liesel stops and turns, with Dedushka's good arm draped over her shoulder. His eyes are bright, alert, though he's drooping a little. I don't think being shot in the shoulder is life-threatening, unless he goes into shock. But it can't feel good.

Liesel studies us, me and Dad, and sets her jaw. There's one more goon left, standing there at the bottom watching us too.

"I can't let you do this," Dad says. He sounds frantic now. "I need you, Jake. You most of all. I need you. I can't let you go.'

There's a lump in Smith's throat. I swallow past it. The gun in his hand shakes ridiculously. Dad takes a step closer. Myk starts up the ladder.

They need to escape. No matter what else happens, they need to escape.

"I'm going to let them get up there safe," Dad whispers, so just Liesel, Dedushka and I can hear it. "Then I'm going to kill Smith. You'll pop back into your body—you've done it before. Then my soldiers will surround you, up there. This is my territory, Jake. Without Smith his men won't fight. I'll have you all back down here before the sun's up." His mouth hardens. "All of you. And you'll be lucky if you ever see the sun again."

Dedushka and Liesel stop, but keep walking towards the ladder, heads together. I'm the one frozen now, like Dad was. I can't move an inch in Smith's stolen body.

I can see it, just like Dad said. He will do that. And then I'll really be done. He won't trust Liesel anymore. He'll never trust me again. There won't be any second chances. We'll all be stuck down here, forever.

"Kill him," Liesel says, soft. They're right next to me. I'm sure Dad can't hear. "Then go. I'll take care of Smith, and the other man. It's the only thing you can do. The only thing that will stop it."

Kill him. She means kill my own father.

I shudder, and almost lose control of Smith again. How could she say that? I can't do that.

Dad laughs. "You know he won't, Liesel. He'd never pull that trigger."

Myk's stopped halfway up the ladder, Mom at the bottom, looking down. They see Smith, but they know it's me. If I pull the trigger they'll know I killed Dad.

He holds his hands up, unarmed. Maybe he did hear— and he's making it harder. Like this it would be murder. Cold, heartless murder of my own father.

But she's right, it would stop everything. All of this, it comes from Dad. The General behind him, but Dad is the one who makes it happen. Without Dad, without Smith, we would all be free. At least of this place. We'd have a chance. With him standing there, we have nothing.

I've wondered before if I could do it if I had to. I've thought how he isn't really the Dad I knew anymore. How he's disappeared, into this creature who only cares about power.

I brace my other hand on the gun, make sure it's cocked. Dad stops, his arms still up, only a foot away. He shakes his head. Just like he used to when I disappointed him with homework, with a million tiny things he didn't like. He's my dad. How can he just want to use me? How can he want to use Lucas, and experiment on Myka? He should want to protect us. He should take care of us.

I despise him.

Smith pushes, hard, and I'm sticking. I'm starting to get lost inside him. Dad's right. Even with the new improved power, I won't last much longer.

I need to do it now. This is my only chance to stop Dad. And then Liesel will stop Smith.

I look down the barrel at eyes just like mine.

"We can work together," he says, his voice breaking. "That's all I want. All I've ever wanted. I can have a power too. We can be partners. We can be a super family."

My fingers—Smith's fingers—feel hot on the trigger. I aim, tighten my finger...

I take a breath. I can't do it. He's still my father.

Before I even loosen the grip Dedushka slides forward, scoops it from my hand, and shoots. No hesitation. Dead-center in the middle of Dad's forehead, just like Liesel shot Eric.

Dad falls, lifeless, to the floor.

Something in me breaks. Time gives up completely.

He's dead. Really dead this time. No hiding in a secret base, pretending. No coming back. Dead. Gone.

Myk didn't see. She's already at the top. But Mom did. She sobs, still climbing up.

I can't breathe properly. Smith pushes against me, strong, making me stagger. I can't stay.

"Hold still," Liesel whispers. "That's all you need to do. Hold still."

I turn. Her gun is out, steady, pointed at me. I swallow, stare into the barrel, keep a firm hold on Smith for a second longer, and hold still.

She fires. It all goes black.

55

JAKE

I Lived by OneRepublic

I open my eyes to the sound of arguing. Male voices, heavy. And a thin, high one. Lucas.

I scramble to my feet, trying to orient myself. It's flat here, the pale stretch of dirt reflecting the half-moon, but with hills all around crowding in. It's hidden. The air is so much cooler, fresher, than down there. Myka and Mom are sitting a few feet away, huddled up with their knees to their chests, with two of Smith's men looming over them.

The other one is struggling to contain Lucas, who's yelling and twisting to get away.

I leap in without even thinking, my adrenaline still pumping. I'm in my own body, and I don't have anything to worry about from Smith or Dad. Ever again.

I launch myself at the Jones, a tackle right at the middle, and take him down, landing hard on top of him. Lucas runs to Mom and Myka, but the other two goons reach out for him.

"STOP," I say. They don't listen, of course. They grab for Lucas. "Smith's dead. He's not coming back. You can just stop."

The man under me frowns and shoves me off. He gets up, quick for a big guy, and is about to go at me again when his phone buzzes, loud. He swears, but he must believe me a little. He pulls it out of his inside pocket, glances at the screen.

"He's right," he says to the other one, his voice distant. "Mr. Smith is dead. Blake is coming up. We can go."

The one with a hand on Lucas smiles, runs a hand over his buzzcut. He glances at me, his eyes white in the moonlight. "Hell yeah. We can finally get away from that bastard."

There's a clattering and the fourth one comes up the hatch, head popping up first like a mushroom. He clasps the hand of the big one, looks at us once. I almost wish the nice-ish one, the one who let me escape–Bradley–was here.

"Good luck," the biggest one says. The blond one. I'm trying to figure out if that's sincere or ominous, but they turn easily and walk off together, down a hill. The four of them together in their matching suits.

I sit, panting, on the dirt. Lucas grins at me. "I guess Mr. Smith didn't exactly inspire loyalty," he says.

I wonder if Smith was paying them well, or if he had some hold on all of them to make them stay. Like Bunny.

Bunny. Vladimir. Dad. Too many people have died. I don't know how to feel about any of it. Mostly I feel numb, as the adrenaline drains away.

"Jake," Myk says. "What happened? We heard two gunshots."

I close my eyes for a second. Swallow. Then I look at them, my mom and my sister, scruffy and tired. But whole, free again. That's the good part. That's what I have to remember. "Dad's dead."

Mom takes a deep, shaky breath. Myk's eyes are too bright. She pulls her knees tighter. "Did you…?"

I shake my head. "It wasn't a choice," I whisper. "He was going to keep all of us there, for the rest of our lives." I don't explain any more than that, for now. They don't need to know that Dedushka did it. It's enough. I go to them, wrap my arms around both of them tight.

"He wasn't himself anymore," Mom murmurs. "He was something else. Something…monstrous, when he wanted to use you. It was all he could think about."

"Jekyll and Hyde," Myka says, low.

I'm still watching the hatch. Liesel and Dedushka should be up here soon too. "It'll be okay," I say. "The other shot was Smith. He's dead too."

Tension goes out of them both. I stand. Lucas is standing too, a little on the outside. But grinning for real now, almost like a kid should grin. "Really?" he asks. "He's really dead?"

"For sure. He's not coming after you ever again. Any of us."

"Thank God," Mom says.

I strain my eyes to see in the dark, hoping for a blonde head and a gray one to appear, and make the family complete.

"Jacob." Liesel's voice floats up, and I launch myself over there, stare down. She's standing at the bottom, one hand on the ladder, alone.

"Here."

"I think you need to come back down."

My gut clenches. That's bad. There are still soldiers down there, and they might still act without Dad, lock me up again. Is Dedushka okay? I know he was shot, but I thought he'd be up here already, growling at us.

I look back at Mom, Myk. "I'll be back in a minute, okay?" Mom nods, one arm still around Myk. Lucas steps closer to them, like he's their protector now.

I take a deep breath of fresh air and head back down to the base. It's harder going down the ladder than going up. My feet keep slipping on the rungs.

When I get to the bottom Liesel is with Dedushka, who's lying on the floor. Dad's body is still lying there too, and Smith's. I stand there for a second, unable to move.

"Get over here," Liesel says, her usual self. "He's fine, Jacob. He just passed out."

I breathe. I kneel on the hard floor, take his hand. His eyes are open, the gray-blue pinned on me. He smiles through the beard.

"Is he going to be okay?" I glance at Liesel, on the other side of him. I squeeze his hand. "I need you, crazy old man."

He squeezes back, his gaze steady. "I will be, da. It is only..." He jerks his chin at his shoulder. "This fool thing. It makes me weak."

"You can't move him out, or take him on the road right now," Liesel says. "I wouldn't even take him up that ladder. He got dizzy when he tried, and lost consciousness. He needs to stay here, see a doctor."

"She is right for one time," Dedushka says, loud, and Liesel flinches. I almost laugh. "I will be all right here without John, without evil Smith. I have no power to use."

"Will he?" I ask her. "Will you stay here with him, make sure he's all right?"

The answer is immediate. "Of course. I will take care of him."

I remember the evil mother taking care of me in Montauk, and I believe her. "I should go," I say. "Get back to them."

"Wait." Dedushka grips my hand, strong. "Yakob. We will be apart for a little while. I have one more thing to say, yes?"

I nod. I wouldn't have made it without him. I would never have made it out of Montauk. He can say as much as he wants. "Yes. Of course."

"Use it for good."

Liesel stiffens. He ignores her, his eyes on mine. "It is all right you have it again. It is part of you—I understand." He smiles, almost a grimace. "It is my legacy. But it is up to you to use it right."

I nod, touch his hand. "I will. I love you, Grandpa." I say it to tease him, to prove to myself that he's really going to be okay. Then wait for the reaction.

He grimaces for real, and flings my hand off. "Do not use that tedious word." Then he waves toward the ladder. "Go. I will see you soon."

I run, climb until my head's in the air again. They're standing there huddled together, waiting. Except Rachel's there too now. She looks bad, beaten by that asshole. Bruises all over, her hand wrapped in a towel sling. But she smiles at me, and my heart flips.

"He's going to be okay," I say. "But he needs to stay here until he is. Liesel is getting a doctor."

283

Relief splashes over their faces. Rachel steps forward to crush me in a hug. I crush back, my face in her hair. "I'm sorry," I say. "I'm so sorry."

She hiccups, and I think she's going to cry. She was hurt because of me. Badly. But he's gone—they're both gone—and she's going to be okay. "We're all okay," she says. "We won."

I hold her closer, looking at my family together over her shoulder. We're together, and we may have broken bits, but we're mostly okay. I guess we did win.

A few minutes later, we hear footsteps on the ladder. We all cringe, in case it's some new danger—we really should get out of here...somewhere. But it's a blonde head. Liesel. She pulls herself up, and brushes off her pants.

"Jacob? May I speak with you please?"

Reluctantly I let go of Rachel. She crushes my hand, once, and heads over with the others.

Liesel pulls me aside by the elbow, out of earshot of the rest of them.

I'm nervous. Talks with Liesel are rarely a good thing. Though she's been different, here—still I know what she wants.

"I want you to work with me." Her voice drops to honey.

"Don't do that," I snap.

She blinks.

"I know you want to work with me. I told you I would, if it made sense. But I'm petrified of getting sucked into..." I wave towards the ladder, the base. The dead bodies at the bottom. "*This* again. Tell me straight what you want, the details. Don't try to play me anymore."

"Fair." She looks me straight on, no bullshit. "I will never bring you underground again, Jacob. I will never mess with your family. No double-cross, no lying. You get to choose if you want to do a job or not—but I promise you, in the long view, every single one of them will help people. I don't have the egotistical goals of John, or the avarice of Smith. I don't care about advancing a project or a department. I just want to *help people.*"

I examine the pine needles on the ground, listening hard.

"You could still go to Stanford," Liesel says. "Rachel too, if she wants. Wherever you want, both of you. All of you. We'll need to set something up...like witness protection. You can't go back home. But it can be done."

My heart starts pounding. I feel like a dog with his ears pricked up.

I told her I would help her, if she helped me. And Stanford.

"Consider it retroactive payment. Your mother and Myka can go to school and work. Lucas can live with them if he wants to. Without Smith, without John, I can guarantee you they'll all be safe."

I look up. "You can't guarantee that."

"I can," she says vehemently. "I will. There were too many mistakes made. Leaks. Strategies. Power-greed. I made mistakes. No one else will know this is active, that you are still even out there, except me and one handler. We'll hide it better."

"You're going to make me die again?"

I'm half-joking, but she nods.

"To the General, yes. You died here. Your brother died here. None of John's men saw, so that's what I'll say. That's the end of it."

I take a deep, long breath, tilt my head back, and look at the sky, the beautiful profusion of stars starting to peek out. I never want to be locked away from the sky again. But she says she won't. And I almost believe her. Except.

"Plus you'll have Dedushka as collateral, to make sure I behave. You'll keep him here."

She shakes her head firmly. "It's not like that, Jacob. I'm going to make him better, and then he'll leave. We'll help him too, if he wants. Only if he wants. I see I went about this all wrong, before. I'm proposing that we'll be partners now. Equal partners." She touches my arm. "You don't have to decide now. We'll talk again, all right? I'll find you. I'll bring the china cat, and we'll find that plane."

She raises a hand to everyone else, strides to the ladder, and disappears.

I'll find you, she said. Because no matter where we go, she's confident she can find me. That's scary, but not surprising anymore. Especially without Dedushka to help us hide, we'd probably be pretty easy to find.

I scratch at the stubble on my cheek, thinking about her proposal. If I accept—if we accept, and we'll all have to talk about it—we'll be protected from anyone who might still know about me, and might still try to use my power for the wrong things. We'll be able to start a new life, together. And I really will be able to use my power for what I feel it's meant for, helping people.

That sounds like something I can work with. I look at my family, together, Lucas talking to Mom, Rachel hugging Myka. They're broken, some. By this place, by being confined, by the trauma of Smith, by the horror of Dad's work, and Dad's death. I'm broken too. But we're here, and we can start again.

We Lukins stick together like glue. Until we shatter, and then we come back together on our own, and put ourselves together. We don't need no stinkin' glue.

Yeah. That's better.

56

RACHEL

UC Berkeley

Dreams by the Cranberries

I look around my dorm room, making sure I've got everything. I'm still not quite comfortable being on my own, in one place. Not responsible for other people. All I have to do every day is get myself up and to class, and then to work at the Institute of Government Studies. It feels too easy, like I'm missing something.

Not that my schedule at Berkeley is easy. After some deep thought, and a conversation with Dedushka, I decided to stay in the political science major I was enrolled in before. To make a difference in government from the inside, from a position of knowledge instead of fear. I don't know if I'll ever actually run for office—that would require background checks I might not pass now—but I can still make things happen.

And I still love it. When I imagine studying something else, like library science or English, it feels flat. This was the right choice.

Liesel says my new identity will pass any background check, that it's made for that. But I don't know if I'd trust it. I'm still getting used to the identity too. No more Rachel Watkins. I'm Andrea Brett, from Providence, Rhode Island. I don't have any family living, but I'm a good student. Good enough for Liesel to pull whatever strings she did to get me here. I just have to live up to Andrea's reputation.

Of course I do have family living. Liesel had me call my parents, both of them, to tell them I was safe and well, that I was going out of the country with the Peace Corps and I wouldn't be able to be in touch. They were awkward, uncomfortable phone calls. Dad said that was great, and then there was silence. Mom cried, moaning about how I was abandoning her, then yelling about how I was a worthless daughter. I stood there and listened, numb, until Liesel took the phone and hung up.

"That's done," she said. "If you want it to be. You're your own person now."

I'm my own person. Andrea Brett. Poly Sci major. Normal. Andrea didn't escape from a secret military base or run from the police in Florida. She's never seen a dead body. Andrea didn't have her fingers broken in a dirty hotel room by a madman. I try to remember that when I talk to other people, when I walk around campus. Andrea has no reason to look over her shoulder in the cafeteria, to have nightmares about guns and knives and big men in suits.

I do look over my shoulder, and I do have nightmares. But I'm here, a fresh start, and I'm determined to make the most of it. To move forward.

There's also still Jake, and all the rest of them. Dedushka, Abby, Myka, Lucas. I get to see them most weekends, and that's like coming home to my real family. I don't have to hide anything with them. I belong.

I send Jake a quick text on my way to American Politics. Even though I've been in classes for a month, it's his first day at Stanford. I know he's nervous. His life over the past year is even harder to shed.

I have a feeling he'll be okay, though. That all of us will.

I grab my backpack, with books and a wallet that say Andrea Brett (normal person), and step into the bright sunshine.

57

MYKA

Safe & Sound by Taylor Swift

I love my new school.

I didn't think there was any way I could like it as much as my last one, but I do. It's called Nueva School, it's in Hillsborough near San Francisco, and it's awesome. There's a design and engineering lab! And a chemistry lab! And music, which I never did at Nysmith but I wanted to. I'm going to do African and Brazilian drumming next year. And in the spring, the eighth grade gets to go to Spain!

I'm Chloe Freeman now. I picked Freeman when Liesel gave us a list of last names to pick from, because...duh. Free.

I said it really should be Freewoman, but I've never heard of that as a last name. And Lucas—he's Oliver now, which is weird—had to share the name too, so Freeman works.

Lucas is at Nueva also, though he's at the high school, so I don't see him during the day. I think he likes it, though he still doesn't talk a lot. About anything. But he smiles more. And I think sometimes he talks to Mom. He's still super shy with Jake.

Mom says we'll get there. I may not ever be able to tickle him like I do Jake, but I'm working up to hugs.

I hug Jake all the time. And Mom, and Dedushka. Sometimes I can't get enough.

The bell rings and I head into math, my second-favorite subject. My new best friend Ming-An is in my group, so it's fun.

The memory of Dad teaching me math all those nights fills my head. His face so serious, so intense. Then his face at the end, so desperate to keep Jake.

"Here I am," I whisper.

I sigh and shove all of it away. Chloe Freeman's dad died a long time ago. I sit with Ming-An, laugh about a picture she sent me this morning, and then we settle in to class.

I can do this. I can do anything now.

58

JAKE

Stanford

The End Is the Beginning Is the End by Smashing Pumpkins

Stanford is both exactly what I expected and not at all what I thought it would be. I guess if you hold something in your head for so long, especially when it seemed impossible, it gets a shiny brochure quality to it. Sitting in the white cell in Montauk, or the gray concrete rooms in Dad's base, I pictured the quad with students sprawled on the grass, all posed in collegiate perfection in the sun.

There are students, and it is sunny. Hot, even. It's Palo Alto in September. But right now at least, on the first day of classes, nobody's lounging on the grass. There's a definite buzz, a sense of purpose. People walk fast, talk fast, seem like they know where they're going. I overhear conversations I don't understand at all, and a couple I do.

I can't believe I'm really here, a backpack on my shoulder, a real enrolled student. It's not a temporary cover or a dream. Not under my name of course, but with my major, my

292

background (roughly), my transcript. Full scholarship. Internship at the California Historical Society next summer already approved. My future back in place, shiny. With just a little detour.

Jason Connors. It has a nice ring to it. I stole the last name from Jimmy, one of my favorite players ever. Maybe it will help me get on the tennis team too.

I lift my face to soak up the sun for a second—I can never get enough sun—then stroll across the Oval to my first class, a freshman seminar: History of Science.

I wonder if we'll cover any psychology, or parapsychology. Probably not. They'd probably say it isn't real, with all the failed experiments. But no one knows about me.

My phone buzzes with a text from Rachel.

`Good luck today. Love you. See you this weekend.`

Love you. It's still new, puppy-awkward, like we're getting to know each other for the first time again, even though we've been through so much. I will see her this weekend. Nearly every weekend—we meet in San Francisco, with the rest of my family.

I text it back, grin like a complete and total idiot, and slip the phone back in my pocket. There are good-luck messages from Mom, Myk, and Lucas in there too. The only contacts in my phone, and the only ones I need.

There's no text from Dedushka. I snort at the thought of it, and a guy with a blue bandanna on his head looks at me funny, then shrugs. Dedushka would never use a cell phone, not in a million lifetimes. But he's okay, recovering, and I know he wishes me well today. That's all he ever wanted. *Use it for good.*

I go up the steps and under the arch of Building 200, History Corner, and swallow down another lump in my throat. My hands tremble a little, but not because I'm inside. This time it's pure adrenaline.

I go up to the second floor, past other history majors, and find the room. It's massive. Tiers and tiers of brown seats, sloping down to a big open space in front. There's a wide desk with four screens behind it. It smells like old books, and a little bit of sweat. The room is about half-full, and the Professor's not here yet. I'm early. Of course I'm early.

I pick a seat about five rows up, a few in. Not ridiculously teacher's pet-ish—Myk would be in the very front row. But *interested*. I drop into the seat and look around, not even trying to be casual.

"Is this seat taken?" asks a musical voice, with a Spanish accent.

I whip my head around. No. It can't be.

But it is.

Ana. She was my first DARPA handler, a lifetime ago, the only one who wasn't tainted by everything that came later. I liked her, even in the midst of everything else. She was kind, but all business. Her dark hair is pulled into a knot at her neck like it always was, though she looks a little younger this time. Less housekeeper, more mature college student. She smiles at me, all white teeth, with real pleasure. She holds out her hand to shake, a new silver charm bracelet dangling from her wrist, jingling. "I am Emma. And you?"

I laugh, a low, short laugh. Too weird. Liesel brought her back to be my handler this time too, my protector. Like nothing else ever happened. But it did. I'm different. And now my talent is mine to control, not theirs.

I have a feeling Ana will understand that. Equal partners. My choices. I shake her hand.

"Jason Connors. Nice to meet you."

We smile again, at all our shared secrets. Then we turn back to the front as the professor comes in and starts writing on the board.

Let the new life begin.

CPSIA information can be obtained
at www.ICGtesting.com
Printed in the USA
LVOW01s0933050317
526180LV00008B/659/P